RISKY BEHAVIOR

L.A. WITT  CARI Z

RIPTIDE PUBLISHING

Witt

Riptide Publishing
PO Box 1537
Burnsville, NC 28714
www.riptidepublishing.com

Risky Behavior

Cover art: Garrett Leigh, blackjazzdesign.com
Editor: Rachel Haimowitz
Layout: L.C. Chase, lcchase.com/design.htm

ISBN: 978-1-62649-565-4

First edition
May, 2017

Also available in ebook:
ISBN: 978-1-62649-564-7

RISKY BEHAVIOR

L.A. WITT ★ CARI Z

TABLE OF CONTENTS

CHAPTER ONE
ANDREAS

"I don't need a goddamned babysitter."

From across a desk covered in reports and folders—any number of which were probably about me—Captain Hamilton shot me a look I'd seen way too many times. Narrow eyes, tight lips, tilted head. The "I've had enough of your shit" look.

"He's not a babysitter." The captain folded his hands in his lap and leaned back in his giant leather chair. "He's a damn good cop and a newly minted detective."

I groaned. "You're sticking me with a rookie?"

Hamilton rolled his eyes. "For fuck's sake, Ruffner. What part of 'newly minted detective' wasn't clear? He's not a rookie."

I snorted. "He knows how to be a beat cop. Call me when he's cut his teeth as an actual—"

"This isn't up for discussion, Detective." He sat up and pressed his elbows onto his desk. "I'm partnering you with Detective Corliss." He inclined his head and stabbed a finger at me. "And I expect you to treat this one as an equal. None of the bullshit like the last two."

"How long am I stuck with him?" I asked through my teeth. "Until he's ready to take off his training wheels?"

"Until I'm good and ready to reassign one of you."

I studied him for a long moment. Long enough to make him twitch and fidget. Then, "What's this about, Captain?"

"It doesn't need to be about anything, *Detective*." He glared at me. "You have your orders. Follow them."

Aside from clenching my jaw, I didn't move. "You want to tell me why you keep pairing me with new—"

"Well for one thing, if they can put up with you, then they can put up with anyone."

"Isn't that considered hazing?"

He exhaled. "For *another* thing, I'm assigning him because detectives work better in pairs. You might see things he's missed. He might see things you've missed. Two heads are better than one. All right?" Before I could call bullshit on that, he said, "Dismissed."

"Captain—"

"*Dismissed.*"

There was no point in fighting him now, so I got up and left without another word. Grinding my teeth so hard my jaw ached, I headed downstairs. Might as well get some work done on my last afternoon as a free man.

This "partner" idiocy was going to drive me insane. On the other hand, Detective Corliss probably wouldn't be a pain in my ass any longer than Detectives Schaeffer and Phillips before him. Schaeffer had held out until he'd heard that one night, instead of staying at my desk to wrap up some paperwork like I'd told him, I'd gone out and collared a suspect we'd been hunting for the past three weeks. Neither he nor Hamilton had been impressed when I'd said I'd known where the suspect was hiding, but didn't trust Schaeffer not to compromise things before I could get close enough to arrest the fucker.

Then there'd been Phillips, who'd insisted at every turn that my refusal to tell her anything was the result of being a misogynist who didn't respect female cops. Hamilton himself had admitted to her that I was just an asshole who didn't like working with *any* cops, and that I gave my male partners the same shit. She'd immediately requested a transfer, and we were both happier for it. And for the past couple of months, I'd been doing quite nicely on my own.

Until now. Couldn't fucking wait.

I glanced at my watch on my way back to my desk. It was quarter after four. Shit. I doubled back and headed for the locker room instead.

When I walked in, there were a few beat cops talking about last night's game over by the sinks. They ignored me, and I ignored them as I continued to the opposite side of the room and opened my locker, all the while keeping my attention trained on them in case one of them came my way.

They didn't seem to be moving, but I worked quickly as always, pulling the small pill bottle from the shaving kit I kept in the back of the locker for those extra-late nights. Checking again that I didn't have anyone looking over my shoulder, I opened the bottle, tugged free the wad of cotton that kept the pills from rattling, and slid one out. Then I replaced the cotton and put the bottle back in its hiding place.

After making double sure no one had materialized nearby, I threw back the pill and washed it down with my water bottle.

There. *Now* I could get back to work.

This time as I walked past the other officers, they noticed me. Their conversation dipped just briefly, pausing midsentence while all three heads turned. I didn't have to look at them to feel them watching me leave, and I wasn't imagining it either. Not when it happened almost every time I left the locker room without being in there long enough to change clothes or shower.

In the name of flying under everyone's radar, I'd kept the pills in my desk for a while. I still had a few there in case I absolutely couldn't get near the locker room, but it was harder to be subtle about popping pills when I was out in the open like that. Especially when the whole goddamned place seemed to be on a low-level alert at all times, everyone poised like bounty hunters to be the one who caught Detective Ruffner red-handed. Sneaking off into the locker room at regular intervals raised suspicion, but I never let anyone actually witness the existence of the bottle or the consumption of the pills.

I kept some on me, of course, but those were strictly for when I couldn't get back to the precinct in time. Lesson learned the hard way.

Properly medicated, I returned to my desk and picked up my coat. I didn't bother telling anyone that I was leaving or where I was going. Never did.

Without a word, I left the precinct.

Two hours later, I parked in the weedy gravel in front of an abandoned warehouse about twenty miles west of town. When I stepped out and slammed the car door, it echoed in the stillness.

In the distance, the last remnants of rush hour traffic ground along, but otherwise, no one and nothing moved.

To be sure, though, I scanned my surroundings. No cars. No people. Good.

And not surprising. I'd taken the most indirect route possible. I'd backtracked. Gone around blocks. Pulled over from time to time. Turned without signaling or even slowing down. Anything to make sure Captain Hamilton hadn't decided to get cute and put some officers on my tail again.

Today, no one had followed me. Well, that cleared one thing up: Corliss was definitely coming along to keep an eye on me. No need to put someone on my ass when there'd be a rookie detective in the fucking passenger seat. Fabulous.

For tonight, I was still on my own, and taking full advantage.

Gravel crunched under my shoes as I followed the familiar pathway through the overgrown weeds toward the crumbling, graffiti-peppered brick building. The hairs on the back of my neck stood on end. All my senses went to high alert, searching for the faintest signs of life.

On the surface, this was a stupid, dangerous place for a rendezvous. That was exactly what I was going for, though. Something that looked like the last place any idiot would want to do business.

For one thing, there were dozens of places where a sniper could set up shop, but I'd know if anything bigger than a pigeon tried to make a perch. I'd combed this building from top to bottom long ago and had placed motion sensors in strategic locations. A lot of shady things happened here, but nobody was getting the drop on me.

Tonight, I knew exactly how many people were inside the warehouse besides me—one. His presence had tripped a sensor, and a message had come to my phone. Ten miles away, I'd remotely checked one of the cameras, and verified that only my contact was here. No one had followed him. No one was waiting to ambush him, me, or both of us. There weren't even any drifters who'd happened by in search of a place to sleep.

Still, I kept a hand on the butt of my pistol as I stepped into the decrepit structure. No such thing as too much caution.

To my left, something crunched under a shoe.

"Jeff?" My voice echoed, even though I didn't shout. "That you?"

"Yeah. Right here."

I turned around just as the kid stepped out of the shadows. His face was partially hidden by a faded red hoodie, both hands tucked deep in its pockets.

I relaxed a little, taking my hand off the gun.

He stayed tense, eyeing me uncertainly. "You got the money?"

"You got what I came for?"

He slid a plastic-wrapped, finger-sized pack of white powder just far enough from his pocket to show me. "Pure. Just like you asked."

"Good." I made a slow, deliberate gesture of reaching into my coat pocket for a wad of bills. We'd done business before, but he wisely distrusted me. A seventeen-year-old who made narcotics runs for gangbangers and conducted clandestine transactions with cops was smart to trust absolutely nobody.

I handed him the cash. He tucked the brick back into his pocket, and we both stood in silence while he counted out the bills. I wasn't worried he'd try to take off—he wasn't stupid enough to believe he could outrun a .45. Not that I would ever shoot a kid, never mind in the back, but I didn't stop him from believing I would.

He shoved the money into one pocket, pulled the brick from the other, and thrust it at me. "It's all here."

"Perfect." As soon as the drugs—pure heroin—were in my possession, Jeff jogged toward the back of the building just like he always did. His boss was not a patient man and would be chomping at the bit by now for that cash.

I gritted my teeth as I headed for my car. Jeff's boss wasn't my top priority right now; there was an even bigger monster with a lot more blood on his hands who needed to go first. That motherfucker wouldn't even make it to jail if I had any say in the matter.

All in good time, though.

I opened my passenger-side door and tucked the heroin into a compartment I'd built into the underside of the seat. It was sealed, insulated from anything that might detect narcotics, including the most sensitive K9 nose. Even if Detective Numbnuts dropped a pen and had to feel around under the seat to find it, he'd never be the wiser.

The thought of him made my blood boil. I was sick and fucking tired of Captain Hamilton assigning me "partners" under the guise of mentorship, making my investigations more efficient, or whatever other excuse he came up with on a given day.

Just say it, Captain.

Just come out and admit they're reporting back to you so you can confirm I'm a dirty cop and a junkie.

Just fucking say it.

But so far, he hadn't said it, and none of my "partners" had provided him with anything damning. So I kept on doing my job.

Tomorrow, I'd get a bead on Detective Corliss and figure out how to fly under his radar until I annoyed him enough to request reassignment. Tonight, with no one in the world aware of the heroin tucked safely away until I needed it, I drove back into town.

"**O**h, sweet baby Jesus." Marla gaped at me as I walked toward Captain Hamilton's office. The blinds were down, but I could see movement through the glass door. It was still a few minutes to nine—I'd come in as early as I could justify before our meeting without making myself look like more of a noob, hoping to get a glimpse of my new partner before the formal introductions were made. "You're wearing a suit."

"Uh, yeah." I made a show of turning my head, looking around the bull pen at the other detectives already at work. I saw a lot of discarded jackets, loosened ties and wrinkled dress shirts, but still. "So is everybody but you. Should I come in wearing high heels and an A-line tomorrow?"

Marla pointed a long, glittery fingernail at my face. "Don't you try to sass me; I'm not your momma. I can throw more shit work your way than you can shake a cat at." Her expression was grim. "A suit, my God. And you shaved today. You look eighteen. Ruffner is going to eat you alive."

"Oh, come on." I smiled, trying to coax one out of Marla in return. "How bad can he be?"

If anything, her frown deepened. "You have no idea. It's like throwing a guppy into a shark tank. I don't know what Hamilton is thinking, pairing the two of you together."

"I can handle myself just fine." What had years of toiling as a beat cop been for, if not to prepare me to deal with assholes? I wanted to get along with my new partner; life would be so much easier if we could be friendly. I was ready for any contingency though. You didn't grow up hearing the stories I did without learning something from them: namely, that the only person you could ever really rely on in the field was yourself. I wanted a good partner, but I was prepared to deal with a bad one, at least for a while.

"Oh, Darren." Marla sighed the world-weary sigh of the enlightened cynic. "It's like trying to warn somebody about a hurricane when there's nothing but sunshine outside. You'll see when you meet him, I guess." She leaned back and tucked a curl of dark-brown hair behind her ear. "Now, how's your daddy?"

"Enjoying his retirement." Enjoying it as well as anybody who'd been a cop for over thirty years could, at least. I thought my mother was two seconds away from flat-out demanding that Vic stop spying on the neighbors, regardless of whether or not he could "prove that they're dealing drugs out of their basement, Jessica—it's obvious!" She'd been encouraging him to spend a lot of time at the cabin lately, where the only things around to spy on were fish and game.

"Uh-huh." Marla looked unconvinced. "Tell Jessica she can come to my place for drinks whenever he gets to be too much. I've got a cupboard full of tequila and a brand-new blender."

"I'll let her know." Not for the first time, I wished that everyone who had been in the force for more than a few years didn't know my entire family. Between my dad's career, my mother's yearly barbeques hosting the entire precinct, and my brother's work in the district attorney's office, there weren't enough people around who didn't remember me from when I was a kid.

Captain Hamilton's door opened with a sudden bang, and both Marla and I started as we turned to look at him. His shoulders were so broad they barely fit inside the doorframe, but from the way they seemed to slump, he was already tired. "Corliss, get in here!" One of the chairs in front of his desk was already occupied. Was that Detective Ruffner? "And Marla, I need—"

"Decaf only until noon," she said, sharp eyes flashing at him. "Or do we need to have a talk about the results of your last physical where everyone can hear it?"

Hamilton sighed. "Fine."

"And if you shatter that door's glass again, I am *not* going to be held responsible for my actions."

This time he winced. "Sorry about that." His vaguely apologetic expression evaporated as soon as he focused on me. "Corliss, inside."

I followed him in and shut the door behind us—quietly—as he took his place behind his desk.

"Sit."

I sat in the spare chair, glancing at the man next to me. There was no way this was Andreas Ruffner. I wasn't going to take shit for wearing a suit from a man sporting a silk pocket square.

"Detective Corliss, this is Detective Thibedeau." He gestured between us with a scowl. "He's going to have the pleasure of riding your ass for the next few weeks."

I frowned, but before I could say anything, Thibedeau chuckled. "Captain, you exaggerate. I'm not here to make things difficult for anyone."

"Tell that to my blood pressure."

I took advantage of the pause. "I thought I was being partnered with Detective Ruffner."

"You are," Thibedeau said. He had his legs crossed and his fingers steepled—a little older and he might have pulled off a Godfather-type demeanor, but instead he came across more like a high-school guidance counselor. "Before you two start working together, though, there are a few extenuating circumstances you should be aware of."

"Thibedeau's with Internal Affairs," Captain Hamilton interjected. He didn't look happy about it.

Less than an hour into my new position, and I was already having a meeting with IA? Fuck me.

Not that I let any of my consternation show. I was a champion of resting nice-face. I crossed my legs to match my interrogator, then looked at Thibedeau. "What sort of things should I be aware of?"

"I'm sure you've heard some of the rumors going around the department about Ruffner."

"No," I said. I didn't even have to play dumb for this part—I'd been so busy busting my ass to make detective that I'd consciously tuned out any and all gossip for months. "I mean, I hear that he can be a little difficult to get along with—"

"He's goes through partners like paper targets," Thibedeau said. "No one manages to stick around him for very long, and we'd really like to know why."

"How many times do I have to tell you, Ruffner is and always has been an asshole?" Captain Hamilton said wearily. "He's also closed more cases than any other detective on the force."

"He's *also* flouted regulations, exhibited poor anger management skills, and has been observed engaging in suspicious behavior both on and off duty."

I had the feeling I'd been shoved into the middle of an argument that had been going on for a long time. "What's that got to do with me?" I asked, redirecting their attention off each other and back to me. Brows smoothed out, tense mouths softened slightly. It was my Bambi eyes; they were killers.

"We just want you to keep an eye on your new partner, Darren— can I call you Darren?" He kept going before I could tell him no. "Detective Ruffner has a proven track record in the department, but his methods have always been unorthodox, and the fact that he can't keep a partner doesn't speak well of his ability to adapt. No one in this force is an island, and no one can go without oversight. How else can we safeguard the public's faith in us?"

He checked his watch, then stood up. "You and I will meet later this week for a casual discussion about what you've observed working with your new partner. You've come very far, very fast, Darren." He smiled at me. I could practically see my reflection in his teeth. "I'd like to help you continue that arc."

I shook the hand he extended. "Sir," I said, as neutrally as possible. Thibedeau left, seeming to take extra care not to let the door slam, and I locked eyes with Captain Hamilton. For just a second, rank fell away, and he was the guy who had picked me up off the ground after my brother told me if I jumped off the swing set wearing a cape, I would fly. "What the hell?"

He sighed. "I know it's irregular, kid, but we have to go along with it for now."

"What's he expecting me to figure out in just a few days? Even if Ruffner is up to something," and holy shit, I really hoped he wasn't, but, "he's been a detective for over a decade. He knows how to cover his tracks."

"I wasn't lying when I said that Ruffner is the best closer on this force." Hamilton looked like he'd bitten into an unripe persimmon. "But he's not perfect. He makes waves sometimes when he shouldn't, and he can't keep a partner to save his life. And that *worries* me, not just because it might end up with him on a slab. I think he's hiding something." He shook his head. "I don't know what it is. For what it's worth, I give Ruffner a lot of leeway because I know he can get the job done, but he needs a partner. He needs someone to have his back."

The look he shot me spoke volumes: Ruffner needed someone to have his back not just in the field, but in the office. "And if there's something there after all? Then we need to know that too."

"Got it," I said quietly. Captain Hamilton dropped his gaze down to his files, and the moment passed. We were back to being boss and underling.

"He's not gonna make it easy on you, either." There was a suspicious gleam in Hamilton's eyes, like he was amused but trying not to let on. "If you can survive being partnered with Detective Ruffner, nobody will say another word about you being too young for the job."

I'd overheard some of those conversations. Never mind that I'd joined up straight out of college, or that I'd worked my beat for seven solid years—two more than required by the department—before taking the exam. I was the stepson of a revered cop and I had unfortunately youthful features: clearly, my success was all the result of nepotism. "I can do it."

"I hope you can."

The intercom buzzed. "Captain, Detective Ruffner is on his way up."

Captain Hamilton rubbed his fingers against his temple. I tried not to take that as a bad sign. "Send him in."

CHAPTER THREE
ANDREAS

On the way up the stairs to meet Hamilton and my new partner, I passed Thibedeau. I knew that motherfucker well, and I didn't like seeing him here. I didn't like *him*, but no one from Internal Affairs came up this way unless they were talking to Hamilton, which meant he'd just come from Hamilton's office.

Wow. I hadn't even met the new kid, and he was already in IA's pocket.

Good to know, assholes.

At the top of the stairs, I stopped, ostensibly to lean against the wall and check my phone. The new pills I was taking made me dizzy as fuck, especially after going up a flight of stairs, and I'd already blacked out twice this week. No point in pushing it, so I stood there as casually as I could, pretending to care what was my screen until the sparkling faded from the edges of my vision. Hopefully that particular side effect would wear off soon—I didn't need it happening at an inopportune moment. Like, say, a foot chase or a struggle to disarm a suspect.

When I was steady, I continued toward Hamilton's office.

"Well hello, Detective," Marla chirped from behind her desk. "How are you, sweetheart?"

"Depends on who my new babysitter is."

She laughed. "He's in with the boss now." She gestured toward Hamilton's office. "They're waiting for you."

"Of course they are."

I didn't bother knocking. Hamilton hated it when I did that, which was exactly *why* I did it.

"Ah, there he is." Hamilton plastered on a grin and leaned back in his chair. "Corliss, meet your new partner—the infamous Andreas Ruffner. Ruffner, this is Detective Darren Corliss."

Corliss stood and extended his hand.

I didn't reciprocate. As I nudged the door shut behind me, I sized him up. He did have one edge over my previous partners-slash-babysitters: he was not hard on the eyes. Almost as tall as I was, so probably six one or so. Built like he made religious use of a gym membership. Bit of a baby face, which made me wonder how many dicks he'd sucked to make it through the ranks as quickly as he had; he couldn't have been more than thirty. Maybe a little older if he came from one of those families where everyone kept paintings in the attic and looked twenty until they were sixty.

I eyed his extended hand like he'd offered me a bag of shit. "Corliss, eh? As in—"

"Yes, my stepdad is Commissioner Corliss." He narrowed his eyes a bit and withdrew his hand. "Well, was."

"Was? I hadn't heard that he'd passed."

"He retired, Andreas," Hamilton said with no shortage of irritation.

I bit back a comment about it being a shame the man was still kicking. I did have to ride around with his kid for the foreseeable future, after all. "Well, if you're the son of Commissioner Corliss, I guess there's no need for this introduction, is there?"

"*Step*son," he said. "And no, I can't say he ever mentioned your name to me. Why? Should he have?"

I started to answer, but the boss beat me to it. "Sit down, Ruffner. You too, Corliss."

My new partner and I exchanged glares as we took our seats. I had to admit, he was ballsier than his predecessors. Most of them seemed nervous when they first met me. That usually wore off in short order. Once they realized my reputation for being an asshole was no exaggeration, they went from nervous to exasperated, and that was fine by me. The sooner they got sick of me, the sooner they were back in here begging Hamilton to be reassigned.

Hamilton had played a wild card this time, though. Corliss was the stepson of a man who blamed me for a significant portion of his gray hair, assuming he had any of it left. While my partner apparently hadn't heard my name, he wasn't nervous or intimidated.

Of course he's got brass balls—they belong to IA. Along with his eyes and ears.

Just what I need.

Hamilton cleared his throat. "You two can get to know each other while you're out on the streets. All you need to know right now is that you're both top-notch cops, and if you can work *together*"—he shot me a warning glare—"then this will work out nicely."

"We'll see about that," I grumbled.

Corliss said nothing.

Hamilton rubbed his forehead, probably exhausted from refereeing the two of us. Then he dropped his hand to his desk. "All right. What's on your docket today, Ruffner?"

I fought the urge to steal a glance at Corliss. "I've got a lead on someone who's working with one of the kingpins downtown. Going to see if I can squeeze a few answers out of him."

Hamilton scowled. "And by squeeze a few answers—"

"By the book, Captain." I smiled sweetly. "Of course."

Beside me, Corliss fidgeted, but he didn't speak.

The captain gave his forehead another rub. "You're on thin ice after that last stunt you pulled. Do not test me, Detective."

Corliss cleared his throat. "Uh, what stunt?"

"Never mind," I growled.

"No. If I'm going to be out there with you, I'd like to know what I'm up against."

I turned to him. "Does it matter?"

That baby face didn't seem quite so babyish as he glared right back at me. "It does when 'stunts' happen in an environment that can get a partner killed."

"Gentlemen . . ."

We held each other's gazes for a moment, then turned back to the captain.

"Look." He put up his hands. "You two don't have to like each other, but you will work together. Ruffner, that means playing by the book. Got it?"

"Yes, sir," I said.

"And Corliss, even if he does do something reckless and stupid, he's your partner. Don't get yourself killed, but have his back. Understood?"

Corliss hesitated. Then, "Yes, sir." He said it with just as much enthusiasm as I had.

Well, wasn't this going to be fun?

The captain dismissed us, and we walked in silence toward the stairs. That silence lingered until we were on the landing, and then the bastard spoke just before we started down the next flight.

"That was a pleasant introduction." He didn't even try to hide the sarcasm.

I halted on the landing. So did he. We faced each other, and without the captain here to moderate, there was nothing tempering Corliss's hostile suspicion.

He folded his arms. "You want to tell me what 'stunt' the captain was referring to?"

"It was all blown out of proportion." I started toward the steps again. "Now let's get downtown and—"

He stopped me with a hand on my arm. "Hey. Answer my question."

I glanced at his hand, then stared him dead in the eye.

Oh, it's gonna be like this, huh?

Shrugging out of his grasp, I faced him fully, and couldn't decide if I was impressed or annoyed that he didn't draw back.

"You know, before we head out on the road," I said, "let's maybe get a couple of things straight between us."

He folded his arms again and held eye contact without the slightest flinch. "All right."

"*You're* joining *me* on my investigations," I said through clenched teeth. "Which means we do shit my way. You're the kid. I'm—"

"Oh for fuck's sake." He rolled his eyes and dropped his arms to his sides. "I had this conversation seven years ago with my FTO. Let me see if I still remember." He glared at me as he ticked off points on his fingers. "I'll call you 'sir,' you're in charge, you're going to remind me at every turn that I'm a stupid fucking kid, you're—"

"And you're going to report everything I say and do back to IA."

That prompted a slight but noticeable flinch. "What the hell are you talking about?"

"Do I look stupid to you?"

He cleared his throat, recovering some of his confident exterior. "Look, Captain Hamilton assigned me to you. I didn't exactly request—"

"Cut the crap, Corliss. I don't like having a partner at all, but I especially don't need a wet-behind-the-ears kid for a babysitter. Partners have to trust each other."

"Yeah?" He swallowed. "So why don't you start by trusting me?"

"Because I know IA was in there with you and the captain before I came in."

Another flinch. Subtler than before, but not subtle enough to slip past me. "So, what? You think I told them where you're keeping your secret weapons stash? Where you buried Jimmy Hoffa?" Despite his momentary loss of confidence, the arrogant little shit smirked. "I just met you. What would you expect me to tell—"

"It's not what you told them," I growled. "I know they're investigating me. Unofficially, of course." I stepped closer, and though he kept his feet planted, he leaned back a satisfying inch. "So let's be clear right now: if I can't trust you to have my back, if you're going to be too busy watching me and taking notes, then this isn't going to work."

"Then why don't you start by telling me what the fuck has you on thin ice with the department? Because if I can't trust you out there, then I will happily go back up *there*"—he gestured sharply up the stairs—"and ask to be reassigned. I don't give two shits if you're the asshole everyone says you are. I just want to know, here and now, if you're going to play by the book, or if you're going to get me killed."

I blinked. This was definitely not the breed of partner I'd had in the past.

Before I could speak, he snarled, "You obviously don't like me already. So tell me now, how do I know *you'll* have *my* back?"

"Because you're my partner."

"Yeah? So?"

I fought the urge to roll my eyes. Or, failing that, grab him by the shoulders and shake some sense into him. "You know how many partners I've had, Detective?"

"Eleven is the last count, I think."

"Twelve. And do you know how many of them have been injured or killed on my watch?"

He gulped. "Uh . . ."

"None." I reached for my hip, and he flinched. "Relax, idiot. I'm not going for my gun."

He eyed me uncertainly, and he sure as hell didn't relax.

I tugged my shirt free from my waistband, and lifted it just enough to reveal the long, jagged scar above my belt. "You want to know how that happened?"

He nodded.

"My 'partner' was too busy keeping an eye on me and didn't notice our suspect was armed."

Corliss's eyes widened.

"He missed a six-inch hunting knife." I pointed emphatically at the scar. "The six-inch hunting knife didn't miss me."

"So, how does that answer my question?"

"Because it wasn't the first time that partner nearly got me killed by focusing more on me than the situation. But even after he got me fucking stabbed, I saved his ass three months later." The memory made my skin crawl, but I forced my voice to remain solid. "He lost his situational awareness and was about to take a bullet to the back, but I took the guy out first. I had to fucking kill someone, and that someone had key information that would have helped my investigation." I tucked in my shirt. "I had to *kill someone*, Detective, because I was watching my partner's back even after he'd failed to watch mine and nearly got me killed." I leaned in closer, deliberately encroaching on Corliss's personal space. "Does that answer your question?"

His Adam's apple jumped. "Y-yeah."

"Good. So we can move on and quit with this bullshit."

Corliss nodded.

Once again silent, we continued down the stairs.

At the bottom, I gestured toward the locker room. "I'm going to get something out of my locker. Meet me in the garage in ten. We've got someone to interview."

He just nodded, and we headed off in separate directions. Five steps later, though, he said, "Oh, Ruffner?"

I turned around, wondering if he knew how badly I wanted to lay him out. "What?"

"Just so we're clear, I'm not calling you sir."

Then he continued toward the garage, leaving me standing there like an idiot.

Yeah. This partnership is going to be great . . .

CHAPTER FOUR
DARREN

Getting some distance from Ruffner made me realize a few things. First, while the man was definitely an asshole, the main thing I was left feeling after our first sterling conversation was guilt. I'd jumped the gun with him, gotten aggressive too quickly, assumed too much. I couldn't exactly blame him for not wanting to take on a new partner when one of them had *literally* gotten him stabbed in the back—or close enough.

There was something about the guy that instantly put me on edge, though. I was good at the long game, and all kidding aside, I knew how to keep my cool during confrontations. But less than ten minutes with Ruffner and I was acting out like a grade schooler. It was something I needed to get a handle on, fast.

The second thing I realized? Glancing back was totally worthwhile—Detective Ruffner had an incredible ass. I wanted to cut those tailored trousers right off his legs.

"Maybe save that for day two," I said to myself as I headed for the garage. "If I survive day one."

It wasn't until I got to the garage that I remembered I didn't know what Ruffner's car looked like. I was stuck waiting at the curb until he showed up, so I pulled out my phone and checked my messages. Three texts: two from Mom, one from Vic. Mom's read, *Good luck today sweetheart!* followed by *Don't listen to your father.*

Vic's just read, *Don't fuck it up, son.* Heartwarming, as usual. Vic wasn't so bad—he treated my mom like gold, as well he should—but he'd never really gotten a handle on how to comfort. I mused texting him back something ridiculous like, *They all love me, I'll be captain by the end of the day*, or even better, the truth: *IA wants me to spy on my partner, who hates me already.* A second later a nondescript sedan screeched to a halt in front of me, and I forgot all about texting. If looks could kill, Ruffner would have just committed murder in the first degree.

"Get in."

I scooted around the front of the car a little warily, still not completely convinced the guy wouldn't run me over just to get me out of the way, and got in. I put my phone away, and he scoffed.

"Sure you can live without it in your hand?" he asked as we pulled out into the drizzly morning.

"I think I'll survive. Sorry," I said with perfect insincerity. "So tell me about the guy we're going to 'talk' to this morning."

"His name is Jake Carter. He's a run-of-the-mill scumbag with slightly more brains than most, which is why he isn't already in a cell." I was a little surprised he'd just answered me without taking the time to throw in an insult or two. "I'm sure something'll turn up at his place to give us reason to bring him in, though. A couple of uniforms are going to meet us there, so you won't even have to dirty your pretty little hands if things get rough."

Aaand there was the insult. "Aw, you think my hands are pretty?" I clasped them in front of my chest. "I'm touched!"

"Touched in the head, maybe."

"I can't imagine why nobody lasts as your partner, with all this sweet talk." My phone buzzed with an incoming text, but I ignored it. "Why do you want to talk to this guy in particular?"

"Because he's connected to Vincent Blake, one of the big players who's losing guys right, left, and center lately. Mostly disappearances at this point, but bodies started turning up a few weeks ago. Nobody's seen Blake in almost a month. There's a shakeup going on, and I want to know who's trying to be the new top dog."

I frowned. "I don't know much about Blake." My phone buzzed again, but I ignored it. "Are there case files I can read to catch up?"

"Sure. Back at the precinct, on my desk." He glanced over at me and smiled. Somehow the expression just made him look angry. And hot. "I can pull over here and you can walk back if you feel like you need some study sessions before you can be helpful."

I can helpfully punch you in the fucking face. Jesus, five minutes in close quarters and he had me on edge again. "I guess I'll just be on hand to keep you from causing another 'incident' then." I smiled back. "I'm a team player." My phone buzzed again. *Shit.*

"You should probably get that. Wouldn't want to make your mommy worry."

I already knew it wasn't my mom. There was only one person it could be, and unfortunately, Ruffner was right. I really didn't want to make him worry. I tried to keep from grimacing while I pulled out my phone and checked the new messages.

Asher: *I'm already an hour late for work and Mom won't even let me out of the house. Did I get drunk last night? Why am I here?*

Asher: *Where the hell is my car?*

Asher: *Darren, call me. Mom and Vic aren't making any sense.*

Another one came in while I was reading, this one actually from my mother. *It's a rough morning for your brother, sweetheart. Come by when you're off work? But don't worry!* Well, shit. The surest way to get someone to worry was to tell them not to.

"You need to run back to the precinct after all?" Ruffner's tone was snarky as ever, but the expression on his face was only half as murderous as it had been a minute ago.

"It's nothing," I said, stowing my phone in my pocket again. I waited for it to buzz, but there were no more incoming messages. Vic must have gotten Asher's phone away from him. I took a slow breath; it was my first day on the new job, and my partner was just waiting for me to screw something up. This wasn't the time for baring my fucking soul. "How long to Carter's place?"

"Not long."

The rest of the ride passed in blessed silence. We stopped in a derelict part of downtown, a subdivision that had fallen apart after the meatpacking plant there shut down ten years ago. There were a few decent places left on the fringes, but the deeper you got, the worse it became. The street felt more like potholes than solid ground, and the cracks in the concrete were all populated with weeds—the only green I saw in any direction. The house we pulled up to had once been a duplex, but the right side of the building was half-collapsed. The left side sported empty flowerboxes and a beater in the driveway. A patrol car was sitting across the street, and two cops got out to meet us.

"Detective," one of them said in a flat voice. "You got an actual reason for dragging us out here?"

"Are drug dealers no longer worth your time, Officer Huan?"

"Only when they're doing something we can actually pin on them," the cop replied. "This guy's been searched before. He always comes up clean."

"Maybe it's time for someone else to do the searching, then," Ruffner said. The cop bristled, but Ruffner was already heading for the door. I followed him, resisting the urge to apologize on his behalf. If I wasn't careful, I'd get all of Ruffner's enemies via osmosis before the week was out.

Ruffner banged on the door. "Carter! Open up."

"Hold your fucking... Just hold on." The door opened a moment later. The man standing in front of us smelled like stale beer and sweat. His T-shirt looked like one big stain, and his hair fell limply over his face. I could see enough of it to make out the guy's smirk, though.

"Deeetective Ruffner," he drawled. "What brings you here on such a..." he glanced up at the sky, "rainy day?"

"I've got a warrant to search the premises, Jake. Go sit down and shut up." Ruffner pushed past the man and headed straight through the living room.

"Nah, don't offer to take your shoes off or nothing," Jake muttered. "Come on in, other cops." He stepped aside. "I'd offer you coffee, except I know you guys can't drink that shit without needing a donut, and I'm fresh out of those."

"Just sit down," Officer Huan said. His silent partner loomed by the door. I pulled on a pair of gloves and headed into the house to join Ruffner.

He seemed busy in the kitchen, so I turned left into the bedroom. It was surprisingly neat, no clothes on the floor or trash anywhere but the trash can. I rummaged through the obvious places, turning over the bedding and looking under the mattress, before moving on to the dresser. Jake's socks were all rolled into individual balls. Shit. Maybe the guy had a split personality or something.

I checked all the drawers, including the balled-up socks, then moved on to the closet. Nothing. The bedside table yielded plenty of tissues and lube, but nothing illegal.

Ruffner met me just as I reentered the hall. "Find anything?" he asked.

"Not in there. You?"

"Not so far, but it's just a matter of time. Try the bathroom next."

The bathroom. Right. Lovely. I stepped into the dingy room across the hall, which was unfortunately not nearly as tidy as the bedroom, and sighed. Toilet first, then.

I'd just finished looking under the sink when I heard a door slam shut. I pushed to my feet and went out to see what was happening, only to watch Ruffner emerging from the bedroom, looking grim and holding something in his hand. *What the hell?* I hadn't missed anything in there. I opened my mouth to ask about it, but Ruffner brushed past me without even pausing and headed back into the living room where Jake and the officers were.

He held up a small, tightly wrapped white brick and waved it in Jake's direction. "In the toe of a sock?" he said scornfully. "I expected better from a clever little fuckup like you."

Jake shot to his feet. "Bullshit!" he shouted. "That's not mine. This is bullshit!"

"When it's nestled in with your tighty-whities, odds are it's yours, Jake." He put the brick down and turned to Officer Huan. "Cuff him."

"Wait," I said, stepping in close. I tried to keep my voice low as I turned to my partner. "Where did you find that?"

"Were you listening for the past minute, or do you have a memory problem?" Ruffner snapped.

I glared at him. "You couldn't have found that in his dresser. I searched it, and there was nothing there."

Ruffner shrugged. "Clearly you didn't search it well enough, Corliss."

"I'm pretty sure I wouldn't have missed a package of fucking heroin."

Ruffner's face darkened, and he stepped in so close I could see tiny flecks of brown in the blue of his eyes. He opened his mouth—

"Fuck *this*!" Jake drove his shoulder into Officer Huan's chest before the cuffs were closed, knocking him back, and ran for the door.

I ran after him. Getting the truth out of Ruffner could wait.

CHAPTER FIVE
ANDREAS

I sprinted out the door behind Corliss. Huan and Simmons were ahead of us, and disappeared around a corner.

Before we'd even turned down the alley to find them, I heard a satisfying grunt. Sure enough, when we entered the alley, Huan had Jake flat on the pavement and was cuffing him.

"That shit ain't mine!" Jake screamed. "I'm being fucking framed, man! That ain't—"

"Shut it," Huan growled. "If it isn't yours, then why did you run?"

Jake glared at me with murder in his bloodshot eyes. To Huan, he said, "I'm being *framed*, man."

"That's for the DA to decide, not me." Huan tightened the cuffs and stood, hauling Jake to his feet. "Jacob Carter, you're under arrest for possession of an illegal narcotic. You have the right to remain silent..."

And that was when the short run caught up with me.

My knees wobbled and the edges of my vision darkened.

"Detective?" Simmons said. "You all right?"

I waved him away. "I'm good. Get him out of here. I'll ask him some questions at the station."

"Will do."

They started walking away, Huan still reading Jake his rights and Jake still insisting he was being framed, and I hoped their voices were getting quieter because of the increasing distance, not because I was passing out. My ears felt like they were stuffed with cotton—everything was muted and far away.

I planted a hand against the wall and breathed slowly, willing the dizziness to pass and the tunnel vision to clear. This new set of pills was screwing me all up. What was going to happen come summer? It was cool and drizzly today, but before the weather turned hot, I needed to get some—

"You sure you're okay?" Corliss's voice was somehow even more irritating when filtered through the cotton in my ears.

I squeezed my eyes shut. "You're still here?"

"Well, yeah." Was that sarcasm? Now? Really? "My partner starts wobbling after a half-block foot chase? I'm not about to leave you alone."

I blinked my vision into focus and glared at him. The edges were still black and sparkling, and I kept my palm against the wall so my balance wouldn't waver any further. "I'm fine. Look after the suspect."

Corliss didn't move. "He's in good hands. You want to tell me what's going on here?" He nodded toward my hand on the wall. "This have something to do with that?"

I looked the direction he'd indicated, and my stomach lurched. My silver medic alert bracelet was peeking out from under my sleeve. I jerked my arm back and tugged my sleeve down over the bracelet.

"Talk to me, Ruffner." Corliss stepped closer. "Because if you can't even run half a block without—"

"I'll be fine." I gave my sleeve another tug, then turned and headed out of the alley. "Now let's get Carter back to—"

"No."

I stopped and turned around. "Pardon me?"

"Before we go anywhere, I want some answers." He closed the distance I'd created, and looked me right in the eye. "One, I want to know if I'm going to be able to count on you if a suspect runs. And two—" he stabbed a finger toward Carter's house "—I want to know where the fuck that heroin came from."

"Funny," I said, and stepped closer to him. "I've got some questions about that too. You said you already searched the bedroom, but you didn't find it? How thoroughly did you search it, *Detective*?"

"Don't try to gas-light me, Ruffner," he snarled back. "I searched it, and I searched it thoroughly. So you tell me—where the hell did it come from?"

"Exactly where I said it came from. And while we're on the subject, don't ever question me in front of a suspect. You want to tag along on my investigation? You play by my rules."

"I'll play by your rules, but not if it means breaking every code of police ethics."

"Yeah, and ethic code number one—you don't throw your partner under the bus in front of a suspect." I turned to walk away again. "Now let's get the fuck out of here. We need to get down to the station and get a statement from him."

I fully expected him to call after me or run up and continue our conversation on the way back to the house. Instead, he muttered something under his breath, then walked back with me in silence.

I just ground my teeth and stared straight ahead.

This was a new record. One hour working together and I already wanted to choke him.

Huan and his partner showed Jake to the interrogation room.

Corliss and I watched him through the two-way glass for a moment.

"You can come in with me if you want to," I said. "But keep your fucking mouth shut."

"Why's that?" he asked under his breath. "He already knows I searched the bedroom before you found the brick. So do—"

"Consider this your first lesson in being a detective," I hissed. "Come in with me, keep your mouth shut, and when we're done, we'll see if you learned anything."

I didn't give him a chance to respond before I headed into the room. He followed and closed the door behind us.

Ignoring Corliss—and hoping he understood I wasn't kidding about keeping his trap shut—I took the chair opposite Jake and sat down. Corliss stayed back. Against the wall to my right, judging by the flick of Jake's eyes.

Jake studied both of us. "So, you got a new good cop for your good cop/bad cop routine, eh, Ruffner?"

"How do you know he's the good cop?"

"Because you always play bad cop."

I laughed. "Just remember, my friend—no matter how bad I am, there's always someone worse than me." I twisted around to glance at Corliss. He stood against the wall, arms folded and jaw tight. His eyes were gleaming with fury. Jake didn't need to know that fury was directed at me.

Facing the suspect again, I folded my hands on the cold metal table. "We need some answers, Jake."

He snorted, trying to look nonchalant, but his eyes kept darting toward Corliss. "If you want to know where that shit came from, I don't know. It ain't fucking mine, man. I'm *clean* now."

"Then where did that brick come from?"

"You tell me!" He threw up his hands. "It ain't mine, you fucking moron!"

I watched him silently for a moment, making a deliberate gesture of drumming my nails on the table so it echoed in the uncomfortable silence. "Possession *is* nine-tenths of the law."

He pinched the bridge of his nose. "I'm being set up. I'm fucking being set up." He dropped his hand to the table with a hard *smack*. "Why can't you see that?"

I shrugged as flippantly as possible. "It isn't my decision to make. I found the dope, and I brought you in. All I can do now is decide whether or not to charge you."

"Yeah?" He narrowed his eyes. "So since you already know it isn't mine, what do I have to do to not get charged? Suck your dick?" He glanced at Corliss. "Or yours?"

It took every ounce of self-control I had not to snicker. The horror on Corliss's face just then must have been priceless, but I didn't dare turn around to see.

Jake looked to me again. "I'm not playing your games. That shit wasn't mine, and—"

"Here's the deal, Jake." I stood and leaned over my hands on the table to loom above him. I already had a few inches on him anyway, and was using every last one to my advantage. As he drew back, gulping, I said, "It's not up to me to decide if that powder was yours. Unless you can prove it's not"—I shrugged—"I have to assume it is, and I'm going to charge you with felony possession."

His eyes were huge. "But I—"

I put a hand up. "Then it's up to the DA to decide. And if she's not feeling particularly charitable toward someone with an established pattern of possession, well . . ." I made a dismissive gesture before planting my hand on the table again. "You're going to be doing time. A lot of time. Am I clear?"

He clenched his jaw. "I want a lawyer."

Corliss moved behind me, and I put up a hand. Never taking my eyes off Jake, I said, "Wait."

"He wants a lawyer," Corliss said coldly.

"Yeah. I know he does." I turned around. "And I'm not quite ready to throw the poor kid to the wolves yet. Are you?"

Corliss narrowed his eyes.

Jake's chair creaked. "What do you mean, throw me to the wolves?"

I faced him again. "Listen, we both know how this city treats junkies and dealers, right?"

He nodded slowly.

"Right. And this isn't your first time being brought in on possession. In my line of work, we call that a pattern."

His jaw went slack. "What? Man, I told you, that shit isn't—"

"Then start talking," I growled. "You have two choices here, kid. One, you want that lawyer, so this meeting is over and you're in the hands of the legal system. You know, the same one that booked your brother for twelve years for selling weed."

Jake wrung his hands on the table. "What's my other choice?"

"Your other choice is you do some talking. You tell me what I want to know."

He narrowed his eyes and folded his arms across his chest, probably so I wouldn't notice how much they were shaking. Too late.

"You're bluffing," he said. "Just like the fucker who did my brother in. You're just going to throw me in prison one way or the other, so what do I care if you get what you want?"

"Ruffner." Corliss stepped closer. "We have to get him a lawyer."

"Not yet." I held Jake's gaze. "You still want that lawyer, Jake? Or do you want a shot at not doing hard time for some powder in your underwear drawer?"

His Adam's apple jumped again. His chest rose and fell rapidly, and sweat gleamed along his hairline. For a moment, I thought he might cry.

Then he set his jaw. "What do you want?"

Slowly, eyes never leaving his, I sat back down and folded my hands again. "I want Blake, and I want the people he's answering to."

Some color drained from Jake's face. "I don't know where he is. Nobody does."

"No, but you know his chain of command. You know people who do know where he is." I leaned forward. "I want names, I want locations, and I want every fucking thing you know about how these people are connected to him. Especially the people above him."

He broke eye contact and fidgeted. Arms folded tightly across his chest, he gnawed his lip, twitching like a jonesing junkie.

I sighed. "All right. I'm done. Corliss, get him his lawyer and—"

"Wait!" Jake deflated. "Okay. Okay. But I want something from you."

I said nothing, but held his gaze and waited for him to go on.

He glanced at Corliss, fidgeting nervously. To me, he said, "Blake's people—they know where my girlfriend and son live. They've told me a million times if I talk to the police, they'll . . ." What little color remained slipped out of his face. "Man, this is my kid."

"I can make arrangements. Tell me where they are, and I'll make sure they're all right."

"No bullshit? Nobody will find them?"

"I'll do everything I can."

"Like, witness protection?"

I nodded. "Help me out, and I'll send you with them." The guys at the US Marshals office would be thrilled that I was sending more people their way, but they owed me some favors, so fuck 'em.

"Okay." Jake took a deep breath. "I'll talk."

Almost two hours later, Corliss and I stepped out of the interrogation room. On the legal tablet in my hand were several pages of detailed information that I'd been trying to get my hands on for months. Names of people connected to the drug ring and the coveted people on high. Just as I'd suspected, everything happening was *way* above Vincent Blake's pay grade. Jake didn't know all the names, but he gave me more than I'd had. It was a damn good start after weeks of spinning my tires.

"How the hell does he know all of that?" Corliss asked. "I thought he was just some two-bit junkie or delivery boy."

"No. He's a lot higher on the food chain than he'd like anyone to know."

"But how did *you* know?"

"Got a tip from an informant a while back. Jake's always been pretty good at keeping his fingerprints off things and making himself look like a small fish. That's why it took so fucking long to get a search warrant."

Corliss held my gaze, his features taut, but he didn't push. The questions were in his eyes. He wasn't stupid. Definitely smarter than I'd given him credit for. That could be a good thing or a bad thing for me: stupid could get me killed, but smart could get me hemmed up.

He cleared his throat. "So what now?"

"Now, I hold up my end of the deal and get in touch with the Marshals about putting Jake and his family under protection." I tapped the notepad in my hand. "Then we start following up on these leads until we collar Blake and his superiors."

"I thought he *was* the kingpin, though."

"You're supposed to think that."

"Oh." Corliss's eyes lost focus. He seemed rattled. Like a rookie after his first time dodging bullets on a routine call gone bad. At some point during the interview with Jake, the hostility had vanished in favor of this uneasiness, as if he'd put the pieces together and realized that regardless of how I'd gotten Jake into that interrogation room, I was getting answers out of him.

He exhaled. "So, um. What should I do?"

I'd recommend having a drink.

I was about to suggest that he could look up some of the addresses Jake had provided and make sure they were legit, but right then Officer Huan appeared beside us.

"Hey, Detective," he said to Corliss, and pointed over his shoulder with his thumb. "Captain wants to see you in his office."

Shit. That's not good.

"Oh. Um." Corliss glanced at me.

I nodded.

"Okay," Corliss said. "I'll be right there."

Huan shot me a glare before he walked off.

"Go," I said. "I need to call the Marshals office anyway."

"All right." Corliss and I locked eyes for a long, uneasy moment. Then, without a word, he left.

Thumbing the tablet in my hand, I chewed the inside of my cheek. I had no doubt what was going on. Huan had almost certainly gone straight to Hamilton and told him about the exchange Corliss and I had after I'd come out of Jake's bedroom with the pack of heroin.

Now would be a good time to prove you won't throw your partner under the bus, Corliss.

CHAPTER SIX
DARREN

My steps dragged as I made my way to Captain Hamilton's office. It wasn't even noon yet and I was already in trouble. That had to be some sort of record. Probably even Ruffner hadn't managed to land himself in hot water this fast after getting promoted to detective. Not that it was my goddamn fault.

I hadn't missed the heroin. I knew that. I'd searched enough people, cars, and houses during my years on the beat to learn the importance of being thorough. So either Ruffner was lying about where he'd found it in the room, or . . . shit. I didn't want to get into the *or*.

But this was what I'd been told to do—watch out for Ruffner's shady behavior. There wasn't much shadier than producing drugs out of thin air and pinning them on a guy who insisted he was being framed. That and not immediately going for a lawyer when Jake said he wanted one. I'd spent too many years listening to Asher bitch about due process to take that without blinking.

Marla shook her head as I walked up. "Jesus, Darren, you didn't waste any time raising hell, did you?"

I tried for a smile. Judging from the skeptical look on her face, she didn't buy it. "In my defense, I had help."

"That's a terrible defense."

"Marla, set Corliss loose already, I need to talk to him *now*!" Captain Hamilton called out.

She pursed her lips but nodded. "You heard him. Go grovel."

"In these pants? Never." That got a reluctant smile from her, but nobody was smiling once I walked inside the office.

"Shut the door and sit down."

I obeyed. Hamilton folded his hands on the desk and stared at me from under his bushy eyebrows for a long moment. I resisted the urge to drum my fingers against the armrests of the chair.

"What the hell happened at Carter's place?"

"Can you be more specific?"

"Don't get smart with me," Hamilton growled. "Officer Huan reported that you and Ruffner had an argument about where he found the drugs that were used to justify bringing Carter in. It sounds like things got heated. I want to know what really happened."

This was it. This was the fork in the road, two possible futures splitting off in opposite directions. If I told Hamilton what I thought had happened, he'd have Thibedeau back down here in under a minute. It would be the beginning of the end of my partnership with Ruffner, and I'd be just one more in a long line of people who hadn't been able to hack it with the guy. Possibly the last one, depending on what they found out when they dug deeper. Did I want to do that? Was I ready to throw more fuel onto Internal Affairs' bonfire?

"I made a mistake."

Hamilton frowned. Looked like I'd surprised him. "What do you mean?"

"I mean I should have been more thorough in my search of Carter's room. I must have missed the drugs, and then I reacted badly when Detective Ruffner retrieved them. It was unprofessional, and I apologize."

"I've never known you to miss evidence before."

"Rough morning," I said with a grimace I didn't even have to fake. "Mom sent me a message about Asher."

Hamilton sighed. "Damn it, Darren. You can't let yourself get distracted in the field by what's going on at home, you know that. Victor can handle it. That's what he's there for." The captain was one of the few people who knew the real reason my stepfather had retired when he did. My mother couldn't deal with my brother's bad days on her own anymore. "Your partner—and I can't believe I'm saying this about Ruffner, given his track record—needs to be able to depend on you. You can't fuck up the trust between you two, not for no good reason." *Like Internal Affairs*, he didn't quite say.

"You're totally right."

"No more fuckups."

"No more." I slashed a quick X over my chest. "Cross my heart."

"What are you, five? Just don't do it again."

"I won't." We stared at each other for a moment. "Are we done here, sir?"

"Yeah, yeah." He sat back and waved me away. "Get back to work."

Music to my ears. I stood up and left with a little nod to Marla, who looked relieved. What had she been expecting, that I'd be fired?

No, I needed to be smart about this. Like him or not, Ruffner had gotten information from Jake that might lead to the arrest of one of the city's most notorious drug dealers. It had the potential to be a huge operation, and I wanted in on the ground floor. I hadn't worked my ass off to become a detective so that I could sit on the sidelines.

I didn't believe that Ruffner was telling me everything. I couldn't, not after I knew I hadn't missed that heroin. But I also didn't believe he was the devil that IA thought he was, and I wasn't about to go crying to Thibedeau without rock-solid evidence. I needed to work on building a rapport with Ruffner, as hair-pullingly awful as that was going to be.

I'd start with a peace offering.

Ruffner's desk wasn't hard to find. It was set back in a corner of the bull pen, close to the doors. The only other desk anywhere near it was mostly bare, with just a computer and a tray for files on top of it. Mine, I supposed. Even though my day had started off bad and gotten worse, I smiled. I had my own *desk.* That was so cool.

Ruffner looked up just in time to catch the Snickers bar I lobbed at him. He glanced from it to me, his perma-glare turned on high. "What the hell's this?"

"It's a candy bar. I thought you might have low blood sugar," I said as I pulled out my chair. "Judging from your dizzy spell earlier." I sat down, and the chair immediately listed to the side. Shit, it was missing a wheel. *Great.*

"I don't have low blood sugar." He tossed the bar back to me.

"That's good to know." I threw it at him again. "Keep it anyway, it's delicious. Lunch of champions."

"A Snickers bar isn't a fucking *lunch*." Nevertheless, he put it down on his desk. I considered it a win. "You're worse than my kids."

Ooh, there was an opening, but I didn't have time to grab it.

"So." Ruffner sat back in his chair. "Should I be expecting a call from the captain?"

"I don't know. Does he usually call you at lunchtime?"

"Don't be a fucking smart-ass, Corliss. You know what I'm asking about."

Yeah, I guess I did. "He won't be calling you."

Judging from the way his brow went up, I'd actually managed to surprise him. "Is that right?"

"Yep. I've always been really good at owning up to mistakes," I said brightly. *Even when they're not mine.* "I'm not so sure that you are, though."

"What the hell is that supposed to mean?"

"It means I'd like to know why you almost fell over when chasing after a suspect." I held up a hand before he could shout at me. "I don't need the details. That's your business. I just need to know what to expect in the future so I won't look for you when chasing down a suspect and find you collapsed on the pavement half a block away."

Ruffner's eyes looked tired. "I've got it under control."

"Really?" I didn't expect my prodding to work, but to my surprise, he didn't tell me to fuck off.

"I'm *getting* it under control," Ruffner clarified. "If for some reason I don't manage to soon, I'll let you know." He smirked. "If you're still around by then."

"Oh, I'm not going anywhere." I carefully shifted around so that my chair tilted upright again. "How'd the call to the Marshals go?"

"Fine. They're moving Carter's family into protective custody. Carter'll go with them once I'm sure we've got all we need from him."

"No issues with the DA's office on that?"

"Not if his leads pan out. They know how to prioritize their targets, and Blake is the biggest target around these days."

"Maybe he is," I said. "Or maybe not. You said his people have been going missing, right?"

"Missing or dead."

"How were they killed?"

"For the most part? Execution style." Ruffner raised a hand and sighted along it like he was pointing a gun at me. "*Pow.* Single shot to the head."

I frowned. "Jesus, this isn't New York or Chicago. Since when have we had Mafia-style killings here?"

"Gangs don't have to be the Mafia to run themselves professionally, although the smart guys organize them that way. You heard Jake—Blake's people have been keeping tabs on his family. If he steps out of line, they pay the price. When you've got leverage on everyone, all you've got to do is maintain the balance to get them to do what you want."

He was right. That was part of what made the drugs he'd found at Jake's place so strange. The guy was used to being careful—he had to be, to keep his family safe. For him to jeopardize them by keeping heroin in his house, if not in his fucking underwear drawer . . .

Something didn't add up. But I'd never figure out what that was if I didn't play along. "It sounds like a lot of his people might be caught between a rock and a hard place."

Ruffner's expression darkened. "It's still their fault. At some point they made a bad decision, and they get to deal with the fallout. Nobody can just wish that shit away."

"But you'd be willing to offer more of these people a deal if they get us closer to Blake."

Ruffner shrugged. "It depends on what they give us. I can't protect everybody like I am Jake. A lot of these guys, they're scum, murderers. They wouldn't take a deal even if I *did* offer it, and I'd rather see most of them laid out on a fucking slab."

Holy shit. "There's not a lot of middle ground in you, is there?"

"There's no such thing as a middle ground most of the time. You either shoot or get shot. You take them down, or they take you down. I haven't survived almost twenty years as a detective by giving criminals the benefit of a doubt." He sounded grim. I guess I couldn't blame him. Still . . .

"But you think more of them might be willing to talk?"

"Maybe." He tapped the list. "Let's find out."

ANDREAS

For a solid hour after Corliss came out of Captain Hamilton's office, I was on edge. As we cross-referenced names and information from Jake's statement, I was so convinced my phone was going to ring, I practically hallucinated the sound.

But the call never came. In fact, when I stepped out briefly to go to the locker room, I passed the captain in the hallway. Aside from a quick look and a grunt, he barely acknowledged my presence. My curiosity was killing me as I went through the motions of taking my pill and tucking away the bottle. What had the two of them talked about? How much did Corliss know? Or rather, how much did he think he knew?

No idea. As far as I could tell, though, he hadn't thrown me under the bus. If he had, then the captain and Thibedeau were keeping the card close to their vests. Maybe holding on to it until they had enough to send me out the door with IA's boot up my ass. I wouldn't put it past Thibedeau to play like that. He'd been after my badge and my hide for years.

There was no way I would ever get them to tip their hand, though. If I wanted to feel out what was happening, I had only one potential source of information: my new partner.

When I got back to my desk, I picked up my jacket off my chair. "Let's take a break. Go get something to eat."

He looked up from the copy of Jake's statement. "Huh?"

"Eat. You know, food?" I draped my jacket over my arm. "You were right. Blood sugar's getting a little low."

He eyed me uncertainly. His gaze flicked toward the candy bar that was still on my desk, wrapped and untouched. I thought he might object, but then he muttered something, closed the folder on the statement, and got up. "You driving, or am I?"

"I always drive."

"Of course you do," he grumbled, but he picked up his jacket and followed me out to the garage. Once we were in the car, there was no chance of anyone overhearing us unless IA had him wearing a wire. Not that I would have put that past them. Either way, I didn't speak yet.

Two blocks from the station, though, Darren broke the silence. "So, now that we're alone. Where did the heroin come from?"

I almost choked on my own breath. "What?"

"Don't play stupid." He turned to me and coolly asked again, "Where did the heroin in Jake's bedroom come from?"

I shot him a glare before returning my focus to the road. "Captain Hamilton wants to know, eh?"

"No. I answered his questions already. Now I want *you* to answer *mine*." He shifted around so he was facing me as much as the seat belt would allow. "Because here's the thing: I got called into the captain's office, had to listen to him read me the riot act, and I looked like a fucking idiot rookie who doesn't know how to do his job—all because I was covering *your* ass."

I glanced at him again. He'd covered my ass? Well, that would explain the lack of an angry summons from the captain. Maybe I was wrong about this kid.

"So," Corliss went on, "since I took the heat for whatever the hell happened back there, I think I'm entitled to an answer or two."

Still guarded, I said nothing.

He huffed sharply. "For fuck's sake, Ruffner, we—"

"Andreas."

Beat. "Huh?"

"Listen." I tapped my thumbs on the wheel. "If we're going to be partners, we might as well be on a first-name basis. So . . . Andreas."

"Oh. Um. Fine. Then call me Darren. But don't change the subject."

"I'm not changing the subject. Here's the thing, Darren—we should be on a first-name basis, and we should trust each other."

"Right. That's what I'm getting at."

"I'm not done." I paused to take a left onto a narrow two-lane street. Traffic was thicker here, so I slowed down, and as I matched the speed of the car in front of me, I glanced at Corliss—Darren—again. "One thing you need to trust me on is that I won't jeopardize your life or your career. If I'm on the wrong side of the people we're trying to collar, it's me in the crosshairs, not you. And if IA or the captain decides to come down on me, it's my ass, not yours."

My skin prickled. Though I didn't look at him, I could feel him watching me.

"So, what?" he said after a moment. "You're not going to tell me where the dope came from because then I have plausible deniability?"

"Call it whatever you want." I shrugged. "But if the captain or that son of a bitch in IA ever ask you questions, you can look them in the eye and say you don't know. They can give you a fucking polygraph, and you'll still come out looking like Detective Perfect. And if I have to take the heat for something, it's me, not you."

Darren exhaled, but didn't push. I knew better than to assume this was the end of it. He was smarter than I'd initially given him credit for, and I suspected he was working out a strategy to get past my defenses to the answers he wanted.

Dig all you want, Detective. You're going to need more than a day to get that out of me.

I pulled up in front of a café I frequented and shut off the engine. We both took off our seat belts, but neither of us opened our doors.

Facing me across the console, Darren said, "Let's get one thing clear."

"All right?"

"You can't have it both ways—either you trust me and we work together, or you leave me out of the loop. And don't feed me bullshit about plausible deniability. Either we work together or we don't."

I looked him right in the eye. "You can call it bullshit all you want. At the end of the day—"

"At the end of the day, you either trust me or you don't."

"I don't even know you," I threw back.

"But you already know I'll take the heat to keep you out of trouble. Could you at least tell me what it is I'm hiding from the captain?"

I studied him. He was right to want to know, but he was also right that I didn't trust him. Not yet. It was much too early, and he was in much too tight with IA.

Exhaling, I took the keys out of the ignition and twisted to rest my elbow on the center console. "Listen, I've spent a lot of years trying to bring down the assholes we're investigating. In the beginning, I played by the book."

"I find that hard to believe."

"We'll see how conventional you are in twenty years. Anyway, I tried doing things on the straight and narrow, and nothing came of it. And all that time, I was going to crime scenes for people who'd died as a result of these fuckers and others like them. Addicts. Bystanders. Women. Kids." I paused. "You ever been to the scene of a crime after someone murdered kids to keep a father quiet?"

Darren gulped and shook his head.

"Give it time. And when it happens, you'll understand why I'm willing to push the envelope if it means getting these people off the streets for good."

He stared at me, but said nothing.

I gestured past him at the café. "Come on. We need to snag a table before this place starts getting crowded."

We got out of the car, and Darren didn't say anything or even look at me. Whether that meant I'd gotten through to him or he was just tired of my shit, I didn't know, but at least that conversation was over for the moment.

The silence continued until after we'd ordered our food. The waiter took our menus, and Darren stared into his water glass.

"So, um." He cleared his throat and met my gaze. "You mentioned you have kids."

Thank God. He'd let the subject drop. I nodded. "Yeah. I've got four."

His eyebrows jumped. "*Four?*"

I laughed. "Is that so hard to believe?"

"No, uh . . . I just, I mean . . ." He shook his head. "You didn't have any pictures of them on your desk or anything."

Good save, kid.

"I don't usually put pictures of my kids on display in a place where we occasionally escort violent criminals."

He sobered. "Oh. Yeah. I . . . hadn't thought about that."

"Neither did I until a few years ago." I paused for a drink. "What about you? Any kids?"

Darren shook his head. "No. I mostly help my mom take care of—" He broke eye contact. "I don't really have much time for relationships, let alone kids. So, it's just me." He paused, then forced a smile as he looked at me again. "So how old are they? Your kids, I mean?"

I was curious about what he'd stopped himself from saying, but he obviously didn't want to go there, so I played along. "Twenty-four, twenty-two, twenty-one, and four."

"Wow." He chuckled cautiously. "Bit of a gap there before that last one."

"Yeah." I picked up my glass and avoided Darren's eyes. "Bit of a gap." I took a swig of water, hoping he would also recognize the signs of a subject that didn't need to continue.

He sat up a little and folded his arms on the table. "So, I have a question. Might be a bit personal, but I'm curious."

Eyeing him, I said, "All right?"

He glanced down at my wrist, and I knew the question before he asked it: "Seriously. What's the deal with the medic-alert thing?" He showed his palms. "You don't have to go into detail. But, like I said before, I should know if—"

"Like *I* said before," I said through my teeth, "I'm getting it under control."

"Yeah, well, it's obviously not under control yet, so could we please cut the crap?" He tilted his head. "Look, I'm not trying to pry. I'm not looking for gossip. But, I mean, if you drop and I've got to call the paramedics for you, what do I tell them? That you're diabetic? That you're a fucking reptilian? I mean, throw me a bone here."

"Well, if something happens"—I gestured at the bracelet—"you know where to get the information."

He exhaled sharply. "Awesome. So my partner is a damn fortune cookie. All I have to do is crack him open and I can read the secret message."

Our eyes locked.

And we both laughed.

Normally, it annoyed the shit out of me when people noticed the bracelet, never mind asked about it, and he'd been pushing for it ever since he'd seen it at Jake's house. But I had to admit, the fortune-cookie thing was pretty funny.

I pushed the bracelet under my sleeve. "Just some seriously low blood pressure. That's why I got dizzy when we ran after Jake."

Darren's eyebrow rose. Mirroring me, he folded his arms on the table and leaned closer, still holding my gaze. "Let me ask you something, then."

"Okay?"

He pointed at his face. "Do I look like the biggest moron who ever walked the earth?"

"Is that a baited question?"

"Whatever." He sat back. "All right, if I have to call the paramedics, I'll take a look. But honestly, I'm just trying to make sure I know how to help you if you get fucked up."

"Much appreciated."

"So is this how every conversation is going to go?" He absently ran his finger around the rim of his glass. "I'm going to have to pry every detail out of you?"

I chuckled. "Consider it practice for when you're interrogating a suspect."

He just shook his head and let it go.

CHAPTER EIGHT
DARREN

Turns out, the best part of the whole fucking day was lunch.

I hadn't imagined that *Andreas* would invite me to use his first name on our first day, not after the rough beginning. He wasn't exactly forthcoming about anything else, but I was starting to get a sense for the guy. If strong and silent was an archetype, then he was its embodiment. Couple that with his mysterious family life—four kids, and the oldest one was only a few years younger than me? Crazy—and the medical issue that I wouldn't get to know about until it was maybe too late, and I sort of felt like I was working less with a detective, and more with an undercover superhero or something. The dark, gritty, complete asshole kind of superhero.

The food at the café was good, the coffee was strong, and by the time we returned to the precinct, I was feeling cautiously optimistic about my future. We could learn to tolerate each other. Andreas would begin to trust me. I'd get my answers, and we'd get a lot of good work done in the process.

Unfortunately, the afternoon lacked both the energy of the morning and the comradery of lunch. The culprit? Paperwork. It's not that I didn't know going into being a detective that there was a lot of paperwork associated with it, but once we got back to our desks, Andreas went to do more work with getting Jake into witness protection, while me? I read case files.

"You said you wanted to catch up," Andreas said after plunking the stack of files down on my barren desk. "Knock yourself out."

By the end of the day, I *wanted* to knock myself out. Parsing through tiny type, looking at pictures of murders so graphic they would turn anybody's stomach, seasoning my brain with conflicting witness statements and sketchy timelines, all while actively keeping my chair from tipping over for four hours—it was like being plunged into a bureaucratic hellscape. Andreas was long gone once I finally finished up with the files.

As I left work, I felt beat to shit, mentally and physically. I wanted nothing more than to head back to my tiny apartment, shower for as long as the hot water held out, and binge-watch *Brooklyn Nine-Nine*. Screw dramas, I needed a comedy right now. But that wasn't in the cards. Instead, I had a quick shower at the precinct, threw on my gym clothes, and drove out to the suburbs, where Mom, Vic, and Asher lived in the house I'd done most of my growing up in.

I frowned as I pulled up to the seventies-era, ranch-style home. The hanging plants looked like they hadn't been watered in days. Mom was usually really good about that kind of thing—she babied her plants. I walked up the steps to the front door, surreptitiously hefting one of the plants as I did. Way too light—the soil was probably dry as a bone. I tried to open the front door, but it was locked. Weird.

"Mom?" I called out as I let myself in. "Vic?"

"I'm in the kitchen, sweetheart."

I followed the well-worn hall to the back of the house. Mom was putting Saran Wrap over a casserole dish, but she stopped when she saw me. "Darren!" She opened her arms for a hug. "How was your first day?"

For a moment, I wanted to tell her the truth. *It sucked. It sucked so hard.* But I looked closely at her face, saw the red eyes and the lack of mascara that meant she'd been crying, and decided that no matter how bad my day had been, hers had probably been worse.

"It was fine," I said, stepping into her embrace. I had almost a foot of height on her, but I still felt smaller than her somehow whenever she hugged me. Safer. "I met my new partner, arrested a few guys, managed to only make Captain Hamilton yell at me twice. It was a good day."

"That man." My mother sighed as she stepped back, her hands still resting on my arms. "It's a wonder his blood pressure isn't through the roof."

"It might be, you should hear Marla talk about it." Movement at the door caught my eye. "Hey, Vic. Everybody says hi."

He scoffed, lumbering into the kitchen with a sigh. Vic wasn't much taller than my mother, but he was a barrel-chested, broad-shouldered beast of a guy. He'd been a state champion wrestler in high school, and had taught me how to handle myself way better than the academy ever could have. "What everybody? I've been gone for a whole month. They've all forgotten me by now."

"Oh, honey." My mom turned to kiss him, which he accepted with a little grumble. "Nobody could ever forget you."

"Eh." He shrugged and opened the fridge for a beer. "Maybe they should. I've forgotten all about them."

I coughed, throwing a muted "*Bullshit*" into my throat-clearing.

"Yeah, yeah, smart-ass." Vic handed me a beer as well, and we clinked the necks of the bottles together. "Here's to surviving your first day as a detective, son. I hope you enjoyed it. That shit won't get any easier."

"Truth," I muttered before taking a sip. "So how's Asher?"

The complete silence wasn't at all reassuring. Mom broke first. "He had a confusing morning, sweetheart. He got a hold of his phone somehow and called in to the office, and when they said he didn't work there anymore he . . . well, he got upset. He tried to leave, and when we said he couldn't, he got a little . . ."

"He almost broke his hand punching a damn wall," Vic said. "He hasn't come out of his room since before noon."

"I set some dinner aside for both of you, if you want to go and eat with him." My mom sounded hopeful. "I'm sure he'd love to see you."

Usually, Asher did. Tonight might not be one of those nights, but I wanted to see him anyway.

"Yeah, I'll take him some dinner." I grabbed the plates, and another beer as well, then walked back down the hall to the room that Asher and I had once shared. I banged on the door with my foot. "Open up, nerd. I've got food." Nothing. I banged again. "Open the damn door before I dump your plate on the ground and keep your beer for myself." Still nothing. "Asher! C'mon, man, open the fucking—" The door swung open before I could knock my foot against it again.

"You," my older brother said as he took a plate out of my hands, "are a whiny bitch, you know that?"

"So I've been told. Repeatedly, over the years." I stepped inside, and he closed the door behind me. The room looked . . . strange. I could never quite get over the transformation it had undergone, all our teenage paraphernalia thrown out to make room for as much of Asher's adult life as our parents could cram in here. His framed degrees were hung above the desk on the far wall—both from pre-law and law school. There were pictures on the walls of people I barely knew: coworkers from when he was with the DA, college friends, trips to places I'd only ever heard about. Of the two of us, Asher was the ambitious one, the guy who was going places. I'd busted my ass to make detective, but he'd been on track for greater things.

Now he couldn't even remember what he'd had for breakfast most days. Early-onset Alzheimer's, the doctors called it. It was genetic, probably passed down from our absentee father, the bastard. Asher had been diagnosed when he was thirty-three, five years older than I was now. It had been the end of his career and his marriage. It had almost been the end of his life.

I sat down at the desk chair, and he mirrored me on the bed. He was wearing suit pants and a button-down shirt, both way nicer than anything I owned, but the shirt was buttoned wrong. I resisted pointing it out. His right hand was wrapped with gauze across the knuckles. "So. You got into a fight with a wall and lost. Pussy."

"Shut up," Asher said, but he didn't sound too upset. "I guess I did. I was angry about work." He chuckled, and shit, *now* he sounded upset. "I didn't remember that I don't have it anymore."

"But you do now?"

"At the moment."

"Good."

"For a given value of good."

"Don't lawyer talk at me. Eat your damn dinner."

"Pasta casserole." Asher poked the plate with his fork. "Must be a Monday."

I grinned. "You remembered that right!"

"Who could forget? It's part of Mom's weekly meal system." We shared a smile, but his dropped off after a few seconds. "I won't remember it forever, though." He put his plate on the bed and shoved it away. "I don't want to forget it. It's a stupid fucking thing to remember, compared to my work and Melissa and all those years of school, but the thought of forgetting which day is casserole day scares the shit out of me."

I put my own food aside and leaned in. "But you haven't forgotten it. It's still in there, same as always."

"But it won't be forever." The way he looked at me, half-scared and half-desperate, let me know that we weren't really talking about pasta casserole anymore. You *won't be in my head forever*, the look screamed. I *won't even be in my own head*.

"Hey." I reached out and took his hand. He gripped me back so hard I could feel my fingers creak. "You think I'm going to let you go just like that? You know me, I'm a tenacious little shit. I will irritate you so hard you'll *wish* you could forget about me, but it's never going to happen. I'm with you for life, dumbass." I let go of him and sat back. "Now drink your beer, and let me tell you all about my new partner."

"New partner? What happened to Ruiz?"

Carlos Ruiz and I hadn't been partners for two years. I kept my face placid, though. "Ruiz took a position in San Diego. This new guy, though, he more than gives Ruiz a run for his money in the asshole department."

"Yeah?" Asher looked a little smug. "Does that mean you've got an even bigger crush on this one?"

"You want to listen, or do you want to make more dumb jokes all night?"

"I'll listen." He leaned back against the wall and crossed his legs, then grabbed his dinner. "Tell me about your new partner."

"You look like shit."

Hello to you too. "Now I'm glad I didn't bring you coffee," I said from where I was crouched beside my chair. Fuck being able to swivel it, I just wanted to sit down without getting an ab workout. "You clearly don't deserve it."

"Good thing I brought my own, then." Andreas sat, but he didn't do anything, just watched me fuss with propping up my chair until the gimpy leg was stable. I took my seat gingerly, then relaxed a little when it didn't immediately fall over again. "Problems with those?" he asked, gesturing to the files.

"Nah, I got through them by six."

"Then why are you so beat?"

I could just not tell him. It would serve him right, frankly, since he hadn't bothered to tell me shit. Plausible deniability aside, I felt the imbalance of information between us like a broken bone—aching, grinding, capable of being ignored for a while but impossible to forget. This was my chance to even the scales a little.

Or I could just not be a sleep-deprived jackass and tell him. "I had a late night with my brother. He needed some help and I didn't want to leave until he was okay."

Andreas tilted his head. I thought he was going to ask for details, but all he said was, "And now he is?"

"Yeah." *Until the next bad day.* "I'll be fine as long as I don't stop caffeinating myself. Who are we going after next? Because I've got to say, correlating Jake's list of suspects with the info in those files? I'm not even sure whether some of the people he mentioned are still alive."

Andreas didn't smile, but he kind of looked like he wanted to, a little tilt at the corners of his eyes. "Well, now that you're up-to-date on all this"—he tapped the files—"let's go get an early lunch and I'll fill you in on the rest."

CHAPTER NINE
ANDREAS

I wasn't all that hungry. In fact, I'd been nauseated ever since I'd taken my meds this morning—probably since I'd taken them on an empty stomach—and the thought of food made me want to gag.

But the department's open-plan office meant we'd either have to talk about this at our desks with too many potential eavesdroppers nearby, or go find a conference room, and I was pretty sure those conference room walls had ears. That probably made me paranoid. Fine. The shoe fit. Just because a guy's paranoid doesn't mean they aren't out to get him.

Which made it almost hilarious that I was taking my in-bed-with-IA new partner someplace else so we could talk without being heard. Except IA wasn't the issue here. They were only concerned with how I handled things and my unorthodox means of acquiring information and arrests.

The rest of the department—my "trusted colleagues"—wanted details about the investigation. I'd heard the gossip. Everyone believed I was just dicking off and dragging this investigation out because it was my only assignment. They were all drowning under enormous caseloads. This—taking down the city's elaborate narcotics ring—was my entire focus. As a result, people wanted to elbow their way in, take it down, and get me back to handling a dozen cases at a time like the rest of them.

I didn't care about the workload or about sharing the glory. I just happened to know from experience that if someone tried to jump in and accelerate things, people got killed. Sometimes cops. Sometimes informants. Sometimes innocent people in the wrong place at the wrong time. And if we didn't take down everyone, if we didn't yank this weed by its rotten, connected roots, it wouldn't make a damn bit of difference. I couldn't just arrest the big players, not even Blake, no matter how many reams of warrants had his name on them, because someone would swoop in and take his place. In ways I wasn't yet ready to explain to my partner, Blake was the *least* of my concerns.

This investigation had to be handled delicately, and the information had to be guarded like nuclear secrets.

So, now that it was time for Darren to learn some of the finer details, I drove us to a small mom-and-pop deli near the river. Ironically, it was a place I'd discovered when an old partner and I had been investigating some bodies found on the riverbank nearby. After canvassing the area for witnesses and scouring the crime scene for evidence, we'd been starving and happened across this place. I'd been coming here ever since.

I parked out front, fished my wallet out of my pocket, and offered Darren a twenty. "Ham and cheese croissant and a large coffee. Black. And get something for yourself."

He looked at the money, then at me. After a few seconds, he must've realized I wasn't kidding. Rolling his eyes, he grabbed the money and got out of the car, but apparently forgot to slam the door until *after* he'd muttered, "Not your damn servant, asshole."

I chuckled. What fun was having a partner if I couldn't fuck with him once in a while?

Minutes later, he returned with the food. As soon as he was in the car, the scents of fresh bread, coffee, and grilled ham and cheese were almost overpowering, and I had to grit my teeth to keep from puking. I'd feel better after I ate. Always did. But man, this part sucked.

Unaware of my queasiness, Darren unwrapped something that smelled fucking awful.

"Jesus." I grimaced. "What the fuck is that? Week-old fish?"

"Well yeah." He looked at me with sarcastic innocence. "You didn't give me enough cash for the fresh fish."

"Jackass," I muttered, and forced down a bite of my own sandwich, which was suddenly a lot more appetizing compared to the ungodly mess in his hand. Then I rolled down the driver's-side window. The river smelled like brackish swamp water, but somehow that was less offensive than whatever he was eating.

"Better?" he asked just before he took a bite.

"All right, new rule—if we're eating in the car, nothing that smells like it came from the morgue trash can."

"Fair enough." He sipped his soda. "Or we could just, you know, sit in the deli next time."

"No. Because the whole point of being out here is to give you some more details about our investigation."

"So?" He took another bite. God, how did people eat that shit?

"This information is need to know." I pointed at the deli. "Nobody in there needs to know."

"Fair enough."

We ate in silence for a few minutes. Hell, maybe we should've eaten inside. That would've saved me from the godawful smell of his food, but I hadn't actually anticipated that, nor had I anticipated being as fucking hungry as I was.

I washed down the last of my sandwich, and admittedly, felt a bit better. The fact that Darren's sandwich didn't smell as strong now—maybe because the window was open, maybe because he'd nearly finished it—probably helped too.

"All right." I put my coffee in the cup holder. "So, the case."

Darren wadded up his sandwich wrapper and tossed it in the bag. "Mm-hmm?"

I rolled up my window, then shifted a bit in my seat, pressing my elbow into the steering wheel and facing him. "I'm probably being stupid, telling you all of this now. You've only been my partner for a day. But you're a good cop. I'm thinking I can I trust you."

He swallowed. "Thanks. I . . . Really?"

"You might be a bit by the book for my taste, but I've been in this business long enough, I can read people pretty well. The only rat I smell here is the one who's got you watching my tail."

Darren's eyes flicked toward the windshield, and some color appeared in his cheeks. "I haven't told them anything."

"I know."

"How do you know?"

"Because I haven't been called into anyone's office yet, and someone followed us here."

Darren looked around. "What? Followed us?"

I laughed. "Red sedan. Over by the dry cleaner."

He craned his neck. "How do you know?"

"Because the higher-ups always have somebody on my ass. If they were getting everything they needed from you, they wouldn't bother."

He scowled. "All right. So you . . ." He glanced at the red sedan again before facing me fully. "So you trust me enough to tell me more about the case."

I nodded. "Here's the thing—on the surface, and as far as most people on the force know, Blake's running a highly successful drug ring and that's it."

"Right."

"It goes deeper than that. Much deeper. If it were just narcotics and it stopped with Blake, I'd have given the green light a long time ago to go in and arrest everyone involved."

Darren tapped his fingers on his pant leg. "So, what else is going on?"

"The short version is that Vincent Blake is working for someone else."

"Who?"

"That's the problem." I sighed. "I'm not sure. I know a few names, and Carter definitely gave me some new ones, but I think there might be more." Okay, that was a bit of a white lie. I knew who was on top of the pyramid. It was everyone between Blake and the top I couldn't get my hands on, and without those, I couldn't make the key arrests.

"More? A few?" Darren shook his head. "What? So there's some kind of conglomerate backing him?"

"If you want to call the city's highest-ranking political figures a conglomerate, sure."

Darren blinked. "Come again?"

"There are some very high-powered people backing him. Whoever's on top is running the narcotics shit show, and he's also got hitmen who are very, very good at making murders look like accidents. Or making intended targets look like innocent bystanders."

Darren's eyebrow rose. I had no doubt he was mentally superimposing a tinfoil hat on my head.

I drummed my fingers on the wheel. "Remember that drive-by last April a few blocks away from the courthouse? When two judges were caught in the crossfire?"

"Of course." He shifted uncomfortably. "It was on the news for weeks. And I went to the funerals."

I nodded. "That wasn't just some gangbangers shooting it out, and those two judges were not bystanders in the wrong place at the wrong time."

"What do you mean?"

"I mean they were the target."

"That's . . ." Darren pressed back against the door, eyeing me warily. "How do you know?"

"Because an informant tried to warn us before it happened. He contacted me and said someone was targeting a couple of judges. He said he'd heard one particular judge's name, but didn't know who the other one was." I shook my head, my gut folding in on itself at the memory. "The named judge was Judge Harrison. She was the one the two victims had been having lunch with."

"Whoa."

"Yeah. She normally walked back with them, but that day, she'd left her purse at the café and had to go back."

Darren's lips parted. "I remember that. She showed up like two minutes after it happened and was a fucking wreck." He paused, eyes losing focus for a moment. "So she was the target?"

"No." I shook my head. "According to the informant, her name had come up, but she wasn't the target. The other two were. Question is, did she just get lucky and not get caught in the crossfire? Or did she know what was going to happen?"

"So . . . are you suggesting she was in on it? Or she was tipped off?"

"That's the problem—I can't prove anything. I know she was connected somehow, but that's it. I can't prove Judge Harrison was taking bribes, I can't prove that Judge Warner knew about it, and I can't prove that she had him killed to keep him quiet."

Darren's eyes were huge now.

"I can't prove it," I went on, "but I have that information from multiple sources. I just don't have enough to get a warrant and arrest a goddamned judge."

Darren focused on something outside the windshield and gnawed his thumbnail. I was quiet, letting him absorb what I'd told him and hoping he didn't decide I was insane.

Finally, he lowered his hand, though he still didn't look at me. "So you think somebody at city hall is running this show. Taking out hits on people for judges and politicians."

"On paper, that's what it looks like. Blake is running the narcotics ring, and he's done hits for higher-ups, but even he doesn't know who's calling the shots. He knows it's coming down from the mayor's office. But we need to know who's between Blake and the mayor if we're going to *prove* Crawford is involved."

Darren took a deep breath. "So what's your game plan?"

"My game plan right now is to find Blake. Because that's one of my—our—biggest problems. I can't find him. No one can."

"And when you do find him?"

I hesitated. This partnership was much too young for me to lay out my entire hand. "When we find him, I'll do exactly what any cop would do—ask questions and dig for answers."

Still facing straight ahead, Darren quietly asked, "Okay. So how do we find him?"

"We've got a better list of contacts now. We just have to put pressure on them like we did with Jake, and keep working our way up until we find Blake. And from there, to the people ordering these hits and pulling the strings for the mayor."

Darren gave a slow nod. Then, equally slowly, he turned to me. "Before we do that, there's something I need you to tell me."

"Okay?"

He stared at me so intently I almost drew back, and in a flat tone, he asked, "Where did the heroin come from?"

I pursed my lips, and it was my turn to look out the windshield.

"Andreas, I think I can trust you too. I trust your instincts. You might be an insufferable asshole, but you're obviously a solid cop." He paused until I faced him. "And you know more about this case than I do. If you really do trust me, then tell me where it came from."

I sighed. How much *did* I trust this kid? My gut said he was different from all the others before him. They'd had alarm bells ringing from the moment we'd met. He had too, but . . . different ones. And so far, he'd covered for me and taken an ass-chewing on my behalf, letting the captain believe he'd dropped the ball on a simple search.

"All right. You didn't miss it in the search."

"Tell me something I don't know."

"It . . ." I blew out a breath. "I needed a reason to bring Jake in, and I needed a way to put pressure on him. He's slipped through my fingers too many times. I had reason to believe there's a bullet out there with his name on it, so I was running out of time. *He* was running out of time." I shrugged. "I had to do something."

Darren's lips tightened, and he focused on something out the window again.

"Look at me, Darren." He did, and I held his gaze. "There are a lot of people on the force who think I'm a dirty cop, and to a degree, they're probably right. Hell, they *are* right. I do shit the rulebook says I shouldn't, and I won't tell you otherwise. But doing things the 'right' way wasn't working." I paused. "So I need you to make a decision. Right here, right now."

Darren swallowed, but said nothing.

"Option one is you're in this for the long haul. You trust that I know what I'm doing and my goal—my *only* goal—is to kill this whole thing from the roots all the way up to the top."

"And option two?"

"You tell IA that they're right to suspect I'm not playing by the rules. You tell them I acquired heroin and planted it during a search so I could arrest Jake Carter and pressure him into giving up his contacts. You do exactly what we both know IA sent you in to do."

Darren's eyes widened slightly.

"So," I said. "What's it gonna be?"

'd been raised by a man who'd eventually become the police commissioner, and who was notorious for being able to pull a confession from damn near anybody. Breaking curfew, cutting class, or stealing gas money from Mom's purse had earned me the kind of interrogations most people only saw in the movies. All Vic had needed was a bright light and a dark room, and he could've made me admit I'd offed JFK and faked the moon landing.

And all that relentless scrutiny had nothing on the intense stare I was getting from across the console in Andreas's car.

The question hung in the air. Did I turn him in for planting *heroin* on someone he wanted to interrogate, or did I trust that he knew what he was doing? Did I join the Rebellion or the Empire?

Andreas's eyebrow rose slightly, and my pulse did the same thing. After a moment, he looked out the windshield, but being out of the interrogation-light intensity of his gaze didn't let me release my breath. If anything, it made me more aware of an imaginary clock on the wall, marking time in gunshot-loud scritches as the silence stretched out.

Well, Darren? What is *it gonna be?*

Andreas opened his mouth to speak, and panic shot through me. Time was up.

Somehow, I gathered my thoughts and beat him to the punch: "The long haul."

He faced me, brow pinched.

I swallowed. "I'm in it for the long haul."

Goddamn. I'd thought his expression was intense *before* I'd answered. For a painfully long moment—probably as long or longer than the space between his question and my answer had been—he watched me. As I held his gaze and waited for him to speak, I was genuinely surprised that I didn't have sweat trickling down my temples or the back of my neck.

Finally, he gave a slight nod, faced forward, and started the car again. "All right. Let's get back to work."

I exhaled. That was it? Apparently it was, because he was backing out of the space, and we were heading in the general direction of the precinct. So why did I still feel like this conversation wasn't over?

Our investigation proceeded into the next few days as normally as any investigation like this could. Phone calls. Dead ends. Interviews. The odd interrogation. Two steps forward, ten steps back.

And mentally, the whole time, I was still in the passenger seat of Andreas's car, parked outside that café with the scents of our sandwiches still lingering in the air. When we were working, when I was home alone, when I was trying to get some much-needed sleep . . . didn't matter where I was or what I was doing. My brain wasn't budging from that seemingly unfinished discussion.

Except how much more could there be? He'd asked me to make a decision. I'd made it. He'd accepted it. We'd moved on. Right?

Shit. No wonder Andreas's previous partners hadn't lasted. He was a lot of gray hair waiting to happen.

A few mornings after our talk, Andreas texted me to let me know he'd be in late. Something about an appointment. Whatever. Admittedly, I was relieved to have a couple of hours to myself.

I decided to spend it down at the gun range a few blocks from the precinct. I didn't need to qualify anytime soon—I'd done my twice-yearly quals less than a month ago—but blowing some holes in an unsuspecting piece of paper was seriously appealing today. It was either that or pistol-whip Andreas just for breathing. Or stapler-whip him, given the amount of time we'd been spending at our desks.

A few other guys from the precinct were at the range. They didn't bother with the ear muffs like I did; they preferred earplugs. Me, I wasn't taking any chances with my hearing. Ditto with my eyes—the rented safety glasses were flimsy at best, so I had a pair of custom-made wraparound glasses that kept out powder, shell casings, or even dust. Kind of the gun range equivalent of a pocket protector, but we'd see who was laughing when an errant chunk of powder got under someone's contact lens.

With my eyes and ears duly protected, I took my pistol out of its holster and laid it on the bench with its action open and the muzzle pointed down range. Then I started loading a couple of spare magazines.

And of course, my brain wandered right back to my partner.

My stomach turned to lead. He'd be finished with his appointment in an hour. We'd meet up. Work together. Continue with this case. Pretend like everything was resolved and there was nothing else to sort out, and maybe in his mind, everything *was* resolved.

I sighed and laid the freshly loaded magazines in a row. Maybe I needed to just put it out there and talk to him about all this. He didn't strike me as the type who'd want to clear the air or talk about feelings, but if we were going to work together, a somewhat uncomfortable conversation might be necessary.

As I hung a target and then sent it downrange to fifteen yards, my spine tingled at the thought of having that conversation. Or any conversation, really. Even though he seemed to be adapting to my presence, and he hadn't been outwardly hostile to me since that tense moment, I was constantly on edge around him. Not just nervous because I was being scrutinized at every turn by someone who was suspicious of my motives, but because I was being scrutinized at every turn by *him*. It was like I was sure I was going to do something to make him roll his eyes, or laugh, or think less of me as a cop . . .

Which made no sense. Why the fuck did I care what he thought of me? Wasn't like I had a snowball's chance in hell with him, so—

A *what*?

I shook myself, swearing under my breath at my own stupid train of thought. Andreas wasn't some potential piece of ass. He was my partner. I didn't need to impress him or charm him or do a goddamned thing except work with him and try not to kill him when he unleashed *his* version of charm. Which, oddly, was annoying me less and less. In its own way, it was almost endearing.

Especially when he coupled it with that slightly lopsided grin, or an upward flick of his eyebrow. Or when I'd say something and get a quiet laugh out of him, and my pulse would go crazy.

Wait, wait, wait.

Was *that* what was going on here? Was I . . . *attracted* to Andreas Ruffner?

Losing your mind, dude. That's what's going on here.

I shook myself again and put a magazine into the pistol. Time to focus on shooting, not on ogling Andreas. Because he was my partner. And kind of an asshole!

But . . . attractive. God, who was I kidding? He was smoking hot. Maybe I'd just spent too much time with younger guys, and guys with the intellectual capacity of a gnat. Now I was spending most of my waking hours with an older one. Someone with a little gray and a whole lot of brains and that hint of arrogance that shouldn't have turned me on but kind of did.

Cocky son of a bitch like that would look amazing on his knees.

I shivered hard, nearly fumbling with the pistol. I shook my head, focused on the target, and leveled my weapon.

After I'd emptied the last magazine, I pushed the button to bring my target up, and as it came closer, I bit back a frustrated sound. My shots were well within the target, but there were a few too many holes in the rings surrounding the center.

Scowling, I put a sticker over the holes so I could try again. I couldn't even blame Andreas for my slightly errant rounds—I'd been trying to tighten up my patterns for years, and this was as good as I'd ever been. There were rookies who could put an entire magazine through the same tiny hole while I was over here shooting like this. Awesome.

Well, practice made perfect, and I still had time, so I started loading magazines again.

I was halfway through loading the second mag when the pressure in the room changed. Without thinking about it, I glanced toward the door.

And lost just enough of my grip on the magazine to send a round flying onto the floor.

It rolled across the casing-littered concrete until Andreas stopped it under the toe of his shoe. As I held my breath—and held on to the magazine and the rest of the rounds—he leaned down to pick it up.

He straightened, raising the round between his thumb and forefinger so the brass gleamed in the fluorescent light. Behind his yellow-tinted safety glasses, his eyes glinted with amusement. "You dropped something."

I gulped as he came closer, and I held out my hand. "Thanks."

He smiled faintly and dropped the round into my palm. When he glanced past me, I cringed, thankful I'd covered the holes with a sticker before he'd walked in. Except did it matter? He'd probably come here to shoot—he had two boxes of ammo under his arm—which meant he'd be here to see my next pathetic attempt. Great.

I thumbed the round into the magazine. "Didn't you have an appointment?"

He shrugged. "Wrapped up earlier than I thought."

"Oh." I paused as I pulled a couple more rounds from the box. "How'd you know I'd be here?"

"Lucky guess."

I eyed him.

Andreas chuckled. "Your safety glasses." He gestured at his own. "They weren't on your desk and you didn't answer your phone. I figured you were probably here."

"Oh. Right. No hiding from you, is there?"

"They didn't make me a detective because of my personality."

I laughed. "No, I guess they didn't." I paused. "So, uh, you came to shoot?"

"Yeah." He glanced down at the ammo as if he'd forgotten he had it. "Figured as long as I was here, might as well put some lead downrange."

He took the booth next to mine—of course he did—and put down the ammo. I stepped back, still loading my magazine. My pulse didn't calm down in the slightest as Andreas shrugged off his leather jacket, revealing the black straps of the shoulder holster crisscrossing his back. Okay, so it was starting to make more sense that I couldn't help staring at him. He was pretty damn fit. And broad in the shoulders. And that ass . . .

I coughed and looked away, hoping like hell he didn't turn around until the heat in my face had cooled a few degrees.

He didn't, though. He was too busy setting everything up so he could shoot. To my surprise, the weapon he pulled from his shoulder holster was a basic Glock. The ammo box beside him was a .45.

I'd half expected him to be carrying some Dirty Harry beast of a gun. A .44 magnum or something. Or maybe something souped up with laser sights or an extended magazine. Andreas shooting an off-the-shelf Glock made sense like James Bond driving a Volvo.

But as he lifted the gun and aimed at the target, my body temperature rose too. Higher still when he squeezed off a few shots. He barely flinched. His hands weren't completely still—the gun did have a moderate recoil, after all—but his stance was rock solid and his hands only moved as much as they absolutely had to in order to absorb the kick. I'd never ogled someone at the range, never really thought there was anything sexy about a man with a gun, but Andreas was disabusing me of that notion with every shot he fired. I couldn't explain it. It just was.

What the hell? It's Andreas!

A casing bounced off the divider between the lanes and landed in a crease in his sleeve. With a barely noticeable shrug, he knocked it free, and it dropped to his feet with a faint *clink*. Not that I watched it fall, because I was busy watching how his shirt held on to his shoulders and—

Dude. Dude. *Eyes on your own lane.*

I pulled my gaze away and returned to my lane. I didn't even care if Andreas saw how badly I was shooting as long as I didn't get an awkwardly timed hard-on right here at the range. Which, fortunately, I'd narrowly avoided, and concentrating on loading and aiming my pistol was enough to pull my focus away from him.

Sort of.

Three shots into my second magazine, I realized he wasn't firing anymore. I couldn't have seen or heard him loading his magazines— the divider between us prevented that—but somehow I knew he wasn't. The hair on my neck prickled.

I glanced over my shoulder.

Yep.

Right there.

Watching.

Fuck.

Which part's the trigger again?

I cleared my throat and adjusted my stance. I concentrated on the iron sights, letting the target blur in the background just like Vic had taught me back when I was eight. When I fired, the recoil smarted, which meant I was holding the gun way too tight and standing with way too much tension in my muscles. Eyes closed, I rolled my shoulders. I could do this.

Behind me, Andreas muffled a cough. "Hey, um . . ."

Equal parts annoyed and relieved, I looked over my shoulder. "Hmm?"

He stepped a little closer. "You mind some unsolicited advice?"

Well, now I was curious. I lowered the gun. "About?"

"Your index finger might be screwing you up a little."

"My . . ." I looked down at my hands, which were still loosely holding the gun. "What am I doing wrong?"

He slid into the narrow confines of the booth with me. "Aim it again."

Heart thumping and skin tingling from being this close to him—*what the hell, Darren?*—I did as I was told.

He reached for my hands, but hesitated. "May I?"

I nodded.

Gently, he nudged my left index finger downward. "You've got your finger around your trigger guard instead of below it."

"I do?" I moved my fingers as he'd suggested. "Damn. I never even noticed that."

A hint of a smile worked at his lips, and he shrugged. "I've seen people do it before. Everyone adapts their grip over time, and sometimes people do it this way because it feels more stable."

"I'm guessing it's not."

He shook his head.

"Well. Now I feel like an idiot." I adjusted my grip slightly. This new configuration was awkward as hell. "I've been doing it wrong for *how* many years?"

Another shrug. "Don't sweat it." He showed me his palm and gestured at some thin scars on the lower part of his ring finger. "I won't tell you how many times the magazine bit me before I figured out how to keep my hand out of the way."

"Really?"

He laughed. "Yeah. Word to the wise—don't let it bite you. The blood blister is painful as fuck."

I shuddered.

"Anyway." He pointed down range. "Give it a try. Might take some time to get used to it, but you'll probably have a better pattern once you do."

"Yeah. Thanks."

Then he stepped out of the booth and back to his own lane.

I aimed, fired one round, and then paused. Yeah, the new grip was awkward as hell, but not nearly as much as this off-balanced, jittery feeling.

What the hell is wrong with me?

CHAPTER ELEVEN
ANDREAS

A s soon as I was back in my own lane, I closed my eyes and pushed out a long breath. In the moment, I'd only been concerned about helping Darren with his form. But suddenly we'd just . . . *been* there. Standing there, absolutely no breathing room whatsoever, with my hand touching his, if only for a few seconds. Now my damn head was spinning, and I couldn't even blame it on the drugs. They were still fucking up my equilibrium, but that was a feeling I recognized from a mile away.

This was a whole different kind of dizzy, and it had been happening a lot lately. It sure as hell had never happened with a partner before, though. Mostly because my partners were more prone to pissing me off than turning me on, but trust Darren to show up and change that.

I scrubbed a hand over my face, ordered myself not to be stupid, and started loading another magazine. Yeah, I'd decided from day one that Darren was attractive, and he'd become considerably more so once I'd realized he was more ally than adversary. Funny what happened when two people were on the same wavelength about something.

But we could be on the same wavelength a million times over, and it still wouldn't mean I had a shot with him. For all I knew, he was straight like the last three or four guys I'd checked out. Or he could be as gay as the day was long. Didn't matter. I hadn't shared a bed with anyone—male or female—since my daughter's mother and I had split, and that was damn near four years ago. I was an idiot if I thought that dry spell was going to end with Darren.

My stomach wound itself into a knot. Another familiar feeling set up shop behind my ribs. That same heavy, depressed feeling that had been my only company on a lot of long, miserable nights over the past few years. It had been a while since I'd felt it come on strong enough to make me want to taste the muzzle of my pistol, but God, it was awful.

I looked down at the pistol, which was lying on the bench, magazine dropped and action open, waiting for me to pick it up and keep shooting. Suddenly I wasn't in the mood to shoot, though. Lifting the gun seemed like too much effort. Aiming it? Firing it? I was exhausted just thinking about it.

Sighing, I loaded a magazine and put it in the pistol, then holstered the gun.

Darren peered around the divider. "You done already?"

I thought quickly, then, "Captain just called. Better go see what he wants to yell about this time."

His eyes widened. "He yelling at both of us?"

"Nope." I picked up my ammo and extra magazines. "Just me. See you back at the precinct?"

Darren studied me, and I thought he might ask questions or see through my bluff, but he shrugged. Gesturing over his shoulder at his target, he said, "I want to finish off this box of ammo, and then I'll meet you there."

I forced a smile. "See you there."

While he went back to shooting, I headed out of the range. In the gun shop, I took out my earplugs, signed out of my lane, and continued toward my car. As I tossed the ammo and my eye protection on the passenger seat, I swore again. There was a dark cloud over my head now, and it was going to be there for a while. Always happened when I let myself entertain thoughts of getting anywhere near somebody. And as a bonus, the somebody I wanted to get close to was someone I couldn't get away from for the foreseeable future.

"I'm in it for the long haul."

Great. Fucking fabulous.

Probably just as well I couldn't drink much with the pills I was taking—I'd have been tempted to call it a day and dive headlong into a bottle.

Oh well.

I started the car and, without looking back, left the gun range.

By the time Darren showed up an hour or so later, the dark cloud hadn't gone away. As we dove into paperwork, scoured files in search of something we might've missed, and drove downtown twice to interview people who might have—but didn't—know something, I couldn't shake it. Not that I was surprised.

At just shy of six, I was done. There was plenty of work left, but I was completely spent.

"I think I'm going to duck out early." I closed a file folder I'd been looking through, leaving a pen in it to mark my place. "You can do the same if you want."

Darren looked up. "So you're telling me when I can come and go now?"

The snide tone caught me off guard. "Uh . . ."

"Just go." He waved me away and returned his attention to the papers spread in front of him. "See you tomorrow."

I hesitated, trying like hell to figure out what had changed since this morning, but I was too fucking tired to read between any lines. So, without another word, I picked up my jacket and keys, and left.

I didn't go home, though.

Down by the river, not far from where Darren and I had eaten our sandwiches a while ago, I found a parking space and got out. The evening was starting to cool down, so I zipped up my jacket as I walked toward the water.

The river wound through the city, and it was dotted with parks where people took their dogs or their kids. I sometimes went to the dog park near the north edge of town. It had been years since I'd had a dog—my job just didn't leave me enough time to give one the attention he deserved—but I liked being around them. Maybe when I retired, I'd get one again.

Tonight, I didn't want to be around dogs, kids, or anyone. So I'd come here—to one of the industrial areas that had foundered during the last few recessions—where most of the buildings were abandoned and nobody really went. We didn't even find all that many bodies down here anymore.

It was deserted, and that was exactly what I needed tonight.

Hands in my pockets, I strolled as close to the lazily flowing river's edge as I could without getting in the mud. As shitty as I felt today,

I wouldn't have been surprised if I were to cap off the evening with a muddy shoe, sock, and pant leg.

With no one around to distract me and nothing to hold my thoughts except making sure I was walking on solid ground, it didn't take long for my mind to wander back to my partner.

There was no point in entertaining fantasies of coaxing him over the boundary of platonic professionalism, but that didn't stop me. There was no point in thinking about all the things we could do without clothes or inhibitions, but that didn't stop me either. I knew how my mind worked. I'd torture myself with the idea that, in some parallel universe, I had a snowball's chance in hell with him, and before long, I'd be jerking off every night until I was ready to lose my mind just being in the same room with him. All because I couldn't quit imagining a night that could never in a million years actually happen.

Naturally, though, the one thing that had even less of a chance of happening was me getting a new partner. Captain Hamilton would laugh me out of his office if I requested someone else, even if the reason wasn't *I'm getting chronic blue balls from being around him*.

Sighing, I gazed out at the river, watching a couple of ducks cruise along the swirling surface.

I was being stupid. I'd get over him just like I'd gotten over the last few people I'd nearly lost my mind over. My ridiculously hot neighbor had moved away a year ago without anything ever happening between us, and I'd gotten over her. Lieutenant Jackson had transferred to another city two years ago, and though I still kept a few fantasies about him tucked away, I didn't trip over my own feet when he crossed my mind now. Hell, after my divorce a decade ago, my roommate and I had actually slept together for a few weeks, and then managed to live together as friends after his girlfriend moved in.

My attraction to each of them had been easily as strong as it was to Darren right now, and I'd made it through without going insane. The same thing would happen with Darren. The only reason I was losing it now was that he was new, and I was frustrated that it had been four years since I'd touched anyone. I'd been fine before. I'd be fine this time. All I needed was to get my head together, get all my thoughts of him out of my system, and—

The ground was suddenly softer than I'd expected, and before I could shift my weight back to solid ground, the mud swallowed my left leg to mid-shin.

"Fuck!" I jerked my foot free, and glared down at the thick mud now coating my shoe.

Great. Now I had something else to think about tonight besides Darren.

Fucking awesome.

The next day was more of the same—interviews, leads, dead ends, and paperwork. Darren and I had gone into the suburbs to talk to a potential witness about some interactions between suspects, but it was yet another dead end. Same shit, different day.

Before heading into town, I pulled into a convenience store to grab a cup of coffee. On the way back out to the car, Darren stopped suddenly.

"All right." He turned to me. "What did I do?"

I blinked. "Come again?"

"Don't play stupid."

"Play— I have no idea what you're talking about."

An eyebrow flicked up, but he said nothing.

Irritation tightened my chest. I quickly ran through a mental replay of the last few hours, but came up empty. "Don't play games. What are you talking about?"

Darren sighed heavily and rolled his eyes. "I thought we were working together. So what's with this cold-shoulder business? You gonna tell me what I did wrong, or what?"

I avoided his eyes.

He sighed again. "Just tell me what the fuck is going on. I mean, we had that talk, and everything was fine. Then yesterday, you helped me at the range—and thank you, by the way—but suddenly when I got back to the precinct, you'd gone completely cold. You've barely said more than two words to me since yesterday, aside from telling me I had your permission to leave early if I wanted to."

I exhaled. "I'm sorry. I . . . I've just been up in my own head. It's not you." *Except it is. Because I can't tell you I want you or why I can't have you.* "Just, uh . . . couple of off days."

He watched me, but his posture relaxed slightly. "So everything is still, uh . . ."

I inclined my head. "You tell me."

"Nothing's changed on my end. I just, I mean, we ended that conversation kind of abruptly, and it seemed like something important, so . . ."

"What more was there to say?"

"I . . ." He chewed his lip. "I don't know. Kinda seemed like we'd left something hanging."

I shrugged. "Not really, no. You said you're in for the long haul and that I can trust you. That's all I needed to know."

"So then . . . the last few days . . . they weren't—"

"Like I said." I tapped my temple. "Just up in my own head. It happens sometimes."

"Oh."

I shifted my weight. "We've got some work to do back at—"

"Yeah. I know." He cleared his throat and played with the lid on his coffee cup. "Okay. Um. Let's go, then." He started toward the car.

"Darren."

He paused, then turned around.

"No one ever said working with me is going to be easy. In fact, I'm pretty sure they warned you about it."

"So did you." He laughed so subtly I almost missed it. "But we do have to work together. So, you know, talk to me."

Hadn't I had this exact conversation with my ex-wife? And my ex-girlfriend? And at least one ex-boyfriend? And just like I had with them, I nodded and said, "All right. I will."

"All right. That's all I need." Then he continued toward the car.

I hesitated for a moment, but finally followed him.

Damn, I definitely had to get my game face on. We had a major case to crack, and we weren't going to have much longer to crack it.

Whatever Darren was doing to my brain and my body, I'd deal with it on my own time. Because dealing with it at work was sure as hell not doing me any favors.

The drug business, I was fast coming to understand, was a fucking bureaucratic nightmare. It *had* to be. Blake either had an army of enforcers he held in an iron fist, or a photographic memory to keep everything untraceable. He controlled the flow of the heroin, but the dissemination? That was down to the everyday pushers, guys like Jake who worked under someone higher on the food chain or struck out on their own while still reporting back to the organization. How much they sold, where they worked, whether law enforcement was getting too close? All that resulted in the kind of mercenary-yet-dull decision making that I associated with dictators, not with drug dealers.

Andreas and I spent the rest of the week running down some of the contacts we'd gotten from Jake's list. We hit brick wall after brick wall on all of them. Some were among the missing, a few were killed in gang turf wars, and yet another died literally minutes before we got to her.

We found Zoe Dugan's body even before the officers sent by a jogger's 911 call did, not far from her last known address. From the look of things, she'd been dragged to the side of the park across from her apartment, shot in the gut, and then finished off with a shot to the head. It had been a hard death, her agony apparent in the withered curl of her body. The jogger was still in hysterics a few feet away, finally distracted by the arrival of the cops.

Andreas was *pissed*. "What the fuck?" he demanded under his breath as he crouched down to examine the body. Zoe's hands had been bound behind her, and she was bent forward over her stomach. The head shot had obviously come second, a simple, final punctuation signifying the end of her life. "This wasn't random."

Well, duh. "No shit."

"I mean the *timing*, Darren. We decided to go after her next last night, and she ended up dead this morning? Outdoors, in this area?" He shook his head and stood up. "It wasn't the safest way to take her out."

"Too public," I said, my mouth playing along as my brain worked to catch up. "Why not kill her in her apartment?"

"They're pretty nice units. A person couldn't shoot someone and expect the neighbors not to call the police. Her back door was open, too. She tried to run for it."

"Who would it be safer to run from than fight?"

He shrugged. "Someone well trained. Maybe someone whose authority couldn't be easily questioned."

My mouth went dry. "You think it might have been a cop?" I murmured, not wanting the two officers behind us to hear.

"We need to consider the possibility. We aren't the only ones with access to Jake's list. We've been going right down the line, and we're getting cockblocked every time. We're going to have to change things up before we lose every lead we've got."

"What do you want to do?"

Andreas opened his mouth, then shut it again before saying anything. "I'm not sure yet," he said slowly. "We could try switching up the order we go after them, but if it really is someone on the inside, then it might not matter."

One of the cops came up to my side, distracting me before I had a chance to press Andreas. "You two done here? The coroner's on the way."

"Yeah," I said after a quick glance at my partner, who didn't meet my eye. "We're done. Thanks."

The ride back to the precinct was silent, which I didn't like. Even during the tense times this week, Andreas had been open— eventually—to talking with me after he'd come clean about his actions in Jake's place. Now he was either deep in thought, or he was brooding over some unexpressed man-pain. Either way, I wanted to know what was going on. I figured I'd give him one ride's grace, then start bugging him again once we were out after the next person on the list—whoever that ended up being.

Instead, I was waylaid the moment we stepped foot inside the station.

"Darren!"

It was Detective Newberry, one of the guys I'd gone through the academy with. He was a few years older than me, had spent four years in the army before deciding to go into law enforcement, and had found his niche in the Major Case Unit. They had their own office in another building—I didn't know what he was doing here.

"Hey, Trent." We shook hands, and then he turned to Andreas.

"You must be this guy's partner. Be careful, man, Darren plays dirty."

"Are you still holding that paintball game against me?" I shook my head in mock despair. "It's been years. Let it go, Trent. Let it go."

Andreas smiled at him. It was the least genuine smile I'd ever seen. "I'll keep that in mind. See you upstairs, Corliss." He left before I could say anything else.

"Wow." Trent watched him go. "He's just as much of an asshole as they say, isn't he?"

"What's up, Trent?" I asked, trying to redirect him without being obvious about it. It didn't work. Trent was a decent detective, and we'd been pretty close once. He knew all my tells.

"Aw, what, are you feeling protective of big, bad Ruffner?" He grinned knowingly. "He is hot, I'll give you that, but I don't think you've got what it takes to grab his attention. The guy's a lady-killer."

After the morning I'd had, I was in no mood to hear that dumbass phrase. "Really, what are you doing here?"

"Just stopping by to see a friend. Speaking of which, Detective Thibedeau mentioned that he wants to meet with you. You should rescue him before he goes looking for you and Ruffner sets him on fire or something. Kidding!" Trent held up both his hands. "He's in his office on the fourth floor. You want me to walk you there?"

"Turns out I'm super good at counting to four. I think I can find it without you."

"Of course you can." Trent left with a smirk and a swagger, and I wondered for the thousandth time since meeting him whether or not it was worth the hit to my record to deck him in the fucking face. And now I was heading up to IA on his say-so?

I didn't want to, but I wanted Andreas and Thibedeau coming face-to-face even less. I chose the lesser evil and headed up to the fourth floor.

Damn, it was cold up here. Wasn't heat supposed to rise? How much air conditioning did our tax dollars pay for just to keep the demons on the fourth floor cool and comfortable? Detective Thibedeau had a private office, and the door was firmly shut. I took a deep breath and knocked twice.

"Come in."

Thibedeau didn't look surprised to see me—that sharp crease in his brow suggested annoyance instead. "Darren. I thought you'd have been here sooner."

"You said you'd be arranging our next meeting, not me."

"But you've had a busy week." He still hadn't asked me to sit. At this point it was probably deliberate, so I didn't bother getting any closer. "Surely you've learned a few things about your partner since Monday that are worth sharing. Even if it's just to clear him of suspicion," he added condescendingly.

"We haven't gotten very far on the case. All the new leads are drying up."

"How is Detective Ruffner taking that?"

"Oh, he's upset about it."

"How can you tell?"

"The constant swearing is a pretty solid tip-off. Look, if I had anything for you, I'd tell you; Ruffner's not such a great partner that I'm eager to spend extra time with him. But I don't. Not yet."

Thibedeau steepled his fingers. "Not even with regards to Jake Carter? Because bringing him in was certainly a lucky windfall. Almost too lucky."

Danger, Will Robinson, danger! "I thought so too at the time, but—" I shrugged "—I was wrong. And we haven't been very lucky since. A week really isn't much time, Detective Thibedeau."

"True." He nodded. "If anything of interest does happen, you know where to find me. I want to know as soon as possible, Darren." Now he was using his *Daddy knows best* voice. It really didn't work for him. "Keeping cops from abusing their power is part of a sacred public trust."

"I understand."

"Good." He smiled flicker-fast. "You can go, then. Have a nice afternoon."

I wasn't Catholic, but I still had the urge to make the sign of the cross as I left Thibedeau's office. He was so oily he could probably walk through a rainstorm without getting wet. I didn't like the guy, but I *did* have to make an effort with him, at least for now. We'd have more than enough evidence to make him back off after we dealt with Blake, but until then I had to look like I was on his side. I wasn't going to give Andreas up, not for the heroin thing, even though I didn't like it. If that was the worst I had to deal with, I'd swallow my worries for now.

Andreas didn't say anything when I joined him at our desks, but his concerned expression spoke volumes. *Later*, I mouthed. When we weren't surrounded by overly interested ears.

Andreas's paranoia might have been catching.

"What a shitty day," I said when we finally settled into a booth at the back of a dim bar off Main Street. It wasn't a cop bar, but it was clean and cheap and it had lots of beer, which was all I cared about. I drank deep from my Guinness, then relaxed with a sigh.

Andreas shrugged. "It could have been worse."

"We found a body this morning. A *dead body*. The body of someone who was tortured and executed in cold fucking blood, from the looks of things. And then I had to talk to Thibedeau, which might have been even worse. I didn't tell him anything, but he's expecting weekly reports at the very least, so now I've got that to look forward to."

"Let's not forget your admirer, Trent." Andreas seemed casual, but his hand was tight around his glass. "Did talking to him make your day better or worse?"

"Trent." I chuckled. "Yeah, it's always a toss-up. On the one hand, he's a pretty fun guy to hang out with. On the other hand, if he's hanging out with you, you know it's because he wants something. I swear, the only reason he was interested in me at the academy was because he wanted to get in good with my stepdad."

"He was interested in you?"

"Sort of. We dated a few times. It was never serious."

"Good." Andreas took a drink. "He's a fuck-head."

Strong words. Andreas seemed bothered. I decided to poke the bear a bit. "Trent's not so bad."

"Clearly you're wrong."

"He's fun to dance with at clubs."

Andreas scoffed. "Anyone can dance in a club—just find the nearest leg and hump it in time to the music."

"He drives a nice car. It's a Camaro."

"Then he's probably compensating for something."

"He's good at pool."

Andreas's eyes gleamed in the low light. "I'm better."

I grinned. "Prove it."

The bar had an ancient pool table in the back room, with a wrinkled surface and two balls missing, both solids. "I'll let you play those, then," Andreas said as he picked out a cue stick. "You'll need the handicap."

"Lots of talk, but I'm not seeing any action so far."

"I'll give you action," he muttered, bending over the table to line up his first shot. I openly admired his ass while he did.

It turned out Andreas really was good at pool. I was better, of course, but not by as much as I'd thought I would be.

"Bullshit," he said when I sunk the eight ball. I did my customary victory dance, a little shimmy that was way easier to pull off when I was on my second beer, and started retrieving the balls.

"Once you're done working through the stages of grief, feel free to try to redeem your honor," I said as I set up for another game. "If you were being nice to me before, I suggest you play to win this time."

Andreas shook his head. "You don't know what you're letting yourself in for."

"Sounds like fun."

What I was in for, apparently, was a fucking masterful series of distractions. It ranged from Andreas casually taking off his jacket just within view as I took a shot, to a stare-down from across the table, to him standing right behind me breathing down my neck as I set up for another shot. If I didn't know better, I'd swear the guy was flirting with me, and it only got worse after I won the second game. The space between us became nonexistent, and when I scratched on my next shot, it was because Andreas's long arms had bracketed me at the edge of the table, making me shiver.

"Too bad," he said, his voice low and amused against my ear. His breath warmed the side of my face, his mouth was right there, and I couldn't help it—I wanted to taste him. Only the knowledge that surprising Andreas would probably lead to him kicking my ass kept me from turning and kissing him right then. But I couldn't be reading this completely wrong.

"I guess it's your turn." I pivoted to face him. He didn't move his arms. He didn't move at all. Our faces were barely an inch apart. When he licked his lips, I almost whimpered. "Or we could play a different game."

Andreas's eyes darkened, fastening on my mouth. Arousal flooded through me, making me ache. I leaned in, and he—

"No." A second later he fell back like I'd shoved him. "We're not doing this."

I didn't even have time to speak, to ask him to stay, to *apologize*. Andreas grabbed his jacket and left, not even stopping to put it on before he was gone.

Fuck my life, what had I just done?

CHAPTER THIRTEEN
ANDREAS

That escalated fucking quickly.

In the cab on the way home—one too many beers to be driving myself—I stared out the window and swore under my breath for the millionth time. I wasn't that drunk. The light-headedness was entirely from my pills—right?—and I'd only had . . . two beers? Three? Shit, I couldn't even remember now. And I probably shouldn't have been drinking at all when I could barely stand without blacking out.

Groaning, I rubbed my forehead. I could blame it on a lot of substances, but the fact was, I'd still been coherent enough that I shouldn't have let things progress as far as they had. Of course he'd tried to kiss me. I'd all but painted *I fucking want you* on my forehead.

Was that all it took these days to let my dick take over where my brain belonged? Just a few beers and some pool-table shit-talking with my new partner? My new hot partner. Who was spying on me for IA's behalf. But had taken the fall for me and, so far, hadn't ratted me out for planting evidence on Jake Carter. But he was still a wild card who could just be saving up all this damning evidence to drop it on Thibedeau's desk later. But who was so, *so* fucking *hot* . . .

Fuck.

Well, apparently I knew how many beers were too many, at least while I was taking these pills. God knew if it was actually the two interacting, or if I'd turned into a damn lightweight, but better not to take any chances. When I was around Darren—one beer. Maximum. Because things absolutely *could not* escalate like they almost had tonight.

And what happens tomorrow?
Tomorrow we discover a whole new circle of awkwardness hell.

Early the next morning, before I'd even finished shaving, my phone vibrated. I cringed, damn near nicking myself in the process. Who the fuck was texting me at six thirty?

So help me, if that's Darren asking to meet up for coffee and talk *about things . . .*

I rinsed my razor and picked up my phone.

The message hadn't come from Darren. My heart sped up—it was from an informant I'd been trying to reach for weeks.

Whse. 730.

I messaged back, *I'll be there.*

Then I quickly finished shaving, not even caring if I cut myself. The warehouse was outside of town, and so was my apartment. Problem was, they were on opposite ends, and traffic was about to start getting hellish, so I had to leave now if I was going to make it by seven thirty. And this was not someone who would wait for me.

With a tiny square of toilet paper to staunch the bleeding on the side of my chin, I grabbed my jacket, ankle holster, wallet, and keys, and hurried out to the car. Fortunately I'd already put on my shoulder holster, so I didn't have to fuck with that while I was trying to drive.

By the time I merged onto the freeway, I had turned into a poster child for road rage, and the freeway had turned into a parking lot. Teeth grinding, heart thumping, I inched along the endless strip of pavement, silently cursing out the road construction up ahead and the traffic reports that wouldn't stop adding new accidents to the mix. If this shit kept up, I'd never make it to the warehouse in time, and it would probably be months before I connected with this informant again. It was one of the few times I wished I still drove a marked car—at least then I could put on a siren.

Every time the song changed on the radio, my stomach somersaulted. Another three and a half minutes had gone by, and I was still too far from the damn warehouse.

Finally, though, the congestion broke up enough for me to get into the left lane and gun the engine. I hovered a few miles above the speed limit—enough to buy me some time without getting me pulled over—and gripped the wheel like my life depended on it.

At five minutes past our designated meeting time, I pulled into the warehouse's rundown parking lot. There were no other cars, but I tried not to read too much into that. Most informants were smart enough not to park their vehicles anywhere near a place they were meeting with a cop.

I got out and started to jog toward the warehouse. Five or six steps from my car, the dizziness caught up with me, so I slowed but didn't stop. Blacking out was a risk I'd have to take. Should've grabbed something to eat on the way out and at least minimized the problem, but it was too late now.

At the entrance to the warehouse, my knees were too rubbery to continue, so I paused and grabbed the decrepit doorframe.

"Out of shape?" Her tone was sarcastic, but somehow carried an undercurrent of genuine concern.

"I'm good." I blinked a few times, and when I was confident my head wouldn't start spinning again and my legs would stay under me, I lifted my gaze.

She was a few feet away, arms folded across an oversized green sweatshirt. The shirt made her seem smaller and thinner, not to mention quite a few years younger. A few strands of blonde hair fell out from her baseball cap, and she wasn't wearing makeup, which made her look paler than normal. Between her job, an infant, and a toddler, she had dark circles under her tired eyes, and when she was dressed down like this, she could pull off the haggard street kid look.

By nine thirty, when she walked into the courthouse, she'd blend right in. Makeup, meticulously styled hair, high heels, a smart suit—typical attorney. If anyone saw her now, she was just another teenager hanging out where she didn't belong.

I took my hand off the doorframe and stepped closer. "All right. I'm here. So what's—"

"You're late," she snapped.

"You didn't exactly give me much warning." I glanced around, double-checking we were alone even though I knew damn well it was just us and a row of pigeons. "You want to meet on short notice, check the traffic reports first."

She scowled.

"I'm here now," I said. "So what's this about?"

"One of Blake's top dogs is appearing in court today." She took a small folded piece of paper from her pocket. "Kenny Walker. Family court at eleven fifteen."

"Family court?" As I unfolded the paper, I asked, "There a reason his name isn't on the docket?"

"He's just there as a character witness. But if you want to grab him and talk to him, he'll be in courtroom six."

I glanced at the paper she'd given me, which detailed information about a custody hearing. On the surface, it wasn't exactly cloak-and-dagger stuff that required clandestine meetings, but neither of us could risk someone connecting her to me. She was one of several sets of eyes and ears I had around the courthouse and city hall, and if anyone so much as *thought* she was collecting data on people above her, she'd be dead.

"All right." I tucked the paper into my wallet. "I'll be there to catch him on his way out."

Lips taut, she nodded. "And if anyone asks how you knew he was there?"

I inclined my head. "After all this time, you still don't trust me not to throw you under the bus?"

She set her jaw. "I don't think any of us can be too careful, can we?"

"Not at all. And yes, I'll have a cover story. No one will know this came from you."

"Thanks." She looked at her phone. "I have a deposition at ten. I have to go."

I nodded, and she hurried out of the warehouse. As always, I gave her some time to get gone before I left, even though there was no one else around. While I waited, I texted Darren.

On my way—will be late.

After the message had sent, I stared at the screen for a moment. This was going to be weird, wasn't it? The best I could hope for was both of us mumbling that we'd been drunk and things had gotten out of hand. Grunted apologies. Blame the booze. Mutter that it wouldn't happen again. Move the fuck on.

But Darren didn't seem like that type. I had a feeling he was the "let's sit down and talk about this over paninis and coffee" kind of guy, and if he was, I'd probably have to toss him off a bridge.

I didn't want to talk about it. At all. Maybe acknowledge it and promise never to speak of it again, but beyond that, it only had the potential to make things really uncomfortable. I couldn't tell him that I'd come on to him because of the alcohol, because then I'd be saying he was only attractive through beer goggles. I couldn't admit that he was insanely attractive, because then I'd have to go into why we'd had to stop, and I was *convinced* he wouldn't accept "because we're coworkers, idiot" as an explanation.

I'd trusted him enough to tell him I'd planted evidence on Jake Carter. I'd trusted him enough to tip my hand about Blake's organization reaching way, way above our pay grades. There were still some things I needed to keep to myself, though.

I rubbed a hand over my face. Yeah. This was going to be weird.

It was almost nine when I walked into the precinct. Darren was at his desk, balancing precariously on that broken chair. I couldn't help wondering when he'd finally call downstairs and demand a decent one, but maybe he didn't want to rock the boat. Or he was working on that six-pack while he combed through papers. None of my business, though I could sure as fuck fantasize about the results.

As I came toward the desks, he looked at me, but quickly dropped his gaze.

"Morning," he said.

"Morning." I put my coat over the back of my chair and sat down. As my laptop woke up, I surreptitiously watched him across our desks. His silence and lack of eye contact were promising, but he was also subtly pressing a thumb against his temples, and he looked like he was barely keeping his eyes open. The hangover was probably what was keeping him quiet. A few more cups of coffee, and he might want to . . . talk about this.

I logged into my computer, and while my emails took their sweet time downloading, I sipped my coffee. Darren still didn't speak. He was poring over a file—probably one of the many I'd given him to review. That was the fucked-up thing with those files. You could read over all the reports and statements a million times, and on the million and first, something would jump out and there'd be a break in the case.

Good luck with that, dude. I've already been through those bastards two million times.

I glanced at the time. Still two hours before Kenny Walker would be on his way into family court, and probably another hour before he'd be on his way out. Which meant with traffic and parking . . .

I cleared my throat. "We're meeting someone at the courthouse. Probably around noon."

Darren lifted his head, and maybe it was the white papers reflecting on his skin, but between his sickly pallor, his bloodshot eyes, and his "you're shitting me" raised eyebrow, he looked like he'd recently spent some time worshipping the porcelain god.

"Or," I said, "I can go while you stay here and . . ." I gestured at the papers.

Slowly shaking his head, he sat up. "No. No, I'm good." He rubbed his eyes with the heels of his hands, then reached for his coffee. "Just, uh, let me wake up a bit more." He paused, the cup stopping just shy of his lips. "When do we need to leave?"

"Probably in the next hour."

"Okay." He drained his coffee and stood, stumbling when the chair wobbled. When he was solid on his feet, he held up his empty cup. "I'm going to go get a refill."

"Good idea." I watched him leave, and when he was out of earshot, I called downstairs.

"Supply and maintenance, this is Bob."

"Hey, Bob. It's Detective Ruffner, third floor. I don't suppose you could spare a swivel chair with functioning wheels, could you?"

"Pretty sure I've got one. I'll send it up today."

"Thanks."

Darren was quiet most of the morning. The coffee did seem to bring some color back into his face and some life back into his eyes, but he didn't say much.

At first, I was relieved. Maybe I wouldn't have to toss him off a bridge after all. As the morning went on, though, and we drove down to the courthouse to deal with Kenny Walker, I started feeling guilty. Was he just hungover? Or was last night really bothering him? As much as I hated the idea, maybe we did need to talk about it.

The courthouse had about seventeen parking spaces that weren't reserved for judges, so I parked a couple of blocks over. As we started up the road, Darren was still silent. Eyes down, shoulders pulled in, jaw tight, and I was pretty sure he wasn't just trying to keep from puking.

This awkward silence was going to drive me insane, so halfway to the courthouse, I stopped. He did too, and turned to me, lifting his gaze.

"Okay." I slid my hands into my pockets. "I get the feeling we should clear the air."

His eyes darted away, and he exhaled. "Yeah. Probably."

And . . . more silence.

Great. I'd taken the initiative to start the conversation, but as per usual, couldn't figure out the next step. It wasn't for nothing that my ex-wife had used my name and "blood from a stone" in the same sentence during our divorce proceedings.

Darren threw up his hands. "Look. It happened. We can't change it. Can we just forget it?"

I blinked. "I . . . Yeah. I was . . . thinking along those lines, actually."

He pursed his lips and kept his gaze down. "For what it's worth, I don't usually drink like that." Color deepened in his cheeks as he added, "And I never show up to work hungover, but I had a few more after you left and . . ." He shook his head. "Anyway. It's done."

"It is. So, um . . ." I swallowed. "We'll just let it go? It never happened?"

"Yeah." He backed it up with a shrug that was stiff enough to make me doubt this was really over. "We should . . ." He gestured up the road.

I nodded. Well, it was a start. Hopefully. In even less comfortable silence than before, we continued toward the courthouse.

Just before we reached it, I turned down a side street. "This way."

"What?"

"Just follow me."

Darren grumbled something, but he followed. At the other end of the street was a small park. There was playground equipment, but no kids in sight. Some gangbangers were sitting on a jungle gym, smoking cigarettes and talking on their phones. A small group of shady-looking guys were huddled near the swings.

Darren fidgeted nervously.

"Relax."

"Right," he grumbled. "So, what are we doing out here anyway?"

"Waiting." I glanced at my watch. "He should be out in the next twenty minutes or so, and I have a feeling he'll come through here."

"What makes you say that?"

"Because I'm pretty sure he left something in the bushes."

Darren craned his neck. All along the edges of the park were thick shrubs. They were trimmed low to the ground, leaving just two inches or so of clearance. Though the city had been telling the gardeners to trim them higher, no one ever did. After all, without the foliage, where would everyone hide their guns while they went in to the courthouse?

He turned to me. "This park is always just littered with guns?"

I nodded and took a seat on a bench. "Can't take them into the courthouse."

"Wow." He sat beside me. "So, what now?"

"Now we wait for our contact to come out of his court date."

"Sounds exciting."

"Very."

The day was getting hotter as the morning wore on, so we both took off our jackets. I still had a loose shirt over the top of my shoulder holster, as did Darren—I preferred not to advertise that I was armed when I was in plainclothes.

We hung around on the bench, checking our phones and ignoring each other to pass the time. As the silence was becoming unbearable, a familiar face appeared.

"There he is." I sat up, nodding toward Kenny and two of his friends.

Darren glanced at me. He was tense, like a bomb-sniffing dog waiting for the command, but he didn't move. Wisely, he was following my lead.

We waited while Kenny and his buddies fished their pistols out from under the bushes. They holstered them—or in one case, stupidly tucked it into the crotch of his pants—and started to leave.

"Think he put the safety on?" I asked.

Darren snorted. "For his future children's sake, let's hope so."

I chuckled and rose, gesturing for Darren to do the same. We started after Kenny.

And the world . . .

Shifted.

Darren grabbed my arm. "Andreas?"

I took a few deep breaths, willing the tunnel vision to clear and the sparkling to stop. "Yeah. I'm good. Sorry." I kept walking because I needed to talk to Kenny, but . . . I wasn't good.

After two steps, I wavered and had to grab the fence for balance. The sharp top bit into my palm, jarring my senses into focus.

Darren touched my arm. "You all right?"

I shrugged away from his touch. "I'm fine."

"You eaten yet today?"

Gritting my teeth, I fought the urge to snap back that I didn't need an additional mother. "We'll get lunch after we talk to Kenny."

"Are you—"

"I'm good. Let's go."

I took two more steps, and my vision darkened. My ears were stuffed with cotton. My legs . . . disappeared.

The world tilted again, and I reached for anything to break my fall. Something bit into my forearm. Then something else cracked against my kneecap.

"Andreas!"

Then nothing.

My vision cleared. I was staring up at tree branches. And the sky. From a bench. I was lying on a bench. How the fuck?

The burning in my arm made my breath catch, but it was the wetness of my sleeve that made me panic. The wetness, and the intense pressure. From Darren. Who was holding a jacket or something around my arm. To staunch the bleeding.

"Shit." I shoved his hands away. "Get off me. Don't fucking touch me!"

He scrambled back. To my horror, there was blood on the front of his sleeve, and even more soaking into the shirt he'd wrapped around my forearm.

I pulled it close to my stomach to keep some pressure on it. Fuck, this hurt. Oh God, I'd really fucked up my arm, hadn't I? "What the hell happened?"

"You passed out." He gestured behind him. "Tried to catch yourself on a sharp edge on the fence."

I closed my eyes for a moment. When I opened them, I realized there were other people around, gaping at us with concerned expressions.

I started to sit up, but Darren halted me with a hand on my shoulder, which he quickly withdrew.

"Don't move." He held out his hand. "Give me your keys. I'll go get the car, and then I'm taking you to the hospital."

I wanted to say we weren't going to the hospital. The amount of blood on my sleeve and the intense throbbing in my arm said otherwise. Stitches, probably. Maybe even an X-ray since this felt suspiciously like the time I broke my arm as a kid.

I moistened my lips. "Keys are in my jacket. Left pocket."

And where the hell is my jacket?

But then Darren picked it up off the ground, searched through the pockets, and spun the keys around his finger. "Stay here. I'll be back."

With that, he was gone.

Well fuck. Because things weren't weird enough already.

"X-rays came back clear." The nurse closed my chart and smiled. "No fractures. Just a mild sprain. Take care of the laceration and follow up with your doctor, but you should be healed in three to four weeks."

I nodded, glancing down at my thickly bandaged forearm. "Thanks."

"Also, here's your bracelet back." The nurse handed me a plastic bag containing my medic alert bracelet. They'd had to take it off before bandaging my arm. It had been cleaned, thank God, though I'd clean it again once I was home. Just to be sure.

"Thanks."

"How's the dizziness?" she asked.

"It's fine." Probably because I was still semireclined on the gurney, but if I told her that, then she'd probably want to give me IV fluids or otherwise make me stay in this hellhole. So I was fine.

"Okay." She smiled. "Well, I'll get your discharge papers started, so you should be good to go soon."

"Thanks."

She left, and not thirty seconds later, there was a knock at the door. Record timing for discharge papers.

"Come in," I said.

Okay, not discharge papers. Shit.

Darren shut the door behind him. "You all right?"

"Yeah." I gestured at my bandaged arm. "Doc didn't even stitch it. Just glued it back together."

"And it wasn't busted?"

I shook my head. "Bit of a sprain, I guess. Must've happened when I landed."

"Good. Good." He rocked from his heels to the balls of his feet. "So when are they letting you out?"

"They're doing the discharge papers now. So, probably next week."

He laughed but didn't sound like he meant it. He sat in the chair beside the door, pressed his elbow onto the armrest, and chewed his thumbnail. He stared at the floor. I gnawed my lip. Apparently awkward silence was going to be a thing now.

Or not.

When Darren spoke, his tone was cold and flat. "For the record, when you came to earlier, I was just trying to stop the bleeding. It wasn't exactly the time to be copping a feel, you know?"

"Copping a—" I cocked my head. "What the hell are you talking about?"

He shifted in the chair. "When you told me not to touch you? I mean, seriously, I know things almost got out of hand last night, but in the park ... I mean ... What the fuck did you think I was doing?"

"I . . ." I glanced down at my bloody shirt. "It wasn't . . . Okay, you know what? Maybe we should clear the air." I thumbed my medic alert bracelet. *Really gonna go there?* "In fact, I think it's less that we need to clear the air, and more that I need to level with you."

Darren watched me, but said nothing.

Well, here goes.

"When I told you to get off me earlier, it wasn't because I thought you were coming on to me." Stomach twisting, I tossed the bagged bracelet toward him. "I was afraid of getting blood on you."

He caught the bracelet and eyed me for a moment. Then he turned it over and read it.

I held my breath, thankful I was no longer hooked to anything that could broadcast my escalating heartrate.

With a shrug, he said, "That's it?"

"That's—" I blinked. "What do you mean, 'That's it'?"

"I mean . . ." he tossed the bracelet back to me, "is this what you've been avoiding telling me? Even before last night?" He shook his head. "That you have HIV?"

The words were like a punch to the gut. I stared down at the bracelet so I didn't have to look at him. "Kind of makes sense I wouldn't want to bleed on you, don't you think?"

"Yeah, I appreciate the concern. And I saw it on the bracelet while you were passed out anyway."

My stomach flipped over. "You did?"

"Uh, yeah. You were out cold and bleeding. Seemed like a good time to see what the deal was." Another shrug, as if he'd just seen some unsightly scar or an ill-advised tattoo and thought nothing of it. "But, I mean, why didn't you tell me from the start? Is this . . . Wait, is that why you get dizzy and why you passed out? Like the meds or something?"

I nodded. "They're doing their job—my viral load's been undetectable for a while now—but the side effects suck. Still trying to get the dosage and everything right, but it is what it is." I swallowed. "And I'd, uh, just as soon no one on the force knew. About any of this."

"Secret's safe with me." He rose, and so did my blood pressure as he came closer. "This is why you put a stop to things last night, isn't it?"

I made myself look him in the eye. "Yeah."

"Not because we were drinking. Not because we're coworkers." He tapped the bagged bracelet. "Because of that."

I nodded.

"For what it's worth, if I'd known, that wouldn't have changed anything."

"What?" I laughed bitterly. "Are you insane?"

Darren rolled his eyes. "I'm from a different generation, Andreas. It's not a death sentence anymore, you know?"

"Your generation is a bunch of idiots, then."

"You're still alive, aren't you?"

I scowled.

"Let me ask you this." He rested a hand on the bedrail beside me. "If this hadn't been a factor, would you have walked away last night?"

Not a chance. And neither of us would be walking at all today.

"No."

"Well, then . . ." A weird smile played at his lips, and when he leaned over me, he murmured, "You'll have to try harder than that to get rid of me."

And then he kissed me.

I put a hand on his chest, fully intending to shove him away, but . . . my God. He knew. Hell, he'd barely blinked. And after I'd spent four damned years steadfastly refusing to get physical with someone, Darren was getting physical with me, and it . . . it felt . . . so fucking good.

So I curled my fingers around his tie and pulled him closer.

CHAPTER FOURTEEN
DARREN

J esus *Christ*, I had never kissed someone like this before. I'd gone in trying for *reassuring*, but by the time Andreas was tugging me into his space, we'd rocketed right past *hot* and into *this hospital bed ain't gonna survive what we're about to do to it.*

It was like our kiss lit a fuse inside Andreas, and I didn't know whether it was attached to a firecracker or a fucking nuclear weapon. Either way, the rising heat of his body and the guttural sound he made against my lips when I wrapped a hand around the back of his neck were more than enough to get me right up there with him. I fumbled for the bedrail, intent on taking it down and making some room for myself.

"Ahem."

Goddamn it, where was the fucking *latch—*

"*Ahem.*"

Andreas registered it before I did. He jerked back like he was on fire, but he didn't quite let go of my tie. We both turned to the nurse standing in front of the door, which she'd been nice enough to close behind her, at least.

"Hi," I said after a moment.

"Hi there." She looked more amused than annoyed. "I've got that discharge paperwork ready, Detective Ruffner. I brought you some water as well." She glanced down at the cup, then back at me. "I should have brought two, it seems. You both look like you could use some cooling off."

You fucked with nurses at your peril. I'd learned that the hard way. "I'm good, thanks," I said, letting go of Andreas and straightening up. Moving away from him was harder than I'd anticipated. *Shit.* I had it bad already, and all we'd done was kiss.

You could be completely screwing yourself with this, my shoulder angel reminded me. It sounded a lot like Asher during his DA days. *Fucking around with a guy who's got kids that aren't much younger than you? Are you crazy?*

My shoulder devil obligingly kicked my shoulder angel in the nuts. I was committed now, at least enough to stick around and see what happened next. Andreas was my partner, and he'd just told me what was, to him, probably the worst thing imaginable. It made me a little limp with relief. His HIV status was a hurdle, but it was far from a deal breaker.

Andreas started signing the clipboard full of papers, and the nurse turned to me. "Will you be taking him home?"

Andreas snorted. I interpreted that as "no way in hell," but smiled anyway. "I'll be with him for the rest of the day."

"He needs fluids," she said. "Lots of fluids, preferably with some electrolytes. Steer clear of alcohol or caffeine. Some food would probably go a long way as well."

"You got it." I was more than a little hungry myself. I'd barely been able to force down a piece of dry toast this morning after drowning my stupid sorrows in whiskey last night. Alone. On my couch. Because I was such a role model.

"We have a pretty good cafeteria," she hinted, then took the finished paperwork back from Andreas and lowered the bedrail.

"I'm not about to keel over," Andreas said, but he was careful getting to his feet.

"It's on the second floor, just take a right off the elevator."

She left, and we looked at each other. My stomach growled. Andreas rolled his eyes. "You're like a puppy."

"A starving puppy," I agreed. "It's not like we've got anywhere else to be at the moment, right?"

"Not anymore we don't." He sounded angry, but I figured it was mostly with himself.

I stepped into his space, fit my hand around the sharp angle of his jaw, and kissed him again. It wasn't as effortlessly hungry as our first kiss, but the fire was still there, just banked behind a layer of interaction with another person.

"You can't use kissing me as a way to shut me up." He only sounded a *little* breathless, but that was enough for me.

"Oh yes, I can. Just not at work. And this wasn't to shut you up—it was because I wanted to. So there." I stuck my tongue out at him. He rolled his eyes.

"So mature," he drawled, but I noticed he was holding pretty firmly onto my hip.

"Maturity is overrated. Let's go get some food."

"Hospital food." We headed toward the elevator, and I was relieved to see that he was walking perfectly fine. "First disgusting fish sandwiches, and now this. You're some sort of culinary masochist, aren't you?"

I pressed the button for the second floor. "Maybe I'm a culinary sadist instead. After all, you *do* have to eat with me."

"Order another one of those sandwiches and that'll change real fast."

"Threat duly noted."

The cafeteria was serviceable, a little better than the cellophane-wrapped microwaveable shit you could get at the corner store closest to the station. It was hot, at least, and the place was busy enough that no one looked twice at us.

"So," I said once we were sitting again. Andreas eyed me warily. God only knew what he was thinking I'd ask him—probably more details about his status, if the way he was gripping his fork like he wanted to stab me with it was any indication. Like I'd be that crass. Yet. "What were you hoping to get out of Kenny?"

Right call. Andreas's shoulders relaxed, and he stabbed his meatloaf instead of me. "Anything. Kenny Walker is one of Blake's bigger fish, but like Jake, he's hard to pin down. We could have arrested him for reckless endangerment after leaving his gun in those bushes, but he'd have been out of custody in under a day. Nothing sticks to him. Get him privately, though?" Andreas's lips curled in a slightly disturbing smile. "He's been known to slip up. Kenny talks a big game, but he really doesn't care for one-on-one time."

"He had two guys with him."

"They weren't going to pull their guns on me."

"Really?" I lowered my voice. "Because if you're right, then these are the people putting out hits on *judges* and getting away with it. It sounds to me like they could have made shooting us look like an accident without much trouble."

"You scared, Darren?"

"I'm cautious. I'd like to know what I'm walking into *before* I step up, when possible."

After a moment, Andreas nodded. "I'll tell you. When possible."

"Good. So how did you know Kenny would be there?"

"I got a message this morning before I came in. Which I would have told you," he said before I could ask. "Except this morning things were fucked up between us."

"They're still pretty fucked up."

"You're telling me," he muttered.

"But at least this time we can clear the air with sex." I got maybe a bit too much enjoyment out of the way Andreas almost choked on his food. "Too soon? What about making out, then? Heavy petting?"

"This isn't a joke." His voice was hard. "There's a lot at stake here. Not just our jobs, but your *health*, you idiot. Do you understand that?"

"I do. There are plenty of precautions we can take to be safe, though. Sex isn't off the table, right?"

"Are you always this single-minded?"

"Only when I see something I want." *And when I haven't gotten off with another person in almost six months.* That had been Phil, my last real date. It hadn't been much of a date, actually: we'd gone out for drinks, he'd blown me in the bathroom, I'd returned the favor in his car, and then he'd dropped me off at my apartment. After that I'd been too busy busting my ass to make detective to take a night off for a friendly fuck.

Andreas stared at me, and I looked right back. I could see the interest in his expression, the assessing gleam in his eyes, but before he could speak, his phone rang. He reached for it with the injured arm, winced, then set down his fork and answered. "Ruffner." A little furrow appeared right between his eyes. "No, Captain." He glanced at the clock on the wall. "Fifteen, maybe twenty minutes. Why?" After a few more words, I could hear the dial tone start up. Well. Captain Hamilton seemed to be feeling a little brusque today.

Andreas pushed his plate away and stood up. "He wants to talk to me. He won't say about what."

"That's . . . kind of disturbing."

Andreas shrugged. "It's not too unusual, actually. If he gives me too much notice, I can usually find a way to get out of meeting with him."

"How have you survived twenty years on the force?"

Andreas smiled grimly. "Persistence. Come on."

I held up the car keys. "Fine, but I'm driving." I could see he wanted to argue with me, but apparently his arm hurt enough that he reined it in. I'd have to enjoy it while I could.

"What do we tell him about your injury?" I asked as I drove us toward the precinct.

"Nothing."

"Right, because *that's* going to fly."

"I have a change of clothes in the back." Oh, hey, so he did. I side-eyed him as he stripped out of his bloodstained shirt and gingerly pulled on a new one, folding the old one up so that the stain was covered and then tucking it into the duffel bag in the backseat. Andreas might be in his forties, but goddamn, he was *built*. "Eyes on the road, Darren."

"We haven't crashed yet, have we?"

"The way this day has gone so far, I wouldn't put it past us."

By the time we parked in the garage, you'd never have known that Andreas had been laid out on his back in the hospital just an hour ago. I'd have admired it more if I didn't know how much pain he must have been hiding. Time and the captain waited for no detective, though.

Marla's gaze narrowed over her cat's-eye glasses as we entered the room. "Where have you two been all day?"

"Working!" I said brightly. "Like we're supposed to. Of course."

"That is not a working face. I can spot a working face a mile away, and that is *not* your face right now, Darren."

"Can we get on with this?" Andreas asked. "The captain is expecting us."

"Don't get snippy with me. You think I don't know that? He's on the phone." Or, at least, he'd *been* on the phone. The door slammed open—Marla winced but didn't say anything this time—and Hamilton glared at us.

"Get in here, Ruffner. Might as well bring your partner too."

We entered his office, and I closed the door behind us as gently as I could. Ruffner sat without being asked. It seemed calculated to come off as insolent, but I saw the faint tremor of fatigue in his arms. "What's this about, sir?"

"I think that's my line," he said. "Do you know a man named Frederic Lee?"

Ruffner frowned. "Not really. He's a clerk at the justice department, I think. Why?"

"Because he was found dead not half an hour ago."

Andreas shrugged. "We're not homicide. What do you expect us to do about it?"

I was no expert at reading Andreas yet, but I'd caught on to a few tells at this point. The way he kept his face perfectly blank and unconcerned despite the frown on it a moment ago made me think twice, but now wasn't the time to ask.

"I was hoping you'd answer a few questions for me. Like why he was found with *your card* pinned to his chest with a switchblade, Ruffner."

My heart skipped a beat, and not in the fun way. *Oh shit.* That wasn't good. Andreas continued to appear unaffected, though.

"I hand out dozens of cards every year. I can't keep track of who they all end up with. Why? Are you accusing me of something?"

Captain Hamilton shook his head. "Of course not. You're not a complete fool, all evidence to the contrary aside. You wouldn't do the equivalent of signing a corpse before dumping it at the old warehouse off Hunt Street." He sighed. "I'm not worried *about* you right now, Ruffner. I'm worried *for* you. This sounds like a message to me, but I don't get the connection. I need you to fill in the blanks."

"I wish I could," he said. "But I don't know the guy. Sorry, Captain. Better luck next time." He stood up, turned, and walked out before either of us could say anything else. Captain Hamilton turned his attention to me.

"Keep a close eye on your partner, Corliss."

"I will," I promised. *For more reasons than you know.*

CHAPTER FIFTEEN
ANDREAS

On the way to the parking garage, I tried my damnedest to keep my usual cool exterior in place, but it wasn't easy. I'd been off-balance ever since last night. Even more so since I'd ripped my arm open. Triply so since Darren had kissed me in the hospital room. I was still shaky from blood loss, not to mention the drug side effects that had dropped me in the first place, and the constant burning and throbbing in my forearm wasn't helping a goddamned thing.

And now Frederic Lee was dead. With my card prominently displayed on his person. In the warehouse where I met with my contacts.

Fuck. Fuck, fuck, fuck. This was *real* bad.

As we stepped out of the elevator into the parking garage, Darren extended his hand, palm up. "Keys."

I gritted my teeth, but handed him the keys.

"So where is this place? Where the hell is Hunt Street?"

"Just outside of town. I'll give you directions as we go."

We got into the car, and as promised, I directed him toward the warehouse. With every turn, my stomach knotted tighter. I didn't want him knowing where this place was. No one was supposed to know where it was, including Frederic Lee and whoever had offed him. They sure as shit weren't supposed to know where my cameras were or how to disconnect them prior to murdering him and dumping his body. I'd tried to access them on my phone, but the signal wasn't working. Hopefully the cameras themselves hadn't been disturbed and I could still get the footage. I wasn't optimistic about it, though.

When we pulled up, the abandoned warehouse was anything but. Several patrol cars and an unmarked were outside. The coroner's van was there, and two news vans were parked across the street. Fortunately, the patrols had been smart and cordoned off the entire place with yellow tape, keeping the vultures and their cameras away. Hollywood celebrities didn't hate the paparazzi like I hated the local media.

Inside, the body was covered and a couple of uniformed officers were standing guard while the forensic photographers documented every inch of the scene. Darren and I split up, wandering around the scene. He checked in with the homicide detectives while I slipped out to check my cameras. Sure enough, they were toast—one was gone and the other had been smashed to tiny bits. The graffiti on the bricks behind it was fresh, too. I wasn't much of a vandalism connoisseur, but the red spray-painted *Die Pig* definitely hadn't been there before.

My heart thumped. Apparently I needed a new place to meet with contacts. Easier said than done, considering it needed to be remote enough I could rough them up if the situation warranted it.

I headed back inside.

"Detective Ruffner?" A familiar female voice turned me around, and Detective Paula Morris extended her hand. "Long time no see."

I shook her hand. "Could've been better circumstances, but good to see you."

She laughed halfheartedly. "Yeah. And under these circumstances, I'm surprised the captain let you come to this scene." She paused. "He told you not to, didn't he?"

"Am I that predictable?"

Another laugh, this time with a little more feeling. "You never change, do you?"

"Not if I can help it." I nodded toward the body, which was in the process of being loaded onto a stretcher. "So I understand you found some evidence tying me to this guy."

"Yep. This is the card we found on him." She pulled a plastic evidence bag from her coat pocket and handed it to me. "You know anything about what's on the back?"

I took it and turned it over. Bloodstains obscured part of the handwritten phone number, but the name was clear as day—*Jeff*.

My own blood turned cold. The name was common, but this wasn't just any Jeff. I'd seen that number on my caller ID enough times to recognize it immediately.

I handed the card back. "I'll be in touch."

"You know something about this?" she asked.

I didn't answer and hurried off to find Darren. He was talking to Morris's partner near a bullet hole in the wall. I didn't bother telling them it was an old one—a .45 cal that had been there since last summer—and motioned for Darren to come with me. "We have to go. Now."

He blinked. "What? But we just—"

"*Now.*"

He stared at me for a second, then handed something back to the other detective and followed me. He didn't say a word until we were in the car. As he started the engine, he asked, "All right. Where are we going?"

"I'm not sure yet." I took out my phone and scrolled through my contacts. "Head back into town." I thumbed a text: *Call me now. 911.*

While I waited for a response, Darren wisely did as he was told, pulling out of the gravel lot and heading toward the city.

A good two minutes later, my phone rang.

I answered, "Jeff?"

"Yeah, man. What's up?"

"Where are you?"

The kid laughed. "What do you think? I'm at school."

I pursed my lips. "You lying to me? This is important."

He didn't answer immediately. There was some movement, and the background noise got a little louder. Whispering now, Jeff said, "I ain't lying. I'm at school."

"Go to the guidance counselor's office. Now. Wait for me there."

"Why? I got class. I can't—"

"*Now*, Jeff."

"All right, all right. What's going on?"

"I'll explain when I get there."

After I hung up, Darren asked, "So, where am I going?"

"North Park High School."

He was quiet for a moment. "You gonna tell me what's going on? Or do I have to wait until we get there?"

I let the surly tone slide. "We're taking someone into protective custody."

"Protective—" Darren shot me a look. "At a high school? Someone you just sent to wait for you with a guidance counselor. Are we . . . are we bringing in a *kid*?"

I exhaled, trying to get comfortable despite the relentless aching on my arm. "A kid whose name was on the back of the card they found on Lee."

"You mean your card?"

"Yeah."

Darren tapped his thumb on the wheel. "What the hell is going on?"

I stared out the windshield. Out of distrust but also necessity, I'd kept a lot of things from my various partners. Darren had proven he could be trusted. I liked him, and not just as a cop. And regardless of how I felt about him, the situation was escalating quickly. The information I had was need to know, and if Darren was going to trust me—and if he was going to stay alive—he needed to know.

I absently played with the edge of the bandage sticking out from under my sleeve. "Lee was one of my contacts. An informant."

"Why am I not surprised?" Darren muttered.

I shot him a glare but let the comment go. "The name on the back of the card is a kid who's been supplying me information too. Among other things."

"'Other things'? Such as?"

I hesitated. "Such as the evidence I planted on Jake so we could bring him in."

Darren's head turned so sharply I was surprised he didn't jerk the wheel and send us into the ditch. "You've been buying *heroin* from a *kid*?"

"I bought it from him one time."

"Oh, that makes it so much better. What the hell is *wrong* with you?"

I narrowed my eyes. "You want the full story before you decide something's wrong with me? Or should we just jump to that conclusion?"

"Oh. Yeah. This should be good." He rolled his eyes. "Do tell, Andreas—what explanation could you possibly have for buying fucking *heroin* from a fucking *kid*?"

I twisted toward Darren. "Because he was *also* a goddamned informant, and when one of Blake's cronies figured out he was talking to me, he got scared and told them I was buying. And they bought it because I've got a reputation in the department for being a junkie and a dirty cop. So, yes, I bought heroin from the kid because if he didn't prove he was supplying me, he was going to turn up in a gutter somewhere."

Darren swallowed.

Speaking a little softer, I added, "It's not an ideal arrangement. Not for anyone involved. But it's kept a target off his back, and it's kept me in the loop with Blake's operations."

"But you think he's in danger now."

"Yeah. Someone's going down the list of people who've supplied me with information."

"How long before they come after you?"

I didn't have an answer for that. And if I did, he wouldn't have liked it.

Darren pulled onto the freeway and accelerated. A couple of mileposts whipped by before he spoke again. "Maybe we should think about putting you someplace safe."

I laughed dryly.

"I'm not kidding. If they've connected you to Lee and to this kid, then there's a damn good chance someone's coming for you."

"So where do you suggest I go? Your place?"

Darren tensed, and I realized what my suggestion had implied.

I cleared my throat. "I mean, um . . ."

"Well, you'd be staying with a cop."

"Yeah, but . . ."

We exchanged uneasy glances.

I coughed again. "Let's get Jeff someplace safe, and then we'll worry about me."

Silence set in.

"Do Blake's people know where Jeff goes to school?" Darren asked.

"Probably, yes."

"Then you probably shouldn't show up there."

I chewed my lip. He had a point. Sighing, I took out my phone again. "I'll send some patrol officers."

"Good idea."

I made the call, dispatching a couple of patrols to pick up Jeff from school, and also to take his mother someplace safe. At this rate, every informant I'd ever spoken to was going to wind up in witness protection, which meant we needed to amp up our investigation and shut this shit down. Whatever was brewing, it wasn't good, and it was going to get bloody.

While I was at it, I texted my ex-girlfriend.

Ask Emily if she wants to go to the zoo this weekend.

On the surface, it was a benign message, but she'd know what I meant. For all our screaming matches and inability to be in the same room, Lisa took me seriously when I sent her coded messages, and suggesting that I was going to take our daughter to the zoo during my custody weekend meant *take her to your aunt's and don't come home until I tell you.* She wouldn't ask questions. By tonight, she and Emily would be well on their way out of town. Thank God her job allowed her to work remotely. My older kids lived in other states, as did their mother, so they were safe. For the moment, anyway.

I put my phone down.

"So, it's taken care of?" Darren asked. "Someone else is picking him up?"

"Yeah."

"Okay. What now?"

I stared at my dormant phone.

"The offer's open, by the way," he said quietly. "About my place."

"Is that offer for my protection?" I turned toward him. "Or something . . . mutually beneficial?"

Darren's cheeks colored. "Does it have to be one or the other?"

I swallowed.

He coughed into his fist and fidgeted. "Look, I'm not suggesting we blow off work and . . ."

"Pick up where we left off when the nurse interrupted us?"

I didn't think he could get any redder, but apparently I was wrong.

"Um. Something like that." He stared straight ahead. "But I can't imagine you're in the mood for much. You've kind of been through the wringer today."

Well, thank God he'd said it. At this point, I was ready to just go home and sleep for a week. Today was not the day to jump into bed with my much-younger partner who *hadn't* bled like a stuck pig and *wasn't* on medication with reams of side effects. And hell, he might've known about my HIV status now, and he'd been all right with kissing me, but I wasn't holding my breath that he'd be as relaxed about it when sex was more than a hypothetical.

I pressed back against the seat and sighed. "Yeah. I'll be lucky if I stay awake past dinner."

"Still." His fingers drummed rapidly on the console between us. "I'm serious. You need to rest after this morning, and I doubt anyone's expecting you to be sleeping at my place."

That included me up until an hour or two ago.

I blew out a breath. "All right. Your place it is."

CHAPTER SIXTEEN

DARREN

Andreas was asleep on my couch. It was four in the afternoon, and he was sacked out on my thrift-store reject, his injured arm carefully slung across his chest, the rest of him spread out as far as he could get on furniture that was way too short for him. His eyes twitched under bruised lids, and every few minutes he reflexively frowned. He might have been asleep, but I wasn't sure he was getting any rest.

I'd been prepared for embarrassment as I showed Andreas into my matchbox of an apartment. It was cheap and close to the precinct, which was the entire reason I'd rented here, but it struck that I'd never invited anyone into it before. Apart from Asher, that was, and he hadn't been here for over a year, not since Vic had taken away his keys for good. The apartment was . . . Okay, so maybe I wasn't the tidiest person, and maybe I hadn't done the dishes in more time than I could remember, but Andreas wasn't going to care about the state of my countertops. Right?

I was righter than I knew. I'd cleared my throat in preparation for a preemptive apology for the mess, but he hadn't stopped at the door, just kicked his shoes off, hung his jacket over the back of a chair, and sat down on the couch with a sigh. "Mind if I take this?"

"Make yourself comfortable."

Five minutes later he'd been asleep.

I wasn't disappointed. No, that wasn't the strange, hot sensation curling in the back of my throat at the sight of Andreas splayed across my couch like he owned it, letting himself get some much-needed sleep in the presence of a person he barely knew. If I had to guess, I'd say I was feeling *possessive*, but fuck that. I wasn't about to mess things up with Andreas by pushing too hard. I could be patient when it came to getting what I wanted. Driven, focused, but patient. A good detective had to be a good hunter too, and I'd learned from the best.

Besides, it wasn't like I didn't have things to do in the meantime. I was a list person—and yeah, I could just imagine what my new partner would say when he realized I had a bullet point fetish, but I'd cross that bridge when I came to it. In the meantime, I was just confused enough right now to be paranoid, and I hated that feeling. A list might bring me some clarity. So I sat down at my kitchen table, pulled an ever-present pad of paper and a pen over, and started writing down names.

Blake's people:
Jake (custody)
Kenny (seen at court, possible contact)
Jeff (a fucking KID, heroin source)

Following them was the growing number of people who had been on our list of possible contacts when we'd started and had subsequently died, or who we hadn't been able to locate. There were too many names there. I frowned and hauled over my personal laptop, logged in and accessed the copy of the file I'd stowed in a private email account. Against the rules, yeah, I knew that, but I didn't feel all that bad about it. Too many people had seen that fucking file already, and one of those people—or more—was winnowing away our list of suspects faster than we could pick them up. I couldn't prove it, but the odds of all those losses being coincidence were just too slim.

I knew what Vic would say. *Talk to your captain.* Hamilton was there to make our lives easier, wasn't he? He was supposed to facilitate the progress of our investigations and keep the brass off our backs, and under slightly different circumstances I'd agree. In this case, though? With Andreas's life possibly on the line, with too many hits and too many disappearances and threats that seemed to come out of nowhere? I couldn't do it. Not without giving away too much, and the more I talked, the deeper IA would dig.

Detective Thibedeau. I started a new list, this one titled *Internal Affairs Assholes*, and put his name at the top of it. I threw Trent Newberry on next, because that was another "coincidence" that grated on me—that Trent had been hanging around a precinct he had no official business at. Why was he even there? Had he seen the file?

Had Thibedeau? The memory of the red car that Andreas had been so wary of earlier in the week surfaced again, and I sighed. Were we still being followed, and was Internal Affairs really behind it?

I rubbed my fingers against my forehead. I'd be accusing Santa Claus of colluding with the enemy next. Thibedeau was the kind of ladder-climber who had filled the DA's office, and Asher had taught me to spot them a mile away. He was opportunistic, but he lived for rules and regulations. If he didn't, if he'd had a shred of creativity and a slightly shorter stick up his ass, he'd have already done what Andreas had: planted evidence to get the result he wanted, only he'd have planted it against Andreas. I just couldn't see it.

Trying to list Andreas's enemies would take way too long, and probably be incomplete regardless. I'd heard the murmurs in the bull pen, seen the glances in the locker room. No one confronted him because he was the living definition of unapproachable, but that didn't mean they didn't talk amongst themselves. After his injury, after the card on Lee's body, and as evident as the shit storm that this case was turning into was, the talk would only get louder. All I could do was ignore it. I had his back on this.

You think you know everything? Oh, my shoulder angel was an insidious little fuck. *You think he's told you all the important stuff? Think a guy like this would open up to* you? *You're not that special, Darren.*

Well, what didn't I know? Apart from anything about his family life, or most of his career on the force, or how he'd been infected and how long he'd been dealing with it. My fingers hovered over the keys, almost ready to do what I hadn't bothered with yet, that low of all lows: Googling his name. It made me feel like a scummy PI just thinking about it.

My phone rang and saved my sanity. I grabbed it and took it out onto the balcony—yeah, I had one, and while it only fit a single chair, it was a nice little addition to an otherwise crappy place. I answered as soon as I slid the glass door shut behind me. "Hey, Mom."

"Darren?" She sounded . . . scared? That wasn't good. "Are you close to home?"

I frowned. "No, I'm still working." Technically that was true, since Captain Hamilton's last words to me had been to look out for my partner. *Bam*, done. I was all over that. "Why?"

"Asher's gone."

My heart stopped beating like it had suddenly forgotten how. I squeezed my eyes shut for a frozen, brutal second before I finally found my voice again. This wasn't the first time Asher had left the house without telling anyone. We had a system in place for this kind of emergency. "Did he take a car?"

"No, they're both still in the garage."

"Okay, so he's on foot. Is Vic out looking for him?"

"Ye—yes, he is, but we don't know how long Asher's been gone! I checked on him twenty minutes ago, and he was there, but . . . I mean, what if he makes it to a bus station, or if he gets mugged? He has his wallet with him, and he's got a little money in there."

"If he's catching a bus, he'll be on camera buying a ticket, and if he's mugged, he'll have something to give up, but—" I had to raise my voice to be heard over my mom's little wail, and seriously, she was breaking my heart here. "But the odds of that are so small, Mom. Seriously. He's probably just walking around the neighborhood, or maybe heading for the DA's office. He's fine. Did Vic rustle up some patrol cars?"

"Yes, a few."

"They'll find him. Just give it a little longer and you'll see, they'll bring Asher home."

"He went out his *window*!" She sounded so affronted. "I don't even know if he's wearing *shoes*, and he's been so angry lately, and what if he hates us? What if he hates staying here with us?"

"Asher loves you, Mom, you know that."

"He used to," she said. "I know he did, but the disease—"

"Just because he can't remember everything doesn't mean he doesn't know who you are. You're his mother, and he loves you. He's just too smart for his own fucking good, the little shit."

That got a watery laugh out of her. "You *both* are. God, you were such hellion children. I don't know how I survived your teens."

"You spoke softly and carried a really big stick."

"Do you think this might be it?" she said, and it was such a non sequitur that I couldn't follow her. She continued before I had to ask what she meant. "The reason your daddy never came back, I mean. Do you think he didn't really mean to leave us, that maybe he just . . .

forgot, one day? He was about Asher's age. Maybe he went for a walk and didn't remember how to get home."

My mother was going to talk herself into a heart attack at this rate. "Alzheimer's comes on pretty gradually," I said as neutrally as I could manage while still wanting to kill the fucker who was my sperm donor. *Went for a walk*, my ass. You didn't just wander away after clearing out your bank accounts and packing a fucking bag. "I really doubt he lost track of things in the space of one afternoon."

"But maybe— Oh!" I heard the doorbell ring. "Oh honey, it's . . . oh, Officer, you found him! Asher, baby!"

I couldn't hear what he said in reply, but if my mother wasn't freaking out about getting my brother to a hospital, then he was at least functional. "I'm going to go, Mom," I said into the phone. "Bye." I'd call back later to talk to my brother, when I was less likely to yell at him for worrying our mother.

I turned around and almost shouted as I saw Andreas right on the other side of the glass door that I apparently hadn't closed completely.

"Fuck," I breathed, opening the door the rest of the way. "If I fall off this balcony, it'll be your fault for sneaking up on me."

"I wasn't sneaking, you were just being loud. Really loud."

I winced. "Sorry, I didn't mean to wake you."

Andreas shook his head. "I don't mind. I was just gonna ask if we needed to go out."

"Go out?"

"To help look for your brother."

I couldn't help it, I gaped. "You don't even know him," I managed after a moment.

Andreas narrowed his eyes. "He's your family. I'm your partner. If you needed to go look for him, then I'd go with you." *Of course, moron*, his tone implied. Rather than feeling talked down to, I got that warm, tight sensation again. I lowered the phone and came back inside, more relaxed than I'd felt in hours.

"He's fine. Someone found him and brought him home."

"Huh. So. Alzheimer's?"

I sat down on the couch with a sigh. It was still warm from Andreas's body heat. "You heard that, huh?"

Andreas nodded at the sliding door. "You left a gap. Loud, remember." He didn't say anything else, but I figured he deserved to know. I knew his deep, dark secret—it wouldn't kill me to share one of mine.

"Asher was diagnosed with early-onset Alzheimer's three years ago. It's extremely rare this young, and tests showed he carries a gene linked to it that he probably inherited from our dad. Not Vic," I clarified, but Andreas just nodded like I wasn't being utterly redundant. "Our actual father vanished off the face of the earth when I was two."

"Do you have the gene?"

"I don't know." I smiled a little and tried to pretend that my hands weren't shaking. We were getting into uncomfortable territory, but I couldn't even remember the last person I'd talked to about this that I wasn't related to. Maybe it would do me some good. "I could get the test, find out if I have it. My mom thinks I should."

Andreas sat down next to me. "What do you think?"

"I think I'd rather not know. If I don't have the gene, great." Except I'd feel ludicrously guilty about escaping that fate when Asher hadn't. He'd never wish it on me, but my feelings didn't have to make sense, damn it. "And if I do have it, then I'm living on a clock. I think it would drive me crazy, always wondering when I was going to start showing signs, whether or not this would be the day I'd finally start forgetting." I forced a shrug. "Right now, I . . . just don't want to know."

Andreas nodded. "I get that."

"Yeah, I can tell." We sat in companionable silence for a while, close enough to touch. I wanted to touch, *fuck* I wanted it so bad, but he still looked like shit and I wasn't feeling so great myself, after my mom's call. "So." I glanced at him. "Delivery and bad TV?" My unfinished lists taunted me from the table, but I just couldn't go back to them right now.

Andreas smiled. It was ridiculously enticing. I had to hold myself back from reaching for his lips and tracing the edges of his smile with my tongue. "Sounds good."

Darren ordered a pizza and pulled a couple of beers out of the fridge. I decided one beer wouldn't kill me, and after the day I'd had, I didn't really care if it did.

We sat on the couch where I'd slept off some of today's bullshit, and though Darren picked up the remote, he didn't turn on the TV. Fine by me—there was an election coming up, so all the news channels would be spewing bullshit, and there weren't any decent shows on right now. Though I supposed he might've had some good things on Netflix; if he was anything like me, he'd have things queued up for weeks before he finally got a chance to sit down and binge-watch them on a rare day off. That was about the only way people in our line of work ever got to watch anything. There were even rumors that Captain Hamilton had called in sick once so he could catch up on a season and a half of *Game of Thrones* because there were so many spoilers floating around at the precinct.

I took a swallow of beer. It was some hipster brand I'd never heard of, and it wasn't half-bad. Somehow I was surprised Darren had good taste in beer. Maybe because his taste in men was questionable.

While I mused over his tastes, Darren stared at the TV screen as if it were on. He took a sip from his beer bottle, but his gaze was distant. His thoughts were probably a million miles away too.

I cleared my throat, and he jumped.

Shifting a little, he glanced at me, as if he'd suddenly realized he'd been staring off into space and was wondering how long ago he'd checked out. "Sorry. Did . . . uh . . . did you say something?"

"Not yet, no. You looked a little preoccupied."

His cheeks colored. "Yeah. Sorry." He shook his head and looked toward the blank TV again. Bringing his beer up to his lips, he muttered, "Just thinking."

"Anything in particular?"

He set the bottle on a coaster on the coffee table. "Would you buy it if I said I was crunching baseball stats?"

"I wasn't born yesterday, Darren."

"Of course not." He smirked. "That would mean I was born this afternoon."

I laughed, nearly choking on my drink. "Fuck you, asshole. I'm not *that* old."

He chuckled halfheartedly, but it faded as he stared off into space again.

"Hey." I turned toward him, slinging my good arm across the back of the couch. "*I'm* supposed to be the quiet, brooding one here."

That prompted a slightly more genuine laugh. "Fair enough." He faced me. "I guess I'm just curious about a few things."

"Such as?"

"Well, after what you told me in the ER this morning..."

Oh God. That.

The beer I'd drunk threatened to come back up, but I forced it to stay down. I reminded myself he hadn't been disgusted by my status. He'd barely batted an eye, actually. Hell, he'd kissed me not thirty seconds after I'd told him. I just fucking hated talking about it.

"What do you want to know?"

"I guess, well . . . I mean, how long have you known?"

"About four and a half years."

"Four and a—" He cocked his head. "Didn't you say you have a four-year-old kid?"

I flinched and nodded.

"Oh."

I drained my beer and set the bottle on the table. "She's negative, thank God. We still have her tested every year just to be *absolutely* sure, but the doctors are pretty confident she's in the clear."

"So, her mother has it?"

I nodded again. "She tested positive during a routine screening while she was pregnant. So I was tested too." I sighed, rubbing the back of my neck. "We're not even sure who got it from who. We both had some wild years before we met—I slept around after my divorce, and she did some heroin in her twenties—so neither of us can pinpoint where we might've gotten it." That old familiar guilt pressed itself against my ribs. "But, statistically, it's way more likely she got it from me."

Darren grimaced. "Jesus."

"Yeah. Great thing for a man to have on his conscience. And let me tell you, I'm probably the only father on the planet who got less sleep *before* my kid was born than after. I couldn't sleep for shit until I knew she'd tested negative."

"I believe that," he said quietly.

"My ex tried to forgive me—especially since there was a small chance she'd been the one to give it to me—but we were already in a rough spot even before she got pregnant. Throw in the stress of a kid we weren't expecting and then finding out we're both HIV positive . . ." I shook my head. "We made it until our daughter was a few months old, and then we called it quits."

Darren watched me for a moment. "Do you still see your daughter?" He winced like the words hadn't come out right. "I mean, shared custody and all that? Or—"

"I see her a couple of weekends a month. I'd like to spend more time with her, but right now, it's all I can do."

He fell silent again. Then, "What about your health? You seem like you're doing pretty well."

I held up my bandaged arm. "You mean aside from blacking out and splitting my arm open?"

"Isn't that from the drugs?"

"It is, but I wouldn't be taking them if I didn't need them."

"Fair enough. But beyond the side effects of the medication, have you had any problems?"

"Not really, no. Ever since I started treatment, my virus load has stayed pretty low. Like I said, it's been undetectable for a long time. Physically, I'd never even know I had it aside from the damn drug side effects." I sighed, running a hand through my hair. "Mentally . . . that's another story."

Darren turned toward me, pulling his knee up onto the cushion between us. "How so?"

I exhaled. "I heard 'HIV' and thought it was a death sentence. I came from the era when AIDS meant two or three good years if you were lucky, and then slowly dying alone."

"That was a long time ago, though."

"Well, as you helpfully pointed out a minute ago," I said with a slight laugh, "I grew up a long time ago."

He chuckled. "Fair point."

"So anyway, I knew nothing about the current prognosis for HIV patients, and I kind of . . . I panicked, I guess. No way in hell was I going through that. In fact, shortly after I found out, before I'd really sat down and let a doctor pull me back to reality, I seriously considered getting myself killed on the job."

Darren's jaw fell open. "Really?"

I nodded. He didn't need to know quite yet that I'd gone a lot further than "seriously considering." Or how much that had altered the course of our current investigation. I was beginning to trust him more than I'd expected to, but I wasn't ready to tip my hand that far—I needed to be absolutely sure before I showed these particular cards.

I muffled a cough. "I basically thought I was already dead, so I just wanted to speed up the process and maybe go out a little less painfully. And I . . ." I dropped my gaze, gut churning as the memories crashed through my mind.

Darren put his hand on my leg, the warm contact sending a shiver through me. "Tell me."

I met his eyes again. Was this really the kid who'd been assigned to spy on me? *And* the guy who'd kissed me this morning, knowing full well I was HIV positive?

This was the first time I'd spoken to someone about all this. I hated thinking about it, never mind talking about it. But I'd been holding on to all of this for four and a half goddamned years, and had never once felt this free to talk about it without fear of someone recoiling in disgust.

I took a deep breath. "I was still in panic mode. Hadn't done a damn bit of research or asked any questions because I was just . . . I was freaked out. All I could think of was how horribly my girlfriend and I were both going to die, and that I might've killed our daughter too. Even if she wasn't positive, I started wondering who'd take care of her after we were gone." I pressed my elbow onto the back of the couch and kneaded my stiff neck. "I was afraid to tell anyone at the precinct because I was convinced I'd lose my job, which would mean my kid would lose all my benefits. And I guess . . . I guess I got this idea that if I was killed on the job, no one would know the truth, and the life insurance would take care of my kids. Not just the baby, but my older kids."

"Wow," Darren said. "I can't even imagine what that was like."

"You don't want to. Trust me. Fortunately, I got my head out of my ass and started getting some answers from doctors."

"And the prognosis is a lot better these days, isn't it?" His eyebrows pulled together. "I've heard they expect most people to live almost a normal life span with HIV now."

I nodded. "Sometimes I'm not sure if that's a blessing or a curse."

"What do you mean?"

"I've been alone since my ex and I split up. It gets a little demoralizing when you meet people, and the minute you mention HIV, they're gone. I mean, I get it. And before I was positive, I probably would've done the same thing. No, I *definitely* would have. But being on this end of it can be . . ."

He squeezed my leg, pulling my focus to where he'd been touching me this entire time. "People can be assholes, but times *have* changed, you know."

"Have they?"

He held my gaze for a few long seconds. Then, with an exasperated sigh, he moved closer to me. "You know, for a respected detective, you suck at picking up clues."

And with that, he kissed me.

My heart thundered against my ribs as I slid a hand around his waist. He shifted, straddling me, and nudged my lips apart with his. The tip of his tongue just teased my lower lip before he broke the kiss.

"I made it past your *delightful* personality," he murmured. "And I'm completely ignoring that this is a terrible idea when we work together." He brushed his lips across mine. "A manageable chronic disease isn't going to scare me off."

I laughed just before he claimed another kiss, and I cradled the back of his head as if he might pull away. He didn't seem to be in any hurry to do that, though—not as he deepened the kiss and reminded me why I'd always loved making out in my past life. His body heat radiated through two layers of clothes, and every time he breathed out through his nose, the cool rush of air across my cheek made me shiver.

I let my uninjured hand drift down to his hip, and when that didn't scare him off, I slid it into his back pocket. He groaned softly, pressing against me, and the thick erection rubbing across mine made me dizzier than I'd been in a long, long time. I'd nearly forgotten what it was like to be naked with someone, and wanted—*needed*—to be naked with him now. If our body heat didn't burn off these clothes soon, I was going to tear them off.

I broke the kiss and went for his neck because it had been too long since I'd done that to anyone, and holy fuck, it was as amazing as I remembered. The warmth of his skin against my lips. The vibration of his voice when he moaned. The way he tilted his head so I could kiss anywhere and everywhere.

And right fucking then, my phone came to life in my pocket.

We both froze.

I swore under my breath and dug the damn thing out. The caller ID said it was the captain. My dick said he could wait.

I hit Ignore and tossed the phone onto another cushion.

"Not important?" he asked.

"Not even a little." I kissed his neck again, and he didn't ask questions.

But then another muffled sound interrupted us—the "Bad Boys" theme from *COPS*.

"Motherfucker," Darren grumbled. He reached for his own pocket.

"The *COPS* theme? Really?"

"Eh." He shrugged as he took it out. "Shit. It's the captain."

I groaned, scrubbing a hand over my face. Of course it was.

He sat back a little, still straddling me, and put the phone to his ear. "Yeah, Captain?"

Any other time, I'd have teased him, trailing my thumb around the outline of his very prominent hard-on. Maybe tugging his shirt free from his waistband, or drawing his zipper down.

But I could hear the captain's voice, and he did *not* sound happy.

Hamilton, you cockblocking son of a bitch . . .

Darren's eyes were unfocused. Then he closed them, and his shoulders drooped. In a resigned tone, he said, "We'll be right there."

I let my head fall back against the couch. Of course we would.

He hung up and tossed the phone in the same direction I'd thrown mine.

"So where are we going?" I grumbled.

"Back to the precinct." He sighed as he stood and adjusted the front of his pants. "Detective Morris wants to talk to us about the murder."

Paula, you're lucky I like you.

I stood too. "Guess we'll pick this up later, then."

Darren smiled apologetically. "Duty calls at the most inconvenient times."

"It does. Let's go."

We got to skip seeing the captain entirely, as it turned out. Detective Morris was waiting for us in the front hall when we arrived, pacing back and forth with a Styrofoam cup of coffee in one hand. Her neat brown ponytail was loose and wilted this late in the day, and her white button-down blouse was untucked. I was surprised that she was still here, honestly. At least now I understood why Andreas had insisted on stopping at Starbucks and ordering something neither of us had any interest in drinking.

"Christ, Paula, don't drink that break room shit," he said as he walked up to her. "You're going to make your ulcers flare up again, and then you'll have to go without coffee for a month and make everyone else miserable." He handed her the vanilla soy latte, and the annoyance on her face melted into pleasure as she took her first sip. Andreas and charming weren't two words I'd ever imagined I'd put together, but he seemed to know how to handle this lady, at least.

"You're a godsend," she said with a sigh. "A mysterious, enigmatic godsend."

Andreas arched an eyebrow. "Excuse me?"

"The card, genius. From the body? And then you running off before you could tell me who *Jeff* was? Is this ringing any bells in that hard head of yours?"

"Paula—"

"Never mind, I think I figured it out." Her teasing expression was replaced with something much grimmer. "I requisitioned a conference room. I need you guys to look at some stuff."

"Lead the way, ma'am," I said.

"Aren't you friendly?" She glanced between us incredulously. "How long do you think it'll take you to wear the shine off your new partner, Andreas?"

"Too fucking long," he said, but he was almost smiling. I took that as a win.

"Well." Detective Morris pulled me up to walk beside her as we started down the hall. "First off, don't call me 'ma'am,' it makes me feel old."

"Didn't you just turn forty?" Andreas asked with a smirk.

"How about you shut your face, Ruffner?" She kept going without missing a beat. "You can call me Detective Morris if you're feeling official, but otherwise it's Paula. Got it?"

I smiled at her. "Got it, Paula. Thanks."

"You're a sweet talker. That's good—Ruffner needs all the help he can get." She ignored his snort and led us into a conference room. Files were spread out across the table, some flipped open, some partially disassembled. There was an open laptop as well—probably her personal one, it looked too nice to be provided by the department. Paula shut the door and took a deep breath.

"So, Frederic Lee's house caught on fire today. The fire marshal suspects arson."

"Was anyone home?" Andreas asked quickly.

"No, his kids were at school and his wife was running errands. The only part of the home to completely burn was his personal office." She gestured toward the laptop. "Pictures are on there. The techs who found his computer said it was unsalvageable."

Leaning in, I could make out the charred plastic outline of what might have once been a computer.

"We're looking into getting warrants for any cloud storage he might have had, but that could take more time than I'm willing to give it. There was no phone on the body, either, so dead end there. I went and got Lee's personal effects from his office in the Justice Department, and while there wasn't a computer, there *was* a copy of his weekly schedule." She pushed over a piece of paper. "After I read through that, I knew I needed to bring you in to consult."

Andreas saw it before I did. "Zoe Dugan."

"She was due in court later this week. Drug possession with intent to sell. How she made bail two months ago, I don't know, but she didn't pay for it herself. This would have been her third time in court. She was let off due to lack of evidence twice already. Lee clerked the case both times. Now she's dead, the same as him."

Wait, was she saying . . . "Are you suggesting Frederic Lee was dirty?"

Paula sighed. "It's not what I *want* to be suggesting, but it's possible. A few years ago, one of his kids came down with cancer. It was pretty heinous, and their insurance wouldn't pay for an experimental treatment she needed. Lee put together a funding campaign that went on for weeks—God, he was fucking relentless. I barely knew the guy and *I* donated a hundred bucks just to get him to leave me alone. He needed almost fifty grand, and he needed it fast. It wasn't happening, though. Then in the space of one day, he went from less than seven thousand to completely funded by an anonymous donor. He never said where the money came from.

"After that, his work habits changed significantly. He started to float from judge to judge, and looking at the statistics, a much higher percentage of his cases ended in a failure to prosecute."

"That sounds like a lot of conjecture," Andreas said. "And it doesn't explain why you need me."

"Apart from the fact that you're working a case in which Zoe Dugan was a person of interest?" Paula shook her head. "We all know about you bringing in Carter—word gets around. I figured you'd be able to shed some light here. More to the point," she addressed Andreas sternly, "I thought you might tell me about *Jeff*. Could the card have been referring to Jeff DeLuca?" She pulled over another file. "A known associate of Dugan's, also never sentenced? He's a juvenile, that makes things harder, but I figure if anyone in this place can draw a line between them, it's you. Especially with your card pinned to the chest of Lee, who's clerked cases where they've been defendants."

"What are you implying?" Andreas didn't sound nervous, but I was starting to feel that way. Paula was a hell of a detective. I didn't approve of all of Andreas's methods, but the last thing I wanted was for him to be accused of something he wasn't guilty of, especially now.

IA would take that as a green light to start railroading him out of the precinct.

Paula rolled her eyes. "Come on, isn't it obvious? Whoever killed Lee might be the same person who killed Dugan, and if they're cleaning house, it's likely that they think you're a threat! We might not always see eye to eye, but that doesn't mean I want you to end up facedown in the damn river."

Oh. That was . . . unexpected.

Andreas opened his mouth, but whatever he was going to say was cut short as his phone chimed. Paula's went off at almost the same time. I stood there like a bump on a log as they checked their messages.

Andreas looked at me. It was like a switch had been flipped: all the warmth I'd been basking in since I'd brought him to my place gone like it had never been there. "I have to leave."

"Fuck yes, you do," Paula said unexpectedly. "That was Joan at the front desk. She says Thibedeau is headed this way. I don't have time to referee a pissing match between you two, so if Darren can fill in the gaps on the case you're working right now, get out of here."

I nodded. "I can do it." Andreas was already on his way out the door. He glanced back at me for a second just before it closed, an almost unsettling intensity in his gaze, and then he was gone.

"So."

I blinked, then realized Paula was talking to me. "Yeah?"

"You're one week in, huh?"

"About that."

"And you haven't tried to kill him yet? Because that has to be a record."

Her humor seemed to bleed away the worst of the tension. I grinned. "He's not that scary."

"Oh yes, he is. He's just not being that scary to *you*, which must mean he likes you. Welcome to a very small club. We have membership cards and go out for drinks every other month."

"Why does he like you?" I asked, then backtracked. "Apart from the fact that you're clearly very likeable, I mean."

"*So* smooth, nice save. And actually, he saved my life back when I was a beat cop. Stupid thing with a drug deal gone wrong." She shook her head. "I was an idiot, went after someone without backup, got pinned. I thought I'd be shot with my own gun. Ruffner got the guy first, though."

"Wow."

"Yeah, after that he couldn't quite shake me, not that he hasn't tried."

"I hear you."

The door slammed open. Detective Thibedeau stalked into the conference room, another IA suit behind him. "Where's Ruffner?" he demanded.

"Gone," Paula said. "It's kind of late, or maybe you haven't noticed?"

He turned to face me. "Then what are you doing here?"

"I'm the newbie. That means I get the shit work."

"Hey!"

"Not that your case is shit," I added for Paula, "just that staying this late is."

"Where did he go?" Thibedeau asked me.

"He didn't say. Home, I guess."

He scowled. "You're on thin ice with my department, Darren. Your inability to keep track of the simplest things with regards to your partner verges on insubordination, and—"

"Whoa, slow down there." Paula managed to interject herself without making Thibedeau snap at her, which had to be a minor miracle. "Neither of us is Ruffner's keeper. He's had this kid running around all day. My eyes would be crossing if I'd done as much work in less than twenty-four hours as Darren here."

"Your defense is noted," Thibedeau said sourly. "Tell me about this case. I want to know about the card you found."

"I don't feel comfortable discussing certain aspects of this case with Internal Affairs at this juncture, Detective," Paula said placidly. "Not until I have more facts. But you can certainly count on me to bring them to you at the earliest possible moment. Now, if you don't mind, we've got the midnight oil to burn."

He wanted to shut her down. I could see the urge well up in his eyes, the twist in his lips that meant he was holding back something he really wanted to let loose. But he couldn't. Not yet, anyway. "I'll hold you to that," he said. "And Darren? Get yourself together. You look like hell." He and the other suit stalked out, and I silently acknowledged Paula as my new hero.

"Holy shit, how did you do that?"

"Blank-faced politeness can get you further than assholery most of the time. That's a lesson Andreas never quite got." She shrugged. "It helps to have advance warning too. My advice to you? Get the admin staff on your side. Joan and I have an understanding."

"I'll buy her a bouquet."

"She likes orchids," Paula advised. She sipped at her coffee, then made a face. "Ugh, too cold. I'm going to go warm this up. You want anything?"

"No thanks." She left the conference room, and I took out my phone. When I dialed Andreas's number, it went to voice mail. Well, that wasn't too surprising. I texted instead.

IA is gone. Paula is a boss. You coming back any time soon?

I got no reply.

CHAPTER NINETEEN

ANDREAS

IA's timing was impeccable. On my way down to the car to avoid that asshole Thibedeau, I jumped on the opportunity to make contact with yet another one of my informants who'd emerged from the woodwork. Or rather, who'd finally returned my fucking call after a few thinly veiled threats about warrants and shakedowns. By the time I started the engine, I had a meeting set up.

Halfway there, my cell phone came to life. I glanced at the caller ID, and guilt made my heart thump harder—Darren.

In the past, if a partner-slash-babysitter tried to make contact while I was taking care of something like this, I'd have ignored the text and not thought twice about it. It should have been easy to do the same with Darren. It wasn't. Of course it wasn't. He wasn't like the other people Captain Hamilton had assigned to keep an eye on me. I wanted to believe the only difference between Darren and the others was that he was the only one I'd made out with, but I couldn't quite convince myself.

It didn't matter, though. Not right now, anyway. Whatever was going on between us could be addressed later. Whatever had gone on in that conference room after I'd left, he could fill me in later, but *this* had to happen now, and it was not a plus-one occasion. I had to meet the informant alone or not at all.

Forty-five minutes after I'd slipped out of the precinct under Thibedeau's radar, after doubling back and driving in circles to be absolutely sure I hadn't been followed, I pulled into the parking lot of a rundown bowling alley. The enormous bowling pin and neon *FAMILY BOWL* sign had been there since roughly 1957, and probably hadn't been cleaned or maintained more than once during that time.

The dilapidated building seemed to be held together by graffiti and prayers. Foot-tall weeds shot up between cracks in pavement that hadn't been painted since the Reagan administration. It was less than two miles from the gleaming financial center of the city, but resembled something out of a postapocalyptic wasteland.

And parked near the side exit was a dull gold-brown Impala with mismatched rims. He was here.

I gave the lot a sweeping glance to be doubly sure I hadn't been followed. Then I went inside.

At the counter, a twentysomething ex-junkie from the halfway house down the road met my gaze. He nodded toward the lounge at the opposite end of the sparsely crowded building. I returned the nod. As I started toward the lounge, the eighties throwback music blasting from crackling speakers got louder. Almost painfully loud. Loud enough to fuck with any bugs, wires, or eavesdroppers.

The lounge was nearly empty. A couple of older guys drinking beer at the bar. A bored bartender who, like the building, had seen better days. A gray-haired woman playing pull-tabs while she vaped.

And in the corner, partially obscured by the back of an oversized booth, was the man I'd come to see.

Without a word, I slid into the booth. He didn't react, and he sure as fuck didn't greet me. After all, Vincent Blake was not a man who wasted time with small talk.

I folded my hands on the table. "I need to know what's going on."

Blake glanced over his shoulder and scanned the room. Facing me again, he spoke so quietly I barely heard him over the thumping music. "The mayor's cleaning house."

"Tell me something I don't know."

He scowled. "Probably don't need to tell you you're on his shit list."

"No, you don't." I suppressed a shudder as the hairs on my neck stood on end. "I need to know who's tipping him off."

Blake slowly shook his head. "That, I don't know. But somebody's spooked him, and he's making sure anyone who's got dirt on him is quiet." He paused, subtly checking our surroundings again. "I don't think it matters who's ratting people out to him—it's time for him to go down."

I sighed heavily. "Yeah, that's a problem. We both know what he's up to, but I don't have enough to arrest him."

"You don't have enough for *you* to arrest him." Blake raised an eyebrow. "If that partner of yours makes a move, though . . ."

"I'm not throwing him under the bus. He's a good cop, and if he tries to arrest the *goddamned mayor* without enough evidence, he's toast."

"Yes. Yes, he is." The burly drug lord leaned forward, narrowing his eyes. "But it's one man's career versus the lives of anyone who's ever crossed paths with Crawford."

I swallowed. He was right. About all of it. No one would ever sign off on an arrest warrant for the mayor if it had my name on it. I'd be reined in so fast my head would spin. Possibly even put on administrative leave pending another psychiatric evaluation.

But Darren . . .

He was a solid cop. The stepson of a respected police commissioner. Someone who took his job seriously, toed the line, and knew how not to piss people off. If he put in for an arrest warrant for someone on high, people would listen because he wasn't a loose cannon. But if the arrest was made, the PR nightmare initiated, and the mayor wasn't convicted? Darren would be a pariah. People loved the mayor. He was one of the most popular, scandal-free politicians this city had ever seen. Short of a bulletproof case, no cop in his right mind would try to collar that asshole, least of all for murder, running a complex ring of narcotic trafficking, and anything else on the laundry list of charges.

My stomach somersaulted. I tried not to consider whether I'd have thought twice about putting a previous partner in this position. I was definitely thinking twice about it with Darren. While I knew beyond a shadow of a doubt that Crawford had blood on his hands—especially after witnessing his involvement with my own eyes—I couldn't prove it. Not yet. Not without names to connect him to the others I knew were involved.

I rubbed my eyes with my thumb and forefinger. "Shit."

"You gotta do it, Andreas." Blake casually sipped his coffee as if we were just shooting the shit and catching up. "You need to bring his ass in, and every corrupt motherfucker in city hall along with him."

"But I still need those *names* in city hall." I threw up my hand. "What good will it do if the charges don't stick? I need more than this. You know I do."

It was his turn to sigh, and he nodded. "I know. He's a slippery one, though." Was he ever. Even someone as high up the food chain as Blake was kept in the dark more often than not. "Tell me what you want me to do."

I thumbed the peeling table edge and thought for a moment. "I need time."

"There *isn't* time, Andreas."

"And if we make a move now, a lot of people could die," I growled. "If we're going to bring him in, and we're going to stop him from taking down—"

"You've *had* time," he snapped. "What more do you need?"

"I need evidence, for God's sake. It doesn't do me a damn bit of good to arrest him if a jury won't convict him."

"Then maybe we need to skip the judge and jury and go right to the executioner."

My heart dropped. "You know I could arrest you just for suggesting that."

He laughed dryly. "You could've arrested me a hundred times over the last few years, but you haven't, and for the same reason you won't now—because you need me if Crawford is going to go down."

"And I need a solution besides assassinating a goddamned politician."

"Then find one," he said. "Or my people will. We're running out of patience, and I'm not going to sit back and watch more of my people's bodies pile up while you make sure all the proper forms are filled out."

"You want to stop him and his people? Or do you just want to take him down and let his successors pick up where he left off?" I thumped the table with my knuckle as I added, "We need to stop the *whole* operation, not just him."

"Then *do* it."

"Just give me some more time."

"How much more, Detective?"

"A few days. Maybe a week. I'll . . . I don't need much more." God help me, there was no way I was bringing Crawford down in a week, but I hoped like hell that could buy me a few days to keep one of Blake's men from opening fire on him.

"One week." Blake sat back, eyes still narrow and fixed on me. "If you don't find a way to stop him in a week, then I will."

I just nodded. We both knew he wasn't kidding. After a moment, I took a deep breath. "When this all goes down, you know there isn't much I can do to keep you out of prison." For all the evidence I didn't have against Crawford, I had piles against Blake and the people who worked for him.

"I know." His voice was calm. "But I still have your word about my family."

"You do. Of course. It might not hurt for you to get them out of town now. As long as I know where they are, I can make sure they're kept safe."

Blake nodded slowly, but said nothing. He took out his wallet, put a wrinkled five beside his coffee, and left without another word.

I stayed behind to put some distance between us. Couldn't risk being seen leaving the same place together, not even when he was incognito in faded old clothes and that piece-of-shit car. Too many people—too many cops—knew both our faces.

While I waited for him to leave, I debated ordering a drink, but thought better of it. Coffee would make me too jittery. I'd already had one beer at Darren's and didn't dare have more—I'd learned the hard way in the past that my medications' side effects didn't go well with more than a small amount of alcohol. After the day my body had had, there was no point in pushing my luck.

Five minutes after Blake left, I got up and left. As I walked out into the muggy night, my mind was fixed on the mission ahead. There had to be a way to do this without resorting to Blake taking the mayor down. I could pull some strings to get a few years taken off his sentence for the mile-long list of charges—though we both knew he was probably going away for twenty-five to life no matter what—but I wouldn't be able to help him if he assassinated the mayor. He'd be dead before he made it to trial.

And, anyway, it wouldn't solve the big problems over at city hall. There was no point in cutting off the head if the beast would just grow a fresh one.

So I had to find another way. Problem was, arresting the mayor or one of his high-up cronies wouldn't be as simple as planting heroin in his office. On the other hand, maybe it would. A judge would never be reelected if he was even suspected of possession.

Judge Harrison was in the mayor's pocket. She was absolutely involved in his illicit activities. If I could threaten her like I had Jake, then I could possibly turn her on him. It would be risky. Bringing in a no-name thug off the streets and holding possession charges over his head—that didn't draw much attention. Even thinking about it with a judge could—

"You want to tell me what the fuck is going on?"

Darren's voice spun me around and damn near gave me heart failure. "What the—"

"I just saw Blake leave," he snarled, stepping closer and glaring at me like he was ready to rip out my throat with his bare hands. "You want to tell me—"

"How did you find me?" Panic sent ice water through my veins. If he knew I was here, who else did? "Answer me, Darren."

His lips pulled tight, and he broke eye contact. He wasn't exactly sheepish, but I got the feeling he didn't have a prepared answer to my question.

It was my turn to move closer. "How did you find me?"

He stared at the ground between us. "I . . ." Then he reached into his pocket and pulled out a GPS receiver. The exact same kind the department issued when we put a transmitter on someone's car.

The ice water turned to pure fire. "You tracked me? How the . . . When the fuck did you . . . Where is the tracker?"

He swallowed. "Under the passenger seat. On the back of that box."

"You son of a bitch. How long have you been—"

"I'm trying to keep IA off my fucking back," he snapped. "I put it in your car the first day we worked together, all right?"

"No, it's not all right! You told me you were—"

"And you didn't tell me you're meeting with goddamned Blake." He gestured sharply toward the bowling alley. "What the fuck is going on, Andreas?"

I narrowed my eyes. "You think I'm going to trust you with anything now? Fuck you."

"Well then, I guess we're both in the same boat, aren't we? Because it turns out that while I'm covering your ass for IA, putting my own ass on the line because, shit, I trusted you for some fucking reason, you're here talking with—"

"You want to say it a little louder? Because that's how cops get other cops shot."

He set his jaw. "Then maybe you need to start talking and tell me what the fuck is going on."

"Yeah? Before or after you tell me how many other bugs you planted on me?"

"For God's sake." He threw up his hands. "What did you want me to do? I've had the captain and IA breathing down my neck since day one, and I—"

"And you put trackers on another cop, Darren. On your *partner*."

He laughed humorlessly. "Oh, please. The day I put that tracker on you, you still thought I was shit on your shoe. But now you're suddenly all righteously indignant and horrified that one cop might not completely trust his *partner*."

"I didn't trust you because I thought you were in IA's pocket. Then you convinced me otherwise. And now—"

"Now it turns out I had a reason to chase you down." He stepped even closer, right up in my face. "What the fuck is going on?"

I held his gaze, not sure how to answer him. An hour ago, I would have thought nothing of tipping my hand to him. Now I couldn't be sure who was looking over his shoulder. What if someone else had gotten their hands on that receiver? What if he'd handed it over to Thibedeau? If he'd put the transmitter in my car to appease IA and convince them he was doing their bidding, then they could have asked at any time to see where I was. What if Thibedeau or the captain had come rolling in while I was conspiring with Blake to bring down the mayor?

I'd promised Blake I'd find a way to arrest the mayor within a week, but that promise had hinged on being able to rely on Darren. Quite possibly putting his career at risk, yes, but having him as an ally had been absolutely crucial.

And now . . .

Shit. Shit, shit, shit.

I couldn't look at him. I was too angry, too betrayed, and I also had a rapidly ticking clock that wouldn't slow down for anyone or anything.

"I'm going to go get some sleep." I turned to walk away, throwing over my shoulder, "You might want to do the same."

He called after me, but I ignored him. I got in the car and slammed the door, cutting off Darren's voice. If he kept shouting, I didn't hear it.

I got the hell out of there, and a mile or two away, pulled over and went around to the passenger side. Now that I knew it was there, it didn't take much digging to find the little transmitter duct-taped to the box where I kept various pieces of contraband.

I ripped it loose, dropped it on the pavement, and ground it under my heel. I didn't check to make sure I'd destroyed it enough to keep him from finding it. In fact, I hoped he did find it, and saw it smashed on the ground as the *Fuck you, Darren* it was meant to be.

And when I got back in the car, my cell phone was ringing.

Darren.

Of course.

CHAPTER TWENTY
DARREN

I had a history of making rash decisions when I got worried.

When my mom first started dating Vic, back when I was seven, it hadn't taken me long to understand that she'd been serious about him. He'd made her happy, he'd been nice to me and my brother, and I'd wanted him to stay. I'd ensured he *would* stay by puncturing one or two of his tires with nails every time he came over. By the time I was sent to bed each evening, he'd have a flat tire and either stay the night, or call a patrol car to pick him up and come fix his car later. Instant insurance that he was coming back. It had taken weeks for Vic to work out what I was doing. Needless to say, neither he nor my mom was happy about it, but they'd understood.

I'd tried to keep my best friend from moving to a new state during middle school by suggesting we run away into the woods together. That had ended in a massive search led by Vic that left me grounded for the rest of the year. I'd tried to keep my brother from forgetting about me when he went away to school by emptying my savings sending him singing telegrams—I hadn't realized at the time the company I'd contacted actually worked primarily as stripper-grams, and that he'd almost been kicked out of school housing for "inappropriate conduct."

Needless to say, my record wasn't fantastic. So I shouldn't have been surprised when the result of my bugging Andreas was him giving me the cold shoulder.

It wasn't that I didn't trust him. Not at this point, at least. Admittedly, when I'd put the tracker in his car, I'd been unsure of how things would shake out between us, but I hadn't done it for Internal Affairs. I'd done it because I hated not knowing things. I hated the thought that he could go somewhere, *be* somewhere, and get into trouble, and I might not know about it. I might not be able to help. I'd bugged his car so I'd be able to provide that help, but I should have told him about it.

Or not, because Andreas had reacted exactly like I'd feared. *"You think I'm going to trust you with anything now? Fuck you."* Which was fucking rich, given that he'd gone off to meet Blake without telling me anything. Hell, I still didn't know what they'd talked about. Why the fuck did they have *anything* to talk about, other than Andreas reading him his Miranda rights? What the hell was going on?

And now I might never know.

I sighed and ground the pads of my thumbs against my gritty eyes. It had been a long day, with too many twists and turns for me to follow at this point. I didn't know if I wanted to fuck Andreas, interrogate him, or beg him for forgiveness. The best thing I could do for myself now was sleep, but I didn't want to go back to my apartment. It was too lonely, and I'd never be able to get the vision of Andreas beneath me on the couch out of my mind.

Home it was.

I let myself in a little after one in the morning. Everybody should have been asleep, but when I stepped into the living room, I saw Vic stretched out in his recliner, one hand resting on the remote, the other scratching absently at his chest as he stared at the muted TV screen. He glanced up at me as I came in. "Hey, son. You look like hell."

"Yeah."

He nodded toward the love seat. "Pull up a chair, tell me about it."

One of the things I'd always loved about Vic—he could handle shit like nobody's business. Nothing threw him. It had made him a popular commissioner, and it had endeared him to my mother like nothing else could. It didn't matter what was going on, it always seemed like Vic could deal.

I flopped down onto the love seat. "Why the late night?"

"Ah, old aches and pains. I couldn't sleep."

I frowned. "Did you take some aspirin?"

"You and my damn doctor. Yes, I took the aspirin. If my blood were any thinner, I'd have hemophilia."

"If you have another heart attack, I'll kick your ass." If I could erase that particular episode from my life, I would. It was the only time Vic had ever been less than capable, and it had scared the shit out of our family.

"I'm fine. Stop beatin' around the bush."

I stared at the television. It was easier than looking at Vic. "I think I fucked things up with my new partner."

"How so?"

"Well, we're working a case right now that's . . . shit, I don't even know how to describe it. Machiavellian, maybe. There are a lot of leads to follow, and more and more of them are ending with people turning up dead. One of those bodies was pretty much a warning to Andreas, and IA is breathing down my neck about him, and I—I misjudged a situation. I think, at least. I don't know because he wouldn't fucking *tell* me anything about it, and . . ."

Vic sighed. "Did you bug him?"

I blinked at him. "How did you even guess that?"

"Because you wanted to do the same thing to your brother. Remember? Putting trackers in all his clothes?"

"And I maintain that if we'd done that, you could have saved yourself a lot of trouble when he ran off earlier today." God, had that just been this afternoon?

"It's a violation of privacy, son."

"It's *practical.*"

"You can't do that to people you care about. Not unless you got no other option, not if you want them to trust you."

"You sound like Andreas."

"And you sound like a sulky little shit," he said, but it seemed mostly fond. "It's rough, I can't pretend it isn't. And trust is a two-way street. So, your partner: do you trust him?" Vic's gaze pinned me in place. "Regardless of what's goin' on that you can't control and don't know about, do you trust him?"

That was the million-dollar question. And in the end, it was surprisingly easy to answer. "Yes. I do."

"Then you've gotta prove that. You've gotta give a little. And you're gonna have to be the bigger man there, kid, because from what I remember of Ruffner, he's never been much for trusting people.

You have to set the tone and hope he follows. You can't force him to, though."

"I'm worried."

"I know you are."

"And I'm *scared*." It felt like setting a broken bone to admit it: painful, but necessary. "Because this case is a big deal, and it could be an even bigger deal if . . . This could go way up the chain. Higher than I would have dreamed just a week ago."

"Within the force?"

"Maybe. I think it's more political, but someone's working against us from the inside."

Vic scratched at the silver stubble on his chin. "You know, years ago, back when your brother was finding his feet at the DA's office, he came to talk to me about something weird going on over there. Cases that could have been prosecuted were being dropped, defendants who should have been sent away for good were getting off light. Nobody was talkin' much about it, but from what he gathered, the DA wanted to focus on the big fish. Only there never was any way to go after the bigger guys, because there were no smaller guys around to get information from. That was back when Crawford was still DA, of course, before he ran for mayor. Ugly race."

Ugly was putting it mildly. Crawford hadn't been favored to win against the incumbent at the time, and had resorted to a smear campaign so brutal it could have come out of Tammany Hall. In the end, the sitting mayor was indicted for embezzlement, and also accused of having an affair with the underage daughter of an aide. He'd committed suicide a month after leaving office, just days before he was scheduled for sentencing.

"Nobody could prove anything against Mayor Crawford, of course," Vic went on. "Nobody even wanted to try. Things have calmed down some since then."

"I think they're firing up again."

"You can't go after someone that high up without protection for you and your partner. Protection or an iron-clad case. You know that, right?"

I groaned. "I do know that, but I don't have it."

"Maybe you're not talking to the right people, then. If you can't go any lower, then maybe you need to go a little higher."

"No lawyer or judge is going to talk to me about this."

"Mayor Kramer has a widow. Nice woman, she and your mom email every now and then. She lives in a rent-controlled apartment over near the interstate." Vic grunted. "Hell of a comedown from the mayoral mansion."

I raised an eyebrow. "You think she knows anything? She didn't say anything during her husband's trial."

"Maybe she couldn't."

It was a thought. If the list of contacts we had was being cut down by outside forces, then maybe it was time to focus on people who weren't on the list. There were a lot of ways for the testimony of a criminal to be called into question, anyway. But Mrs. Kramer had avoided personal fallout from her husband's takedown. It was possible she knew something or could point us in a new direction.

Of course, for her to point *us* anywhere, I had to be on speaking terms with Andreas again. I'd called him ten times since he'd driven off, and he hadn't picked up once.

That was a problem for tomorrow—later today, actually. I needed to sleep, but I didn't fit on the love seat anymore. "Think I'll wake Asher up if I crash with him?"

Vic waved a hand. "He won't mind. When does he ever mind you?"

"Hey, it happens."

"Not these days. Go, get in there, go to sleep."

"You should too."

"I will in a few minutes, son."

I left him in the living room and walked down to Asher's door. It wasn't locked. I let myself in, quietly got rid of my shoes and jeans, and then settled onto the close side of Asher's enormous bed. I was trying to be stealthy, but his eyes opened just before mine closed. "Darren?"

"Yeah, 's me."

"Are you okay?"

I smiled a little. "Just tired. Can I sleep here tonight?"

"Sure." He reached out and ruffled my hair. "Tell me about it in the morning, huh?"

You won't remember to ask me in the morning. "I will," I said, then buried my face in the pillow and tried my damnedest to fall asleep.

It still took far too long.

The direct approach had failed me with Andreas. I tried calling him once after I woke up the next morning, and got nothing. Okay, fine. I had ways around that. I drove back to the deli Andreas had taken me to earlier that week and grabbed a ham and cheese croissant. Then I went by Starbucks for coffee for three. By the time I got to the precinct and was actually face-to-face with Paula again, I felt pretty calm.

She, on the other hand, looked like she'd been there all night. "Omigod coffee, oh fuck, give it to me," she moaned as soon as I stepped into the conference room.

"Why are you still here?" I asked as I handed over her latte.

"My brain." She tapped the side of her head. "It's too busy to go home. Don't worry, I caught a few hours of sleep." She pointed at the folded jacket in the far corner of the room.

"You slept on the floor?"

"You make it sound like a bed of nails. Nails. God. Can you imagine sleeping on a real bed of nails? Like, I wouldn't be able to stop thinking about all the hands that were *missing* them, y'know?"

My nose wrinkled with involuntary disgust. "I don't think those are the nails the metaphor is referring to."

"Well, either way it would be nasty. Where's your dark and gloomy shadow on this fine . . . whatever day it is . . . morning?"

"Ah." I gave her my best grin. "Actually, I could use your help with that."

"Oh really?" Despite her obvious fatigue, Paula managed to impart an impressive level of disdain. "You fucked it up? In the space of one evening?"

"How do you know *he* didn't fuck it up?"

"Because if it was Ruffner's fault, you wouldn't be looking at me like a guilty puppy. Which, stop that, your eyes are criminal." She considered it for a moment. "Fine. But only because you're going to bring me a latte every day for the next week."

"Service with a smile," I promised her.

"Yeah, I wish. Hang on."

She pressed the Call button on her phone, and of course he picked up on the second ring with her. Of *course* he did. I literally had to clamp my lips together to keep from speaking while she talked to Andreas. A minute later he was on his way, and Paula took her jacket to catch a few more hours of sleep in the break room. I was nervous—of course I was nervous—but all I really needed to do was keep Andreas from walking out the door the instant he saw me. That was where the food came in. It smelled good, I had to admit it. If my mom hadn't made me waffles before I left, I'd have bought one for myself.

Shit, I really *was* spoiled.

I was ready when the door opened. "Son of a *bitch*—" Andreas began. I cut him off before he could get going.

"I'm sorry." It was best to get that out there first, because I really was. "I shouldn't have put a tracker in your car, I get that. I didn't do it for the captain or IA, I swear to God. I did it because I was worried you'd try to ditch me and go do everything on your own, and lo and behold, I was kind of right, *but*—" I raised a hand in a placating gesture "—I know you were doing it because you felt like you had to. There's stuff going on that you haven't explained to me, and I'd really appreciate it if you would, but I'm not going to push. Okay? Not now. We need to work together and I need to trust your judgment, and I need you to believe you can rely on me. So. Let's chalk it up to me being an insecure jackass and get back to work."

No reply. Time to move on to step two. I tilted my head toward the food. "I brought you lunch. More like brunch for you, probably, because I doubt you've eaten." Andreas looked tired. He was still wearing yesterday's clothes, and they were rumpled—had he slept in his car? It still probably wasn't safe for him to go home right now. If I thought he'd let me get away with it, I'd offer to give him a massage, because I'd seen boards less stiff than he looked right now. "And I had an idea about a new line we could take on the case." *Sit down, c'mon, just please sit down. Don't walk out. Don't make me leave you alone.*

He finally sat and grabbed for one of the remaining coffees first thing. "Fine. Talk."

I sat across from him and pulled out everything I'd dug up on the late Mayor Kramer. "First things first: how are you at sweet-talking widows?"

CHAPTER TWENTY-ONE
ANDREAS

I could sweet-talk my four-year-old. On occasion, I could even pull it off with my older kids, though they didn't really fall for it anymore. Anyone else could go fuck themselves.

Most of the time, anyway. Today, we needed an audience with a woman who'd sworn to spit in the face of anyone on this city's payroll, including cops. *Especially* cops. If we were going to get more than five seconds of her time, someone with some actual charm and tact needed to talk to her.

My puppy-eyed partner with the smooth voice and the soft smile—he was definitely the man for the job.

I sat on the conference room table, working my way through the ham and cheese croissant he'd bought, and listened while he made the call.

"Ma'am, I understand completely." He paced back and forth while he talked. "We'd be happy to meet you wherever is convenient for you. Yes, yes, I understand. No, ma'am, I promise we're—" He rolled his eyes and mouthed *Are you fucking kidding me?* at the ceiling.

I suppressed a laugh, as much to keep her from hearing it as Darren. I didn't need him thinking I was in the mood for joking or anything other than strictly business. The croissant and coffee might've melted some of the ice, but I was still pissed about the tracker in my car, not to mention rattled that he'd shown his face. If Blake had seen him and recognized him, Darren and I would both be washing up on the riverbank right about now.

But I couldn't explain that to Darren without going into detail about my relationship with the kingpin. Or that no amount of apologizing or buttering me up with croissants—goddamn, this was a good croissant—was going to change the fact that he'd nearly fucked up that relationship and with it, our investigation.

With a huff, Darren shoved his phone in his pocket and turned to me. "All right. She's meeting us at the Grand Royal Hotel at four."

I raised an eyebrow. "The Grand Royal?"

"Yep. As she put it, if she's going to talk to us, she's getting a good meal out of it, and the city's footing the bill."

I grunted. "Given Mrs. Kramer's history with the city, I suspect this isn't just about scoring a three-hundred-dollar lunch on the taxpayer's dime for spite."

"Oh yeah?"

"Yeah. In her shoes, I'd want to do this in public. As visibly as possible." I crumpled up the empty croissant wrapper and tossed it at the trash, but missed. "Hiding in plain sight, in a way—no one with anything to hide would talk to the cops out in the open like that."

"You think so?"

"Call it a hunch."

Darren leaned down to pick up the balled-up wrapper, and dropped it into the trash can. "You think she knows anything useful?"

"It's entirely possible." I absently rubbed my arm, which was sore as hell and itchy where the doc had glued it. "I hadn't thought about asking her before, but your stepdad's right—Crawford's shit probably started well before he was elected, and the widow of his opponent might know something."

He relaxed a little, as if my approval meant something.

I glanced at the clock on the wall. "We've got a couple of hours. We should probably—"

"Use that time to clear the air about last night?"

Son of a bitch.

"Which part?" I asked through gritted teeth. "The part where you bugged me, followed me, and jeopardized my meeting with a contact?"

"Jeopardized—" he sputtered. "Do you hear yourself? You were meeting with—"

"And do you think you're the only one using trackers and listening devices?" I hissed, stepping up in his face. "Breathe a word in this building about what you saw, and I'll make sure you're reassigned so fast—"

"Do you really think the captain would reassign me?" he threw back. "On your request?" With a humorless laugh, he added, "Pretty sure you already tried that. How'd it work out for you?"

I narrowed my eyes. "Just be discreet, all right?"

"Fine. But," and he sounded serious about it, "I don't appreciate surprises like last night any more than you do, and I'd like to suggest that you tell me what the hell is going on before we have any more misunderstandings."

"Oh yeah? Before or after you start trusting me?"

He exhaled sharply and turned away, throwing up his hands. "I apologized already. What more do you want?"

"You think an apology cuts it? Do you realize what could have happened last night if—"

"No, Andreas." He spun around, his face angry but his eyes pleading with me. "No, I don't realize what could have happened, because I don't know what the fuck is going on. You've kept me in the dark since day one, and only give me little nibbles here and there to keep me placated. I'm *trying* to work with you. I'm trying to *solve* this case." He showed his palms. "I fucked up. I admitted I fucked up. But would you believe for one second that I was trying to do the right thing?"

I held his gaze. Admittedly, I couldn't argue with him. In a way, he was the equivalent of an eager golden retriever who chased after a stick and brought back an angry rattlesnake. He was only trying to do what he was supposed to do, and he didn't actually *mean* to make things worse.

"All right." I picked up my jacket and keys. "Let's get out of here."

"Wait, what? Where are we going?"

"Someplace where the walls don't have quite so many ears."

Someplace where the walls didn't have quite so many ears was a park down by the river. At least this was out in the open. Any eavesdroppers would have to be experts at camouflage to avoid detection on this sprawling, treeless riverbank.

I was admittedly extra paranoid. After what happened at the bowling alley, I'd spent two hours last night combing my car and my apartment for more bugs, and found two. One of them I didn't recognize. The other was made by the same company as the tracker Darren had used. They could've been planted by anybody—one of Blake's cronies, a double agent informant, the captain, IA, Darren. There was no telling for sure who was listening on the other end, but right now, they were both being treated to the sounds of an endless loop of exceptionally terrible and moist-sounding porn, coupled with a recording of a barking dog.

With the sounds of potential bestiality keeping the eavesdroppers entertained, Darren and I left my car and walked toward the river. We found a weathered, graffiti-covered picnic table, and I sat on it with my feet on the bench.

Hands in his pockets, Darren faced me. "Think we're out of earshot of anybody who might care what we're talking about?"

"That depends. You bring anyone with you?"

Groaning, he rolled his eyes. "You want me to strip down and prove I'm not wearing a wire?"

"Look, I get it—you want me to trust you, and you apologized. But you've got to understand why I'm so paranoid."

He sighed. "Yeah. I do. And I swear, I'm not wearing any wires."

I studied him for a moment and decided I believed him. He'd been pretty damned contrite all morning, and I suspected it wasn't an act. "All right. So . . ." Shit. Where to start? "Okay, let me start at the beginning. Trust me—it's relevant."

Darren nodded, shifting his weight. "Okay."

"I told you when I was diagnosed, I self-destructed."

"Right . . ."

"I basically tried to do the opposite of suicide by cop."

"You tried to get killed on the job."

I nodded. "I'm not proud of it. I was panicking, and I was worried about who would put my older kids through school and take care of the little one."

"Understandable."

"So I . . ." Heat rushed into my cheeks, and I lowered my gaze. "I knew there was some shit going down with Blake's crew. Something big."

"Even back then?"

"Yep. And I got it in my head that if I went in and singlehandedly busted them, I'd go down and, with any luck, so would they."

"Whoa."

"I didn't want to get my partner killed, though, so I waited until she'd gone home for the night. Then I went in."

Darren folded his arms loosely across his chest. "What was your game plan? Go in guns blazing and hope for the best?"

"I wasn't *that* reckless." I laughed dryly. "Doesn't really say much, does it? Anyway, I knew Blake was receiving a big shipment at the regional airport. Montrose. We had plenty of evidence, but kept getting shut down when we tried to obtain a warrant."

Darren's jaw went slack. "Wait, what?"

"Stay with me. I knew something was up. And no matter how many times the DA's office told us we didn't have sufficient evidence to search the airport or any of the aircraft, I knew damn well there were narcotics moving through there. So, I took one of the body cameras that patrol officers wear, faked a call from an informant who wanted me to meet him there, and planned to 'happen by' when the drugs came in."

"Jesus." Darren joined me on the table, sitting a few inches away from me, but close enough we could lower our voices.

When he was situated, I continued. "The plane came in right on schedule. I took cover and made sure the body camera was catching everything. But then . . ." I stared out at the river, eyes unfocused.

"What happened?"

"Mayor Crawford showed up with Blake's younger brother. The merchandise was exchanged. And . . . something happened. I don't exactly know what, but suddenly everyone was agitated. Weapons started coming out." I rubbed my hand over my face. "It's all a bit of a blur after that—even the body camera couldn't catch much because I took cover."

"I thought you were *trying* to get killed."

"I was. But then suddenly the mayor was about to get killed, and I . . . I froze. I thought maybe I could save him. Right up until I realized he wasn't the one in danger."

Darren blinked.

"Like I said, it's all kind of a blur. One second, everything was in chaos. The next, Crawford's security detail had the brother and the pilot on their knees, and they were about to take them down execution style."

"You . . . Are you serious?"

"As a heart attack. I couldn't save the pilot. By the time I realized what was happening, he'd already been shot. I opened fire, and Crawford and his boys ran."

"So you saved him? From the mayor?"

"Yeah." I leaned back on my uninjured hand, cradling the other across my stomach, and looked up at the mostly clear sky. "I grabbed him and got him out of there. Blake got in touch with me after that, and I guess he decided I was on his side. Or something. Anyway, he told me everything he knew. Which was basically that he wasn't the kingpin we all think he is. He's just a middleman like everyone else, and he's caught up in enough wheels that he can't get out."

"Sounds like the fucking Mafia."

"Pretty much. And it all goes back to corrupt government. The mayor is running the whole shit show, and he has no qualms about killing people in the process." I turned to Darren. "In a way, it kind of gave me a new lease on life because I suddenly had this big thing that I had to stop or it would haunt me in Hell or wherever I ended up."

"Wow." He paused. "Why haven't you told anyone?"

"Because I don't know who to trust." I hesitated. "The man who executed the pilot? He was a cop."

Darren's breath hitched. "Are you sure?"

"One hundred percent. There were others there who I recognized too. When I went in the next day to try to turn in the body cam's footage, I realized I didn't know who I could trust. For all I knew, the entire force was in the mayor's back pocket."

"Where are those cops now?"

"One's dead. Took a round to the face during a routine traffic stop. Shooter was never caught."

Darren straightened. "So you think . . ."

"Pretty obvious, isn't it? The other one's doing twenty-five to life for killing his wife."

"No shit?"

I shook my head. "And somebody's got some dirt on him, because I've tried talking to him. He knows something—he damn sure knows something—but he won't say a word."

"Not even when he's already in prison?"

"Nope. My guess? He was going to blow a whistle, but someone took out his wife, framed him for it, and threatened to go after the rest of his family if he talked."

"Jesus Christ." Darren ran an unsteady hand through his hair. "No wonder you're so paranoid."

"Yeah. I mean, I had a reputation for not playing well with others long before this, but after I watched a cop kill a man in cold blood on the mayor's order . . ." I shook my head. "I have to watch my back."

Chewing his lip, Darren stared at the grass below us. "Now I see why you didn't trust me."

"I probably still shouldn't."

He eyed me.

"I have to protect myself." I shrugged. "I can't trust anyone just because they say I can."

"But you're telling me now, so you must . . . You do trust me?"

I locked eyes with him, then nodded. "Yeah. Probably more than I should. But my instincts . . ."

We held each other's gaze for a long moment.

Then I cleared my throat and focused on the river again. "I can't do this by myself. Things are about to blow up, and we have to shut it down before people get killed. I *have* to be able to trust you."

"You can," he said softly. "I promise. That shit with the tracker—it won't happen again."

"I know." We were both quiet for a while. Then I took a breath and went on. "Blake knows he's going to jail when all this is over. He's caught up in the wheels just like everybody else. The only reason he stayed involved is the same reason I stayed alive."

"To take down the mayor."

I nodded. "As long as Blake is working for him—delivering the goods, keeping his boys in line, doing the mayor's dirty work—his family is safe. The minute he tries to disappear, Crawford will make sure anyone who's ever had so much as a three-minute conversation with Blake winds up dead in a ditch."

"Including you," Darren breathed.

"Including me."

"Does Crawford know you're involved?"

"I'd like to say no, but somebody knows."

"How do you know they—" His teeth snapped together. "The business card."

"Yep."

"Shit. Any idea who made that connection?"

"Could be anyone. And it wasn't just the card that was meant to send a message. That warehouse is where I've met with a number of informants. I might've had a few . . . informal interrogations in there too."

Darren's eyebrow rose. "'Informal interrogations'?"

"Sometimes the end justifies the means."

"Right." He drew back slightly, and the uneasiness in his eyes was palpable.

I sighed. "Listen, no matter what IA or anyone else has told you, I'm not a dirty cop. Yes, I've done some things that could get my ass terminated, if not shot in a back alley. I've roughed up suspects when no one could hear us. I've threatened people. I've—"

"Bought heroin from kids so you could arrest someone on false pretenses."

"Yeah. But do you understand now why I did that?"

He stared down at his hands as he tugged a stray thread on his sleeve. "I get it. But goddamn, Andreas. There's lines, you know?"

"There are. And I tried to walk those lines for a long, long time." I paused. "I'm *not* a dirty cop. You've got to believe me, Darren."

"You need me to trust you."

I swallowed. "Yes. I need you to trust me."

He turned his head and looked me right in the eye. "I do trust you. I have from the start. Probably more than I should have."

"But do you still?"

He nodded. "As some crotchety old detective once said—instincts."

We both managed a quiet laugh.

"Trust your instincts, then." I resisted the urge to give his knee a gentle squeeze. We were out in public. Too out in the open for one man to put a hand on the other. And after last night, God only knew where I stood with Darren anyway. That was something we'd have to sort out later.

"Well." Darren cleared his throat and hoisted himself up off the table and onto his feet. "We should go. We've got a widow waiting to chat with us."

CHAPTER TWENTY-TWO
DARREN

he Grand Royal Hotel downtown was a monument to the decadence of an earlier age. Built in the 1920s, it looked like someone had stolen it out of Italy and then dumped it, slightly more dilapidated, in the middle of a bunch of soulless square skyscrapers. We arrived just in time to meet Mrs. Kramer for the hotel's famous afternoon tea.

"Afternoon tea," Andreas muttered for probably the fifth time as the hostess escorted us to our table in the all-pink Rose Room. "Jesus Christ."

"Just think how jealous your daughter will be when you tell her you ate tiny sandwiches and petit fours at a fancy tea party," I teased. "You could bring her next time. It would probably make her day."

"There won't be a next time."

"Well, not looking like that, maybe. You'd need to dress up, put on a suit . . ." Actually, the thought of Andreas in a suit was almost enough to make me forget how to walk. I would have run right into the hostess if Andreas hadn't grabbed my arm.

"Your party, ma'am."

"Thank you." Mrs. Kramer gestured to us from where she sat on the other side of the lace-covered table. "Do sit down, gentlemen. You're attracting enough attention as it is, looking that way."

"What way?" I asked as I pulled out my chair. I had to stop myself from pulling out Andreas's as well. Injured or not, he wouldn't appreciate it.

Mrs. Kramer smiled. It didn't seem natural on her. She looked like ancient, disdainful elegance wrapped in a mothball-scented tweed dress, and not the sort of person who made a habit of smiling. "Why, looking like undereducated, roughneck cops, of course."

Oh yeah, this was going to be great. A woman who hated the police and a partner who hated politicians. I'd be lucky if they didn't smash me to pieces between them by the time tea was over.

A silent waitress came by with a plate of pastries and set it down. Mrs. Kramer used a pair of silver tongs to take one of them. "The madeleines are excellent, by the way."

"This is bullshit." As the waitress passed by again, Andreas motioned her to a stop. "You serve sandwiches here?"

"We have cream cheese and cucumber—"

"No, I mean real sandwiches. With meat."

"Um . . . I could get you a chicken salad sandwich?" she offered. "It's just, the kitchen is kind of in high-tea mode, so all we've got are things that don't need to be heated up."

"That's fine. We need two of them. And coffee."

"Is black tea okay?"

"If that's the best you can do."

She thought about it for a moment. "I think we've got Nescafe in the break room."

"Perfect." She walked off, and Andreas turned to stare at Mrs. Kramer, who had one eyebrow raised. He matched her expression flawlessly. "Problem?"

After a frigid moment of silence, she started to chuckle. I breathed a sigh of relief. "You remind me of my husband," Mrs. Kramer said as she added milk to her tea. "He couldn't stand this sort of thing either. Take my advice, dear." Now she was looking at me. "Don't let people railroad you into doing things you're not comfortable with. It's better to stand firm than be beaten down. Unless, of course, you're the one doing the beating."

It was an imperfect segue, but I'd take it. "Your husband lost his last election and was indicted at the end of it. How did that happen?"

"It happened because Wendell Crawford is a dirty son of a bitch who might as well have been running a Mafia as a political campaign." She said it like someone might say, *Hey, the sky is really blue.* Like it was simply accepted fact. "It wasn't that we weren't used to playing hardball. My husband was a career politician who had already weathered a recall campaign six years earlier. I thought we had seen it all. I thought we'd prepared for everything. But . . ." She shrugged daintily. "It turns out you can't prepare for the devil."

"You're saying he was framed."

"I'd have shouted it from the rooftops if I thought anyone could have helped us at the time. Yes, of *course* he was framed. Embezzlement? Pssht. Jonathan was a professional accountant before he was first elected. If he'd been embezzling money, no one would have ever found out about it. And I would be a lot better off than I am right now," she added before eating a tiny dark chocolate truffle.

"He was found guilty," Andreas said.

"During a trial overseen by Judge Carmilla Harrison, yes. Carmilla. God, what were her parents thinking?" Mrs. Kramer tutted. "Of course he was found guilty. Between the evidence that she didn't allow the defense to present, and the witnesses Crawford bribed or coerced into lying for him, a guilty verdict was inevitable."

Well, it sounded good, but sound wasn't substance. "Can you prove any of this?"

"No. Not precisely." When she spoke again, Mrs. Kramer sounded less prideful and more simply tired. "I know that you were hoping for more from me, but I don't have a silver bullet that will take down Crawford and his gang of thugs. If I did, I'd have used it years ago to save my husband's life."

"Then you don't believe he committed suicide."

Mrs. Kramer rolled her eyes. "He was found lying on our couch with a hole right in the middle of his forehead. The gun was still in his hand. Of all the insulting ways to stage a suicide, I have to admit that it rankled. It's like they didn't even *care* whether I believed Jonathan killed himself or not. I'm telling you, it's a slap in the face."

Andreas and I exchanged a brief *Is she fucking serious?* look. "So it's not that suicide wasn't a possibility, it's the way he did it that you don't buy?" Andreas asked.

"Jonathan was very low after the trial. Very, very low. People thought the worst of him, his lifelong friends wouldn't speak to him, and the fact that Veronica Martin—she was a young woman interning in the office that summer—had actually testified that he'd molested her was the last straw. He thought the world of that family,"

Mrs. Kramer said sadly. "We both did. He would never have touched Veronica that way, never. She lied, and it just about broke his heart."

"So suicide *was* on the table," I prompted.

"Yes, I suppose so, but shooting himself in the head? Moreover, using his left hand to do it?" She scoffed. "Jonathan had a mortal fear of guns, gentlemen. He had a bad experience with a handgun when he was a child, accidentally wounding a friend while playing with his father's revolver. Jonathan refused to handle them, or to have them in the house at all. And while we kept it out of the papers at the time, the reality is that my husband suffered a minor stroke one year before the election. He recovered quickly, but he was significantly weaker on his left side afterward. He could barely lift a pen, much less raise a gun, steady it in front of his head, and then pull the trigger. Lazy, I tell you. Just plain lazy."

I could hear Andreas gritting his teeth. "This is interesting, but it doesn't actually *help* us."

Mrs. Kramer delicately wiped her lips with the edge of a linen napkin. "How much do you know about the way a Mafia is run?"

Andreas grimaced. "More than I'd like to."

"The concept of loyalty is paramount in the Mafia. Loyalty can be reinforced in a number of ways, but the best way to do it is with blood. Family rarely turns on family. One person, if he or she is clever enough, can use those family connections to manipulate people into not only giving them their loyalty, but becoming so tightly bound to them that they would never dream of trying to break free, for fear of losing the people they love."

I followed, but . . . "How does that help us?"

"It's just a matter of finding the weakest link. Judge Harrison is tighter than a blood-filled tick. She is very cognizant of her own strengths and weaknesses, and mitigates them accordingly. You could rummage through her trash and you wouldn't find a single receipt. You could break into her house and search for incriminating files or documents, and find nothing at all. She's too careful. Her family, on the other hand?" Mrs. Kramer smiled her not-smile again. "Not so careful."

Andreas leaned forward a bit. "Go on."

"You know, Veronica died a few years ago. She was only nineteen. Another suicide." Mrs. Kramer shook her head. "She apparently shot herself through the head. Right between the eyes, actually. Gossip at the time said it was because her boyfriend broke up with her. Their relationship was a bit scandalous; he was a decade older than Veronica."

"Who was she dating?"

"Oh, I think you might know him, actually. His name is Trent Newberry. He's a detective with the Thirty-Second Precinct. He is also—" Mrs. Kramer paused for a moment, making sure we were both completely focused on her "—Judge Harrison's nephew. She never married, never had children of her own, but she's always doted on that young man."

I knew my mouth had dropped open, but I couldn't quite coordinate myself enough to close it. Trent? Really? Bro-tastic, ass-kissing, ladder-climbing Trent? Trent who I'd spent a pleasant few weeks exchanging blowjobs with years ago?

Andreas certainly seemed to like the news, if the wolfish grin on his face was anything to go by. "You think Newberry killed both Veronica Martin and your husband."

"I'm almost sure of it. The guns used in both shootings had had their serial numbers filed off. I'm willing to bet that they were stolen. Perhaps from one of your evidence lockers," she added. "It probably wouldn't be too difficult for him, or someone else on Crawford's payroll, to 'misplace' a weapon or two. Perhaps mark them as destroyed when they really weren't." She sipped at her tea. "It's a starting place, at least."

I finally found my voice. "Why are you telling us all this? Why speak now, when it's too late for it to do you much good?"

"How could I speak out before, when in all likelihood I'd just end up like my husband? I may not have much of a life, Detective Corliss, but that doesn't mean I'm in a hurry for it to be over. I've been waiting for a bloodhound to come around asking the right questions." For the first time, her smile looked real. "And now there's a pair of you."

The arrival of the waitress was so jarring I actually jumped. "Two chicken salad sandwiches and two coffees!" she announced, setting down the plates. She'd used the same fine china as the pastry dish, and prettied them up with a sprig of parsley and a radish cut in the shape of a rose.

Mrs. Kramer was still smiling as she toasted us with her teacup. "Bon appétit, gentlemen."

Hours after we'd left the pretentious tea party, and after we'd paid a brief visit to Trent's brother, Trent's father, and Trent's ex-roommate, Darren dropped onto his sofa and handed me a beer. In theory, we should've been back at the station, but after everything Mayor Kramer's widow had said to us, I wasn't so sure that was the safest place. The walls there had ears. I just didn't know where or how many. My apartment was still on too many radars, so we'd come back here instead. Didn't mean we hadn't checked the place over just to be on the safe side, though.

"Well, that was a, uh, productive afternoon," he said as we clinked the bottles together. "Still not quite sure what the point of all that was."

I chuckled as I brought the ice-cold bottle up to my lips. "I don't know. I thought it was pretty clear."

He eyed me. "But we didn't get anything useful out of any of them. You just asked them a few questions that were benign even by my standards, and then we left."

"Mm-hmm."

"So . . ." His eyebrows rose.

I took another drink. "And what do you think every single one of them did as soon as we left?"

"Called Trent and asked him why the hell a couple of detectives were sniffing around."

I grinned.

Darren's eyebrows climbed even higher. Then he rolled his eyes and laughed into his beer bottle. "So we were just antagonizing Trent."

"I don't know if that's the word I'd use."

"What word would you use?"

I considered it for a moment, then shrugged again. "Fine. Antagonizing."

Sighing, Darren lowered his beer. "Okay, but fill me in here. What exactly was that supposed to accomplish?"

"Here's the thing. Trent's involved in something shady. He's connected to Crawford and this entire scandal. And I want him to know that we know that. Or, at least, that we know something."

Darren tilted his head. "Isn't that something we don't want him to know? He can cover his tracks if he knows."

"In theory, yes. But we're tipping our hand just far enough that he doesn't know *what* we know. He'll get nervous. Start watching his back. Quite possibly try to cover his tracks. All we have to do is keep him twitchy, and then keep an eye on him until he makes a mistake." I idly rubbed an ache out of my throbbing wrist. "And even if he doesn't slip up, when we start making noise about going to see his dear old aunt Judge Harrison to ask a few questions, I have a hunch he won't be able to keep his poker face."

Darren regarded me silently for a moment before laughing. "Wow. If that's not the most Ruffner-esque form of detective work I've ever heard of . . ."

I laughed too, and took another drink. "You'll see. He'll tip his hand."

"Is it wrong that I'm looking forward to seeing it?"

"Not at all."

We exchanged glances, chuckled, and sipped our beers.

And then . . . silence fell. Awkward silence. The kind of silence that reminded me of the drive home last night after Darren had followed me. How weird things had been when I'd walked into that conference room this morning.

My stomach tightened. We hadn't really put that whole thing to bed, had we? Yeah, he'd apologized, and yeah, I'd agreed to share more information, but last night had been following us around all day long. Now that we had some downtime, there was no avoiding everything that had been semi-patiently waiting for attention.

"Listen, um . . ." Darren stared into his beer bottle, tapping his fingers rapidly on the side of it. "About the tracker. I really am—"

"Darren. We've been over this."

"I know, but it's killing me. I'm sorry. It . . ." He sighed. "Just . . . I'm sorry. The captain and IA—they just want me to keep an eye on you. Report back anything that's not a hundred percent by the book."

"So, basically everything I do."

He laughed humorlessly. "Basically."

"Have you told them anything?"

Darren shook his head. He cleared his throat, and goddamn if he didn't break out the puppy-dog eyes. "I'm sorry, though. I do want you to trust me. The tracker in your car . . . It won't happen again."

"I know it won't. I do trust you."

"Even after that?"

"Yeah."

Darren's eyes shifted away, then back to me, and he squirmed on the cushion. "I guess I'm just really freaked out about things getting weird between us."

"They've kind of been weird from the start, haven't they?"

"Yeah, but . . ." He paused and locked eyes with me. Barely whispering, he said, "It hasn't always been weird in a *bad* way."

Oh, wasn't that the truth. In fact, now that he'd mentioned it, I liked the way things had been weird-but-not-bad between us, and that had a hell of a lot more appeal than this weirdness.

Heart thumping, I slid closer to him. Darren sat straighter, but he didn't recoil away, and he didn't stop me when I took the bottle from his hand and set it on the table.

Facing him again, I slid my arm around him.

Drew him in.

And kissed him.

Oh God, yes. This kind of weird, I could live with. He was my partner, and I'd wanted to wring his neck last night, and now he was kissing me back. Pulling me closer. Taking over. He pushed my lips apart with his tongue in the same moment he shifted around to straddle me, and we were back to the very first time we'd made out on his couch. I was just distracted enough that I kept pressing the sore spot on my arm against him. Oh well. I could live with it. Some pain was well worth having my hands on Darren.

Abruptly, he broke the kiss and murmured, "Turn off your phone."

"Huh?"

"Your phone. Turn it off." He shifted a bit and took out his own cell phone. "Off. Now."

"What are—"

"I am not getting cockblocked by the fucking captain again. Turn. It. *Off.*"

"Yes, sir." I pulled it out of my pocket, put it on airplane mode, and tossed it on the table. Darren's clattered on top of mine a second later, and he hauled me into an even deeper, hungrier kiss.

When he met my gaze again, his eyes were absolutely on fire. I'd seen him turned on before, but not like this.

He swept his tongue across his lips. "We should really move this into the bedroom."

"Yeah?" I grinned up at him. "Why's that?"

"Because that's where I keep the condoms and lube."

My whole body broke out in goose bumps. *Yes, please.*

I couldn't speak, though, so I just nodded. We got up and headed for the bedroom, but we hadn't even made it out of the living room before Darren grabbed me, pinned me against the wall, and claimed another demanding kiss. This side of him blew my mind—I'd never imagined him being this aggressive.

As he kissed my neck, I panted, "Didn't . . . didn't think you had it in you. To be this . . ." Words. What were words?

"I can be," he said against my throat. "When I want something."

Before I could come up with a playful retort, his hand slid over the front of my pants, and my vocabulary disintegrated to "Fuck . . ."

"We will." Teeth grazed my neck. "Don't worry, we will."

I squeezed my eyes shut and tilted my head, completely overwhelmed by his mouth and his body and his presence. Was this real? Was I fucking hallucinating?

And did he really just drop to his knees in front of me?

I stared down at him. Oh yes. God yes. He was kneeling, and he was unzipping my fly, and if his fingers brushed my cock one more time, I was going to lose my mind.

Then . . . holy shit. He closed his fingers around my cock. Skin on skin. Stroking. *Fuck.*

Our eyes met, and he grinned. As he leaned forward, he licked his lips. I knew exactly what he had in mind, and God, I wanted it, but I nudged him back. "We can't. Remember, I'm—"

"I know you are." He stood and kissed me again. "I know, and I haven't forgotten, and I still have every intention of seeing how much of your dick I can take down my throat."

I shivered hard. This crass, brazen side of him was so . . . new. And hot. Christ, it was hot. "But we should—"

He silenced me with a deep, non-negotiable kiss, melting every bone in my body and making my cock impossibly harder in his hand. "It's safe."

I shook my head. "Not completely, and I—"

"Andreas, I've been on PrEP for months." Another kiss, gentler this time. "Just relax and enjoy it."

He knelt again, and I didn't stop him. If he wasn't worried, then I wasn't. Everything I'd read had said oral sex was extremely low risk even without PrEP, and I shouldn't have been surprised he was taking that pill. He had his head screwed on way too straight to not take advantage of that kind of preemptive protection against HIV, even if he wasn't sleeping with someone he knew was positive.

And now here he was, knowing damn well I was positive, and he wasn't joking about seeing how far he could take me into his mouth. It had been years since anyone had gone down on me, but I was pretty fucking sure none of them had been as skilled or enthusiastic as Darren. Just the way he swirled his tongue around the head of my cock almost sent me through the roof. And, Jesus, did he even *have* a gag reflex?

I combed my fingers through his hair, alternately watching him and letting my eyelids slide shut. As he stroked my cock and teased all over with his lips and tongue, he moaned like he was the one on the receiving end. I couldn't fucking believe it—all this time spent being certain no one would ever want to touch me again, and now this.

"Oh God." I shivered, arching off the wall. "F-fuck, you're gonna make me come."

Abruptly, Darren stopped. "Can't have that."

My heart sank. Right. He was probably willing to suck my dick, but asking him to finish a blowjob was too much. Understandable. Still . . .

He stood, pressed me against the wall just like he had before, and kissed me again. "Much as I want to make you come," he murmured between kisses, "I don't want this to be over yet. Not till I get to fuck you."

It took my brain a few seconds to catch up. Wait, *that* was why he'd stopped? Not . . . Really?

Darren drew back and met my gaze. "What's wrong?"

"What?"

"You tensed up." His eyebrows pulled together. "Maybe I should've asked—*do* you bottom? Or—"

"It's been fucking years since I've been touched." I cradled his face and kissed him. "Turned on as I am right now, there is literally nothing I can imagine saying no to."

He grinned against my lips. "Good. Because I'm a top. And I really, *really* want—"

The kiss happened. I wasn't sure if he moved in or if I did, but somehow he was speaking, and then we were kissing, and he didn't need to finish the thought because we both got the message. I wanted him. Right fucking now. If his dick was as thick as it felt through his pants, then I definitely wanted—

Bang! Bang! Bang!

Darren and I jumped like it was gunfire, not someone pounding on the front door.

"Open up, Darren!" an all too familiar voice boomed from outside. *Bang! Bang! Bang!* "I know you're home!"

We both froze.

"Is that—" I looked at Darren, whose gaze was fixed on the door. "Is that *Trent*?"

His Adam's apple jumped. He nodded, then shifted his attention back to me. "Yeah. That's Trent."

"You have got to be shitting me."

"Open up, asshole!" Trent shouted.

I glanced at the door. "How the hell does he know where you live?"

"Uh. Well." Darren's cheeks colored. "He's . . . spent a night or two here."

"Spent—" I blinked. "Like . . ."

"Yeah."

Bang! *Bang*! *Bang*!

"Come on, Darren!"

Darren's face darkened even more, and he started to pull away, but I wrapped my arms around him and drew him back in. Chuckling, I said, "You have terrible taste in men, you know that?" Then I kissed his throat, and he relaxed a little.

He leaned into me, sucking in a sharp breath. "So I guess a threesome is out of the question?"

"With him? Absolutely."

"Fair enough." He lifted my chin and claimed a kiss.

Bang! *Bang*! *Bang*!

"Don't fucking ignore me!"

Darren scowled at the door. Then he met my eyes. "We should go in the bedroom. There's way too much noise out here."

CHAPTER TWENTY-FOUR
DARREN

The last time Andreas had been in my apartment, I'd been worried about what he thought of the place. This time, I made sure he was too fucking desperate to notice the pile of clothes he almost tripped over as I shoved him toward my room. It wasn't hard. Andreas barely took the time to breathe, trailing his hungry mouth over every inch he could reach of my skin as we stumbled through the door and toward my bed.

We both stopped long enough to take off our holsters. With those out of the way, he dropped onto his back, and I followed, pinning him against my rumpled sheets with my body and finally getting my hands beneath his shirt. He moved his own up to my back, bare now that I'd abandoned my button-down somewhere on the floor, and pulled me tighter to him. I felt more than heard the grunt of discomfort in his throat. "Don't hurt yourself," I mumbled against his lips.

He gripped me even harder. "Don't care if it hurts."

"You'll care if it affects your grip tomorrow."

"Jesus fuck, don't—don't go easy on me." That was the closest thing to begging I'd ever heard from Andreas, and it made my dick throb inside my slacks. "I don't need that, I don't want it, just . . . don't *stop—*"

I leaned back and laughed. "You think I'm going to stop?" He was splayed out and flushed against the blue cotton of my bedspread, nothing but his rigid cock exposed. He looked like a fucking *gift*. "You think you could do anything that would make me want to stop now?" I brushed his red, wet mouth with my own, catching his lower lip between my teeth and pulling until he groaned, then released him and licked the tender skin. "You aren't going anywhere until I've come inside of you."

Andreas's cock actually jerked against my leg when I said that, and he had to shut his eyes and breathe through his nose for a moment. I bit my own lip to regain a little control. It had been a long time for him, four fucking *years* since Andreas had been touched like this. It would be easy for me to push him over the edge, but I didn't want things to end before I'd reminded him of how it felt to be wanted like I wanted him right now. Having him in my bed, under my control . . . if I bit my lip any harder, I'd draw blood, because I was worried I was in a fucking dream. That wouldn't do, though. I didn't want to make Andreas any more nervous about having sex than he already was.

I slid back so I rested on his thighs, then tugged at the edge of his shirt. "Get this off."

He took a few more deep breaths, then opened his eyes. They devoured me as I stood up, coming to rest on my bulge as he complied.

Holy shit. I couldn't remember the last time I'd had someone so gorgeous in my bed. It had been nothing but club hookups for months before I buckled down to study for my exam, and before that . . . well. I'd been with guys my age, guys who had youth and good looks on their side, but none of the sheer magnetism that had captivated me the first time I saw Andreas. There was nothing yielding about this man, nothing soft, but here he was, naked and wanting, all for me.

I was so goddamn spoiled.

I knelt, not to go down on him again, although his breath hitched hopefully. I got him out of his socks and pants instead, making sure his briefs came away as well. His thighs were heavily muscled, and I wanted to bite down and leave my marks all over them. I needed to be careful with my teeth, though. Instead, I raked my nails from the bend of his hips down to his knees, leaving bright-red lines behind. Andreas groaned again, his quads jumping. Good. I hoped they throbbed.

"Shit," he muttered. "You look . . ."

I grinned. "Yeah?"

"Dangerous."

The breathiness in his voice let me know he wasn't exactly bothered. "It figures you'd find that hot. Sit up." He leaned forward off his hands, and I stood up and finally, *finally* got my pants out of the way. I ran my hands through Andreas's thick hair, dark strands clinging to my fingers as I tilted his head back. "How long has it been since you sucked a guy off?"

Andreas licked his lips. The blue of his irises was almost completely gone. "A long time," he said. His voice was hoarse.

"Well. Let's hope it's like riding a bike."

I didn't even get to guide him in; Andreas was fucking eager to get his mouth around my cock. His technique was straightforward, taking me as deep as he could before pulling back with a long, slow suck. I kept him from going too deep but otherwise just enjoyed it, the way he threw himself into going down on me like it was his purpose in life. I was thick enough that his lips stretched beautifully around me, and I traced the edge of his mouth with my thumb as he worked.

"Fuck," I muttered. My balls were already tightening, drawing too close to my body for less than a minute's time. I wanted this too much. "*Fuck.*"

I pulled him off, and Andreas glared up at me like he wanted to kill me. It made me chuckle. "Roll over and lie down."

"What, you can't come more than once a night?"

"Keep pushing it and I'll just jerk myself off," I warned him. "See how you like looking but not touching." It was an empty threat—there was no way I wasn't fucking him at this point—but it got Andreas moving. He shifted away from me and rolled onto his stomach, and I exhaled shakily. God damn, I wanted him so badly I'd have to be careful not to go off before I got into him. Someday I'd wear a cock ring and fuck him until he couldn't hold himself up anymore, but not now. Not the first time.

His ass was gorgeous, the kind of perky that twinks would kill for. It was almost funny, seeing an ass like this on such a hard man. I was in an ideal place to appreciate it, and as I ran my hands over his smooth skin and felt him push back into my grip, I decided to revise my stance on biting. I leaned in and huffed a breath over one cheek, pressing my mouth to the spot just below the dimple in his lower back. I smacked his ass just as I dug the edge of my teeth into his skin.

"*Uhh.*" Andreas sounded drugged, not moving away from me, not moving at all as I bit him hard enough to leave a bruise, then soothed the spot with my tongue. He'd feel that tomorrow. I wanted him to.

"Is that far enough from easy?" I asked. "Probably not, for you." I trailed my fingers down his crack, pressing the pad of my index finger against his anus. He clenched down against nothing, and I smiled, then swatted his hole. "You want it so bad, don't you?"

"Can't tell me you don't." Andreas's voice was ragged, but the challenge in it was clear.

"No," I agreed, feeling the throb in my groin quicken. "I can't. Stay there. Don't touch yourself." I let go of him and rummaged through my bedside table drawer, frowning when I came up with condoms but no lube. Come on, *c'mon* . . .

"Those are enough."

I tried to ignore the way the pure sex of Andreas's voice made ridiculous things seem reasonable. "They're lubed, but it won't be enough."

"It has been before."

Oh shit. I could imagine it, Andreas in the stall of some seedy club bathroom, so desperate for it that he dropped his pants and let some guy slide into him with no prep, just the lube on the condom easing the way into his ass.

No, Darren. Bad.

"Yeah, but I bet you were having more sex back then." Under my bed, it had to be under the bed; I'd used the damn stuff only a few days ago. I crouched down to check. Where— Aha, *there*. I emerged triumphant to lock eyes with Andreas, who was looking at me over his shoulder.

"I haven't fucked another person in four years. That doesn't mean I haven't fucked myself plenty."

My breath caught in my throat. Now *that* was a pretty picture. Way better than someone else fucking him. I settled onto my knees between his spread thighs and popped the top on the lube.

"I wanted," I said, dragging the words out as I slicked my fingers. "To fuck you." I put the bottle down. "Over that goddamn pool table." I pressed two fingers against him, felt his muscle give and take me inside. He was so tight I could barely fit both of them in, but Andreas didn't want it easy, and I didn't want to give it to him that way.

"You were being such a bastard, and I wanted to kiss you so bad." I pressed deeper, loving every moan that came out of his mouth.

It didn't take long to loosen him up some, enough that I could move in and out of him without feeling like he was going to break my hand. "I wanted to do more. I thought about that later, once I knew I hadn't fucked us over completely. I thought about how it would have felt to push your face down against the table and jerk your pants down and just plow right into you." I'd come really hard to that little fantasy, actually.

"God, do it now."

"Too late, I've already got these—" I spread my fingers apart, and he groaned, twitching but not pulling away "—inside of you. Maybe they're enough, huh? Maybe you want to come on my hand."

"I want your *dick* in me, Darren. *Fuck*, what do I need to do?" Andreas demanded. It wasn't as intimidating as his demands usually were, given that he was pressing back against my fingers like he was afraid I'd take them away. "Give you an engraved goddamn invitation? Please fuck me like you fucking mean it, all right?"

"Well." I slowly withdrew my fingers and pretended that my hand wasn't trembling. "Since you asked so nicely."

Getting the condom on took way too long, and adding more lube was just asking for trouble, the pressure of my own hand felt so good. I spread Andreas's legs a little farther apart as I moved in close, swept my hands from his shoulders down to his hips, got a grip, and pressed the head of my cock against his ass.

He opened up and let me in. Not easily, not without a grunt of what might have been pain, but steadily. A few seconds later, I was buried in Andreas, and I had to tug on my own balls to keep from coming right there.

"Wait," I ground out when he started to move. He didn't stop, and so I smacked his ass again. *That* got him to settle down.

Once I was confident my body wouldn't embarrass me, I pulled back until I was barely in him, then slammed home almost hard enough to drive his face into the bed. Andreas had his weight balanced on his knees and forearms, the injured one on top. He was breathing like a marathoner at the end of a race, huge gulps of air, as though he were overwhelmed. Good. I wanted him overwhelmed. If he was coming off a four-year dry spell, I wanted him to fucking drown in sensation now.

"I like a guy who says please." I drove into him like I might never get the chance again, hard and fast. Part of me wanted to do better, to really draw this out, but Andreas wouldn't thank me for slowing down right now. I didn't know if I was capable of it, anyway. He felt so tight around my cock, squeezing hard enough to make my eyes cross. I jerked his hips back with every thrust, forcing his body to match my rhythm. Andreas let me move him, gave up all control of his body to me, and I reveled in it.

I wasn't going to last much longer. I had no idea how Andreas hadn't come already. I ground in tight against him, then reached around and closed my hand on his cock. He was wet, slippery pre-come slicking my fingers, and I instinctively tightened my grip.

"Oh *fuck*," he gasped, and that was it. Andreas came in my hand, his hips shivering in the vise of my hold on him. I pressed my forehead against his back and let go, unloading into the condom and almost lightheaded with the pure, ecstatic relief of it. I couldn't remember the last time I'd come so hard. Maybe never.

I had just enough brain power left to pull out before I collapsed onto Andreas. I staggered to the bathroom and got rid of the condom, rinsed off my hand, and after a moment's consideration, grabbed a towel.

Andreas was lying on his side, slightly curled, like his muscles couldn't quite figure out how to release all the way. His eyes were closed, but they opened as I joined him on the bed. I spread the towel out over the wet spot, then lay down and wrapped an arm around his shoulders. Screw being big and tough right now; I wanted a cuddle. I was a little surprised when Andreas didn't object, just rolled a little farther into me and put his head on my shoulder.

"Fancy." His fingers plucked at the towel. "What are you, a college kid?" He didn't sound annoyed, though—honestly, he sounded drunk.

I was too tired to even think about prevaricating. "I only have one set of sheets, and I don't feel up to washing them right now. Tomorrow." I yawned. "C'n do it t'morrow."

"You falling asleep already?"

Wasn't it obvious? "Mm-hmm."

"Hey, Darren."

Oh crap, was he already regretting this? Was he going to pull away, run back to his place, cool things off between us? Had all of this been a terrible, horrible idea? I opened my eyes and found him looking at me—not his usual intense glare, but an expression I'd never seen on him before. "Yeah?"

"Thanks. That was good."

I smiled. "Don't thank me for giving me exactly what I wanted."

"How much of that do you think Trent heard?"

"If he's lucky?" My smile turned into a grin. "All of it."

Darren and I both dozed for a while. I probably would've slept for a few hours if the alarm on my phone hadn't nudged me fully awake. The alarm was relatively quiet, but shrill enough to carry into the bedroom.

Moving as stealthily as I could to avoid jarring Darren, I got up, pulled on my boxers, and went into the living room to silence the alarm. Then I went looking for my jacket.

It had landed in the hallway, about halfway between the living room and the bedroom, and my skin broke out in goose bumps just thinking about that moment. Darren had been getting more aggressive by the second. His kiss had been so demanding it was almost painful. Every time he'd grabbed a handful of clothing, it was either to tear it off me or to physically pull me toward the bedroom. Or closer to him. As if I'd wanted to be anywhere else.

Grinning to myself, I picked up my jacket and fished out the packet of pills I carried for when I couldn't get back to the precinct. In the kitchen, I found a clean glass and ran some water from the tap.

This was a new prescription. Still the same type of drug, but a slightly different dosage. Or something. The only thing that had mattered to me was that with any luck, the change would kill the dizziness that had been driving me crazy lately. Though if it gave me the headaches I was getting before I'd changed scrips the last time, then I'd take the dizziness with a smile. At least I could function with that.

I was just worried as hell it would have a whole different set of side effects.

I chased the pill around the center of my palm with my thumb.

"You all right?" Darren's voice spun me around, and I nearly dropped both the glass and the pill. He was standing in the kitchen doorway, his thumb hooked casually in the pocket of the black gym shorts he'd put on.

I cleared my throat. "Yeah, I . . ." I glanced down at the pill. "Just needed to take this before I forget." With that, I threw it back and washed it down with the water. As I set the glass in the sink, I added, "Did I wake you up?"

"Nah." He stepped closer and slid a hand down over my ass. "I was coming around when you got up." He pulled me in and kissed me. "Didn't want you sneaking out before I had a chance to fuck you again."

His comment went straight to my balls, and so did his hand. I couldn't help groaning as he cupped me through my pants.

"Jesus . . ." I pressed against his palm. "You're full of surprises, you know that?"

"How so?"

I grinned. "For starters, the day I met you, if someone had told me you were an aggressive power top with a thing for biting—"

He burst out laughing and shrugged. "Don't lie, Andreas. You still wouldn't have liked me."

"No, probably not." I slid my hand beneath the waistband of his shorts. "You're kinda growing on me, though."

"Likewise." He kneaded my dick through my clothes.

"Horndog," I said, almost groaning.

"I finally got you into bed. What do you expect?"

"Fair enough." I couldn't help laughing, and shook my head.

"What?"

"Oh." I smoothed his hair. "Just realized the captain told me to try to get along with you more than I have my last several partners. I'm not sure this is what he had in mind."

Darren snorted. "No, probably not." He lifted his chin and kissed me. "But if he asks how we're getting along, I'll be sure to give a glowing review."

"I should hope so. Especially if I let you fuck me twice."

"Let me?" He stroked me through my pants again. "Pretty sure I could make you beg for it."

I had a witty remark ready to fire, but his thumb traced the head of my cock, and . . . whatever. I leaned in to kiss his neck. "You have more condoms, right?"

"Plenty. I haven't worn you out yet, have I?"

"Worn me out?" I nipped his collarbone hard enough to make him grunt. "I'm not *that* old."

"Good. Bedroom."

Returning to the real world was bizarre. After one night and a hot, lazy morning together, I felt like I'd been vacationing in another dimension for years. And what a vacation it was.

But it was over now, at least for the moment. If the looks Darren kept shooting me in the car were any indication, though, there was a rematch in my future.

But for now, we had an investigation to continue. So, clinging desperately to cups of coffee, we walked from the parking garage to the elevator up to the precinct.

"Listen, um . . ." Darren glanced at me. "We, uh, should probably keep this between us."

"Yeah." I nodded. "Especially if Trent is . . ."

Darren flinched. "Someone I used to fuck?"

"Mm-hmm."

"I, uh . . ." He stared at the floor of the elevator. "Guess I should've told you about that. Before we—"

"Don't worry about it." The elevator lurched to a stop, and the doors opened. As we continued down the hall, I quietly said, "Your past is your business. Especially since I'm pretty sure you weren't aware he was involved with anything shady."

"Besides me, no."

I laughed, and Darren relaxed.

We fell into our usual routine. Well, as much routine as any detective ever had. In this case, phone messages, emails, follow-ups, and all that usual bullshit. And, on top of all that, making calls to try to get a few minutes of one Judge Harrison's time.

While we worked, the bitter, semiburnt coffee from the break room kept me grounded in the present, and the aches and twinges kept me from believing last night had been a dream. It had definitely happened. Especially since every time I sat at my desk and winced, Darren snickered. Arrogant bastard. Not that he was walking any less gingerly than I was, though I was pretty sure he didn't have a visible bite mark on his ass cheek.

I pushed a file folder aside after looking through it a million times, and Darren slammed his phone down.

"Finally!"

"What?"

He held up a Post-it note like a captured flag. "We've got a meeting with Judge Harrison at two thirty."

I grinned. "Well done. I didn't think we'd get in for a few days."

"Yeah, well." He laughed. "When you've got Darren Corliss's patented sweet talking on your side . . ."

"Uh-huh."

He chuckled, but then sobered. "So what's the game plan?" He absently scraped the Post-it back and forth on the edge of his desk. "I've, uh, never tried to rattle a judge's cage before."

"Well, we don't want to tip our hands too far at this point."

"So, don't bring up anything we talked about with Mayor Kramer's widow."

"Don't even mention that we've talked to her at all. Nothing about Veronica. Nothing about Trent."

"And I assume nothing about Crawford, Blake . . ."

I shook my head. "At this point, I think the best way to get under her skin is to let her know she has something to lose."

"Such as?"

"Such as the press and the public finding out she was tipped off about Judge Warner's shooting. Not just a lucky survivor."

Darren's eyes lost focus as he kept playing with the Post-it. "Won't look good during election season."

"No, it won't. Even if we can't prove she was involved in anything shady, or that she had something to hide that Judge Warner would've publicized, the mere fact that she knew not to be there—"

"And didn't warn Judge Warner or Young."

I nodded. "Exactly. So I say we start there. See how she reacts. Once we've got her attention, then we get some names out of her."

"You think she'd roll on whoever she's working for?"

"If my suspicion is right and she's only taking bribes and turning a blind eye to criminal activity? Yes. If she's in any deeper than that—if she's actually got blood on her hands besides Judges Warner and Young—we might have to try something else. But either way, she's going to get nervous."

"And so will her nephew."

"Exactly."

Darren was quiet for a moment, but then he nodded. "All right. Sounds like a plan." He met my gaze. "I'll follow your lead."

Before we left the precinct an hour or so later, I swung into the locker room.

So far, the new medication was doing all right. My temples had been throbbing a little, but it wasn't as bad as the headaches I'd had before. With any luck, it would stay this way. The dizziness was . . . well, it wasn't worse. It would take time to get better if it happened at all.

Anything was better than those fucking kidney stones, though.

Alone in the locker room, I took the pill bottle out of its hiding place. As I pulled out a tablet, the door opened, and someone came in. I tracked them, listening to the sharp steps.

Damn it, just my luck—they came down this row of lockers. Right up to my open locker. And stopped.

The hair on my neck prickled, and I quickly but casually slipped the pill bottle back behind the box. Then, with as neutral an expression as I could muster, I shut the door.

"Trent." I gritted my teeth, but smiled at the motherfucker. "What a nice surprise."

"Fuck you, Ruffner," he growled.

"My, my." I spun the combo on my lock. "Someone's testy."

"Cut the crap. You want to tell me why you're harassing my family?"

"Harassing? Is that what you call it when a detective follows leads and—"

"What leads?" he hissed. "You're harassing my family, asshole."

I glared at him. "If you think it's genuine harassment, take it up with IA."

"Didn't I just say to cut the crap?" Trent's lip curled with what I could only guess was barely contained fury. He stepped closer, almost into a normal person's comfort zone, which put him well inside mine. "If you want something from me, come and get it from me. Not my parents. Not my brother. And *not my aunt.*"

"Who says I want anything from you?" I just kept myself from adding *besides what I already have.* Whatever had gone on between him and Darren was obviously over, and whatever was going on between *me* and Darren wasn't something I was going to dangle in front of his ex. No matter how priceless it would be to see the fucker get pissed off about it.

Trent set his jaw. "I don't know what you and Corliss are up to, but you've questioned three of my family members in the last twenty-four hours, and a little bird told me you're on your way to meet with my aunt. How is that not harassment?"

"Seeing as it's part of an active investigation, how is it any of your business?"

His lips thinned, and he stabbed a finger at me, very nearly hitting my chest. "I would suggest you watch your step, Ruffner," he snarled, his face inches from mine. "Because I wouldn't want anyone to start fucking with *your* family."

Ice water trickled through my veins. "My family has nothing to do with anything here—"

"And mine does?" Trent narrowed his eyes. "Leave. My family. *Alone.*"

Without waiting for a response, he stormed past me and disappeared around the last locker. His dress shoes cracked against the floor until the door banged shut behind him, and I slowly released my breath.

This was what we wanted. The whole point of questioning his family was to shake him up and get him to make a mistake. Hostility was to be expected.

But God help him if he fucked with my family.

CHAPTER TWENTY-SIX

DARREN

armilla Harrison had a private office only a block from where the DA worked. It felt kind of odd, being so close and not stopping by to check in on Asher. Just a few years ago, I'd come here all the time. We'd get together for a beer after work, or I'd run him a slice of leftover pizza when he was working late on a case. The pace of his life had been frenetic, but Asher had loved it.

"Problem?" Andreas asked after I hesitated a little too long getting out of the car. He managed to make it sound concerned instead of chiding, though. It was amazing the kind of leeway a few excellent orgasms could get you.

"No, I'm good. Just." I shook my head. "It's a little weird being here to see someone other than my brother."

"I get that." There was a touch of sympathy in his voice, but mostly he sounded impatient. "Is your head in the right place for this today? Because I can always go in by myself."

I laughed. "Oh, she would throw you out so fast."

"She might try."

"No, she would, because she's a judge and she's got security officers to help her out, and the last thing you need is the captain finding out you were in a brawl with a bunch of rent-a-cops. I'm fine." There was no way I wasn't going to see this through.

"Good." He turned and led the way into the building. It was pretty fancy, with marble floors and brass fittings and dark, gleaming wood walls. It practically screamed *Lawyers work here. Flee, puny mortals!* Andreas marched right past the doorman like Van Helsing on a mission, leaving me to deal with his spluttering attempts to refuse us entry.

"We have an appointment with Judge Harrison, we're good!" I called, giving the guy a little wave as I hustled to keep up. "Jesus, you can slow down a little, it's not a death march," I said under my breath.

"Not yet it's not." He stopped in front of Judge Harrison's door and knocked loudly. "And it won't be if she can give us what we need."

I narrowed my eyes at him while we waited for a response. "Be honest. You wanted to grow up to be the Punisher, didn't you?"

"The who?"

"The Punisher?" Andreas looked blank. "You know, with the skull T-shirt and the—"

"Enter."

Enter? Who even said that anymore? The office we stepped into was just as archaic as the greeting: walls lined with thick books that could more accurately be called *tomes*, a huge wooden desk with a green leather writing surface, and a sconce—an actual fucking sconce—on the wall. Behind the desk was a woman of indeterminate middle age, her hair cut in a careful brown bob, her expression cool. She pointed at the single chair in front of the desk.

"Sit."

I held back and let Andreas have the seat. I was following his lead here, after all, but it was an asshole move on Judge Harrison's part to expect people and not let all of them sit down. *Note to self: passive-aggressive behaviors.*

"Say what you came here to say."

That was all the opening Andreas needed. "I know you're throwing some of your cases."

She scoffed. "How could you possibly know that?"

"Data. Statistics. Correlations between the people who've gotten off with a slap on the wrist at your bench compared to the records of those who haven't, and their criminal actions following their appearance in your court." And God, those stats had been a bitch to crank out. The office computers ran the numbers slower than a toddler ran a marathon.

"I don't need to tell you that correlations by themselves aren't indicative of any wrongdoing on my part."

"No, but they're another piece of the puzzle. I know you aren't doing it alone, that's for sure."

Judge Harrison sighed. "If all you've come here to do is throw around baseless accusations, Detective Ruffner, then you can—"

"I know the fact that you survived that shooting in April was no accident."

If I hadn't been watching her so closely, I might have missed the way she paled a little, the wrinkles around her mouth deepening as she bit back her initial response. I caught it, though, and if I could see it, then Andreas had as well.

"You escaped unscathed, so lucky, while Judge Warner and Judge Young were gunned down in the street. But it wasn't luck. You *knew* there was going to be a shooting."

"More baseless accu—"

"You went to lunch with those two men, your colleagues, people you worked with for over a decade, and you ate with them and joked with them and looked them in the eyes, and then you let them walk into their own assassinations." Andreas whistled lowly. "Damn, I know I've got a reputation for being a son of a bitch, but I can't even imagine how cold you'd have to be to send your friends to their deaths like that. And now your clerk is dead. Who'll it be next, your stenographer?"

"You have no proof." She sounded certain.

"Are you sure of that? Because I know you got a call that day. Someone telling you you'd left your wallet behind, ostensibly, but it wasn't that, was it? It was someone telling you to get out of the way. Who called you, Judge Harrison?"

Her lips were bloodless now, pressed together so tight I could almost see the outline of her teeth beneath them. She didn't say anything, and Andreas pushed forward. "You think we can get a subpoena for your phone records? There has to be a judge left in city hall who isn't dirty or dead yet."

"You know nothing. You have no evidence, and no way to compel it. If you had a case, we wouldn't be here."

Andreas leaned forward, both hands pressing into the rich, dark leather of the desk. "I'm trying to save lives. Maybe your life, the way things are going lately. Maybe even your *nephew's* life. Do you give a damn about Trent? Because if you do, you're gonna need to speak up,

Judge Harrison. People are going to die, and soon, and the only way to stop it is to stop the person who's got you in a choke chain."

I watched her the whole time Andreas spoke, mostly because I had nothing else to do. The look that flitted across her face when Andreas mentioned Trent—that was weird. It wasn't worry or affection. It was something else entirely.

"I won't listen to your ridiculous allegations any longer." Oh shit, she was getting ready to kick us out. "The two of you can—"

"It's hard, isn't it?" My mouth moved before my brain really told it to. I was aware of Andreas's stare, of Judge Harrison's venomous look, but they didn't really register. I had to follow my hunch before my momentum died. "Having someone you love change. I get it. It happened with me too. You remember my brother, Asher Corliss?"

Judge Harrison took a deep breath. "I do, yes. He was an excellent lawyer before he got . . . sick." She seemed uneasy. "I'm sorry about what's happened to him, but—"

"It's hard in a way because it's so gradual," I barreled on. I couldn't give her a chance to grab the reins again. "Some days it's like he's barely changed at all. He remembers cases and court dates and the names of all his coworkers. Other days he doesn't even remember who *I* am. He gets angry and defensive and downright *mean*. It feels like I'm talking to a different person altogether. And it's hard, because I remember him the way he used to be. That isn't who he is now, though. I love my brother, but we don't really know each other anymore." I paused, then added, "At least he's not a murderer. Not like Trent."

She flinched. I kept going. "How long has it been since you went from protecting him to being afraid of him? Maybe since that thing with Mayor Kramer? Or a little further down the road, after Kramer's former intern killed herself. Except she didn't kill herself, did she?" *We all know that isn't what happened.*

Judge Harrison closed her eyes with a heavy sigh. "I can't give you anything." Andreas started to object, but she held up a hand. "I *can't*. I have no concrete evidence of wrongdoing on the part of anyone, not myself and certainly not the person behind this situation. One of the reasons I was encouraged to be a part of this is because I have a special talent, Detectives: I have a photographic memory. I don't need hardcopies or memos to remember what I need to do."

"But your testimony—"

"Just because I don't have any evidence against myself doesn't mean other people don't, Detective Ruffner. My own nephew has vowed to speak out against me if it comes to that."

"Why would he do that?" I asked.

Her lips thinned again. "Because he can. He was so . . . I had so much hope for him, early on." She shrugged helplessly. "He got into a little trouble here and there, but he had such a bright future ahead of him! I couldn't let him throw it all away thanks to a few mistakes, and so I helped him."

"You covered for him."

"I facilitated his continued career as a police officer."

"You covered for a criminal and gave him the means and opportunity to abuse his position." There was no forgiveness in Andreas's voice. "You helped him get away with murder, literally."

"I don't know for sure—"

"But you suspect!" He slammed the palm of his hand down on the desk. "You could know if you wanted to, but you buried your head in the sand instead, went on brushing off the cases you were told to and hoping, what, that Trent would get *better*? See the error of his fucking ways? Why would he, when he has you for an example? All the power of your office, and you acting like God up on your throne. Sounds like the sort of thing a fucking sociopath like Trent would want to emulate."

"No, it isn't like that!" The last of Judge Harrison's cool had finally slipped away, revealing her desperate worry. "They told me they'd kill me!"

"Who? When?"

"In April, at the café. I don't know who called me, but they told me—they said I needed to watch myself, or bad things would happen to me. I didn't know about the shooting until afterward. I would never have led them into that, they were my *colleagues*." Probably the closest thing she had to friends.

"You have to help us bring down Crawford." She was already shaking her head, but Andreas persisted. "You have to, or everything you're telling yourself that going along with his plan is going to prevent? It'll happen. It's going to happen anyway, do you get that?

There are people out there who are tired of being played with, tired of being targeted. A lot of people are going to die if we can't bring Crawford to justice."

"He's too careful. And that's not an excuse, it's the truth! I know he's monitoring my computer and my phone. He'll know if I'm turning on him, and he'll kill me before I can accomplish anything. If you want to catch Mayor Crawford, then you're going to have to do it in the act. That or break into his home and search for his own records, which," she frowned, "apart from casting the legality of everything found into doubt, would probably just result in your death. That place is a fortress.

"Catch him in the act. Get independent, incontrovertible proof of wrongdoing, and you'll have the makings of a case. If you can get that . . ." Her voice wavered for a moment, but she pressed on. "If you can get that, then I'll help you to the best of my ability. Until then, though, my hands are well and truly tied."

"You're a coward." Andreas's voice was quiet, but it still cut like a scalpel.

Judge Harrison squared her shoulders. "I'll be brave when the gain outweighs the loss, Detective Ruffner. Now." It was her turn to command. "Both of you get the hell out of my office."

Darren slid into the passenger seat and shut the door. "So what's our game plan?"

"Exactly what she said—we need to catch Crawford in the act. And soon."

"But how do we do that?" Darren tapped his nails on the console. "And make sure we take down the whole organization?"

I started the engine but didn't put the car in gear yet. "I'm not sure we have time for that anymore. Crawford is the man in charge, but Trent is the other key player." Pieces were falling together in my head. Yeah, it was Trent. Of course it was Trent. And wouldn't a cop have been thorough and smart enough to disable my cameras in the warehouse before dumping the body? Add a little anti-cop graffiti to throw off the scent? Yeah, it was all making sense now. "If we take down the two big dogs that are left, the organization won't collapse, but it'll fall into chaos. At least temporarily."

"So, drop Crawford and Newberry, then round up as many as we can before they have a chance to regroup?"

"Exactly." I stared out the windshield for a moment. "Things are about to go down. Whether we initiate it or those assholes do, shit's about to get real." I turned to him. "You ready for this?"

He gulped. "This is what we trained for, right?"

"Yeah. But they usually let you throw a few grenades before they saddle you with a nuke." I patted his thigh and laughed dryly. "Hang on tight."

Darren chuckled. "I will. So, if we're going to initiate it, what do we *do*? We can't just send in SWAT and hope for the best."

"No, but we might need to have them on standby."

"I was joking."

"I'm not." I broke eye contact and shifted into reverse. "We're going to have to set up something big." I paused to pull out of the parking space, and as I drove down the street away from the courthouse, I continued. "Crawford isn't going to want to get involved in a few people swapping powder in a back alley. If he's there, it's got to be important."

"Like when you busted him at the airport."

I nodded. "He's more cautious now. He doesn't even come to high-dollar transactions anymore."

"So how do we flush him out?"

"My best guess is we make him believe someone's stealing from him."

"Someone like Trent?"

I flashed him a grin. "You're getting good at this."

"What? Reading your mind?"

"No, because I hadn't even thought of that yet." We exchanged glances before I focused on the road again. "But it's perfect. Might take a few days to arrange, but it can be done." I paused. "We should get Blake involved. Nobody knows this organization like he does."

"Okay. I'll follow your lead."

"Good. I'll get in touch with him. He's not easy to reach, but I'm pretty sure he'll want to meet if we're talking about an endgame."

"I would hope so." Darren was quiet for a long moment. Then, "I think we should put Judge Harrison in witness protection."

I chewed my lip. "Probably not a bad idea. Even if she convinces Trent she didn't say anything, he might not be willing to take chances."

"And we need her."

"Yes, we do." I tapped my thumbs on the wheel. "All right. I'll pull some strings and get her somewhere safe. Then we start putting together our plan to flush out Trent and the mayor."

"Awesome. Let's do this."

By the time we made it back to Darren's place, it was almost ten thirty and we were both absolutely spent. As much as I'd been looking

forward to spending some time between the sheets, the only thing we'd be doing in that bed tonight was sleeping.

My body was exhausted, but apparently my brain wasn't done yet. While Darren snored softly beside me—lucky bastard—I stared up at the ceiling.

Things had changed now that we had a judge on our side. Though she hadn't been thrilled about going into witness protection, she'd eventually agreed to it. As far as anyone in the courthouse knew, she'd flown to New Mexico to comfort a friend whose husband had suddenly passed. My friends at the US Marshals office made sure the story was airtight, complete with an obituary that would appear in two Albuquerque newspapers. If Trent were to call and check up on his aunt, he'd have no way of knowing, even if he traced the call, that she was speaking to him from a small, secure apartment wherever they'd put her up. Even I didn't get the details.

After we'd set everything up for her, Judge Harrison agreed that once Crawford and Trent were in custody, she'd testify against them and name drop every dirty judge in the state to go down with them. With Judge Harrison in our pocket, we were golden.

Blake had been his typical difficult self to reach, but I'd finally gotten him on the line late this evening. Tomorrow night, we'd meet with him. He wasn't thrilled about my partner seeing his face, but he'd deal with it. Nobody had time to be picky right now. Which was also why Darren and I couldn't afford to hold out until we had warrants for everyone who worked for Crawford. Arresting Crawford and Trent would be a crippling blow. A lethal one if we didn't give the organization time to get their shit together.

Where could we do this? How? Did we set up an entire warehouse and make it appear to Trent that Crawford was running another shop without giving him a cut? Convince Crawford that Trent was meeting with a hitman to have him killed? A million scenarios rattled through my head. The smaller the operation, the less opportunity for innocent bloodshed, but also the less likely Crawford himself would show up. He had to believe that he and only he could deal with this, and that he needed to deal with it in person.

Blake. Blake would know. Like nobody else, I reminded myself, he understood the inner workings of the organization. He and his brother—who was also safely in witness protection—would know how to flush out both men.

I wiped a hand over my face and exhaled.

"You still awake?" Darren murmured.

"Can't sleep." I turned my head, searching for his silhouette in the darkness. "I didn't wake you up, did I?"

"Eh." He rolled over and draped his arm across my stomach. "I'd offer to fuck you to sleep, but . . ." A second later, he was snoring again.

I chuckled and kissed his forehead. "Tease." Eyes closed, I tried to keep my mind off the mission and instead focused on the warmth of Darren's body against mine. Maybe I was too tired for sex, but I was not too tired to enjoy finally having someone to sleep next to for the first time in too long.

Running my fingers through his hair, I smiled into the darkness. I still resented the shit out of Captain Hamilton's insistence on sending partners to babysit me, but I had to admit—it had worked out pretty damn nicely this time.

Eventually, I drifted off, but it seemed like I'd barely shut my eyes before my phone chirped to life. I blinked a few times. The goddamned sun wasn't even up. Feeling around, I muttered, "You fucking kidding me?"

"Who the hell is calling?" Darren grumbled into his pillow.

"I don't—" But then my groggy brain cleared enough to recognize the ringtone, and I was suddenly wide awake. I snatched the phone off the bedside table and sat up. "Hey, kiddo."

"Hey, Dad," my oldest daughter, Erin, said. "I didn't wake you up, did I?"

"Hmm?" I rubbed my eyes. "No. No. I was . . . getting ready for work." My heart was thumping—any time one of my kids called out of the blue, I immediately expected the worst. "What's up?"

"Well, I need to come to town for a couple of days. I know it's kind of on short notice, but can I stay at your place?"

My instant reaction was always to tell her or her siblings they could stay with me, but even I wasn't staying at my place right now. Too many bullets flying, and potentially with my name on them.

I cleared my throat. "My complex is actually fumigating right now and dealing with some black mold. I'm staying with a friend."

I paused. "But I can pay for a hotel room for you. What's bringing you to town?"

"An interview for an internship. I guess I was handpicked for it, so it sounds like I'll get it."

"Oh really?" I smiled despite my sleepiness. "That's great!"

"Yeah, I'm excited." I could practically see her grinning from ear to ear. "It's definitely not the job I was expecting. I was looking into banks and that kind of thing."

"So where is this one?"

"It's at city hall."

Ice water shot through my veins. "Come again?"

Beside me, Darren sat up.

Erin went on. "Yeah, I don't know what I'll be doing yet, but it sounds like I'll be working in the mayor's office."

"Oh."

Darren put his hand on my leg and mouthed, *What's wrong?*

I held up my finger. *Just a second.*

To Erin, I said, "And, um, when's the interview?"

"This Thursday." She clicked her tongue. "I know it's short notice. Mom said she'd pay for a train ticket as long as I could nail down a place to stay."

I swallowed hard. My mouth had gone dry. "Okay. Yeah. I'll . . . I'll work something out for you. Just . . . email me when you know when your train comes in and how long you'll be here."

"Okay. I'll let you go. Thanks, Dad!"

"Anytime, sweetheart. I love you."

"Love you too."

She hung up, and I dropped the phone onto the covers. "Fuck."

"What's going on?" Darren asked.

"That was my daughter." I turned to him. "She's got an interview at city hall."

His eyes were suddenly huge. "For what?"

"An internship." Gritting my teeth, I added, "She was apparently handpicked for it."

"Isn't she going to school out of state?"

"Yeah." I swung my legs over the edge of the bed and rubbed my stiff neck. "Fuck. This is Trent. I know it is. Son of a bitch threatened to fuck with my family if we didn't back off."

"Jesus. But you're going to let her do the interview?"

"What can I do? If she doesn't, he's going to know for a fact that we're onto him, and he'll step up his game."

"Shit."

"I'm gonna kill him," I said through my teeth.

Darren squeezed my shoulder. "No, we're going to bust him and put him in prison for all the shit he's involved in. Him and everyone else."

"He's fucking with my *kids*, Darren."

"I know. And you've said yourself we either bring this thing down starting at the roots, or we don't bring it down at all."

I closed my eyes and slowly exhaled. "You're right. You're right." Leaning forward, I pressed my fingers into my temples. "I swear to God, though, if anything happens to one of my kids . . ."

"I'll be right there with you to fuck his world up." The growl in his voice told me he wasn't lying.

"Thanks," was all I could say.

He got up. "Guess we'd better get to work."

"Yeah. Guess so."

"I'll put the coffee on."

The second we walked into the precinct, I knew something was wrong. Something besides my daughter suddenly being a candidate for an internship at city hall.

It was one thing to catch someone's eye as I walked past. It was another when conversations stopped and heads turned. In the parking garage, in the elevator, in the hallway—people halted midsentence and stared at Darren and me.

"Do I even want to know what that's all about?" Darren asked under his breath.

"Probably not, but I have a feeling we're going to find out anyway."

"Detective Ruffner!" Captain Hamilton's voice boomed from stairwell. "My office. *Now!*"

I rolled my eyes. "Well, that answers at least part of it."

"Am I coming too?"

"If you want to." I turned and headed back toward the stairwell where Hamilton was waiting. Darren hesitated for a second, but then he followed.

As we approached, Hamilton glared past me. "This doesn't concern you, Corliss."

Darren halted. "Uh . . ."

"Don't you have work to do?" the captain snarled.

I looked over my shoulder and met his *What do I do?* gaze. I nodded toward our desks. Darren gulped, but then he headed back the way we'd come.

Once my partner was out of earshot, I faced the captain. "What's going on?"

"My office," he repeated, and stormed up the steps. He didn't say another word until he'd slammed the door shut behind us. "Sit down."

"Where?" Both of the chairs in front of Hamilton's desk were occupied.

Thibedeau, of course.

And Trent. Oh, wasn't that a shock?

Should've let Darren come up here with me. He might actually stop me from killing this son of a bitch.

I looked back and forth between the two assholes, then turned to the captain. "I guess I'll stand."

"I guess you will." He took his own seat behind his desk.

"What's going on?" I asked.

"Detective Newberry came to me with some information that's a little disturbing."

It took all the self-control I had not to laugh out loud and tell him that everything I knew about Trent was probably a million times more disturbing. But I needed a poker face right now. This was a man who'd proven his tentacles could reach my kids.

I glanced at him, and his expression offered nothing either. He was as icy and blank as Thibedeau.

"What information?" I asked.

Hamilton sat up, resting his elbows on the desk. "I understand you've been taking some . . . medication. During working hours."

My stomach lurched. "Half the precinct lives on antacids and ibuprofen. Why would I be any different?"

"Prescription ibuprofen?" Thibedeau asked, his voice flat and chilly.

That poker face was getting tougher and tougher to maintain. I guarded my HIV status like a state secret. Though I knew now that no one could fire me for it, that there really weren't any legal, tangible consequences for people knowing I was positive, it wasn't something I wanted to advertise. "I wasn't aware that I needed to inform the department if I was taking—"

"Bullshit," the captain snapped, catching me completely off guard. "You know damn well the department needs to know if you're taking narcotics."

"Narcotics?" I blinked. "I'm not taking any—"

"Detective," Thibedeau said in the most condescending voice imaginable, "if you've got a drug problem, we're here to help."

Yeah. Help me find my way to the unemployment line.

"I do not have a drug problem."

"I saw you taking pills at your locker, Ruffner." Trent spoke with such concern, he was probably fooling everybody who didn't know he was a murderer. "Denial isn't going to help you."

I rolled my eyes. "Those weren't narcotics."

"Then what are they, Detective?" Captain's patience was clearly down to its last frayed thread. The vein on his forehead was throbbing close to the surface, and the red in his face was beginning to match his nose.

This line of questioning was probably all kinds of illegal, but I didn't have time to figure out the intricacies of HIPAA and all that shit while IA, a dirty cop, and my boss were waiting for an explanation.

"Fine." I blew out a breath. "They're antiretrovirals."

Thibedeau and Trent exchanged puzzled glances.

Hamilton blinked. "Anti-what now?"

"Antiretrovirals." My stomach twisted into knots. So much for keeping my status to myself at work. "They're for—"

"Treating HIV," Trent helpfully interjected.

I shot him a murderous glare.

"What?" Hamilton shifted in his chair. "Is that true, Ruffner?"

I'm going to choke you with my bare hands, Trent.

"Yes." I faced him again. "I'm HIV positive. The pills I've been taking are to keep that under control."

Exhaling slowly, he sat back and folded his hands on top of his belt buckle. "And those are the only drugs you're taking."

"Yes, Captain." I hated the heat in my cheeks as much as I hated the men to my left and right. "I'm not taking anything else."

"Well." The captain rolled his shoulders. "Apparently this was much ado about—"

"Captain, I know what I saw!" Trent sat up.

Thibedeau sighed impatiently. "How could you tell a pain pill from an antiretroviral?"

"The bottle was sitting on the bench in the locker room," Trent insisted. "I saw the label, clear as day. It was Dilaudid."

"That's horseshit," I said.

"Detective." Thibedeau sounded bored now. "We can't demand access to your locker without a warrant, but if you take us down there now and give us a look, then maybe we can put this whole thing to bed."

"For fuck's sake. Fine." I waved a hand at the door. "Let's go." I'd already shown one card I hadn't wanted to play at work. What was letting them see my locker too?

"All right." Thibedeau stood. So did the captain.

A little slower, Trent rose, and as he did, our eyes locked for a split second.

And just like this morning when Erin told me she was interviewing at city hall, my blood turned cold.

One by one, they filed out of the captain's office, and what choice did I have but to follow them? I'd already given them consent to see inside my locker. Technically, I could rescind it and let them get a warrant, but my credibility would be shot.

Downstairs, all our footsteps seemed to echo menacingly on the locker room's tile floor. Of course, there must've been half a dozen other cops in there, and like everyone else in the building today, they stared.

Dread twisted my gut into knots as we approached my locker, and I'd never had to fight this hard to keep my expression blank. It was entirely possible Trent was fucking with me. He wanted me to lift the veil on some paranoia. Even when my locker came up clean, Hamilton and Thibedeau would have every reason to expect I was hiding *something*. They just had to figure out where.

Willing my hands to stay steady—*not playing your game, Trent*—I dialed in the combination. When the lock clicked, I pulled open the door and stepped aside.

Thibedeau looked first. He scanned up and down, inspecting every inch he could see without pawing through my belongings. "Where are the drugs you usually take?"

I gestured at the top shelf. "In the shaving kit behind the box."

"Keeping them hidden?" Trent asked with a hint of a sneer.

"Newberry," Hamilton growled.

Thibedeau pulled the small bottle from its hiding place. He read the label, then handed it over to the captain. "I can't pronounce it to save my life, but it's no narcotic I've ever heard of."

Hamilton took the bottle and scrutinized the label as well. My skin crawled.

Guess I can take these out in the open now. No point in keeping it a big secret.

"Looks fine to me." He handed it back to Thibedeau, who replaced it in the locker.

"What about the bag?" Thibedeau pointed at my gym bag. "Mind if I look in there?"

"Have at it," I said. "Didn't think you boys were that interested in my jock strap, but all right."

He glared at me, then reached for the bag.

And as he pulled it out of the locker, a distinctive rattle made me freeze.

Expression hardening even more, he dropped the bag on the bench. "Open it."

With my heart in my throat, and everyone in the room staring silently at me, I unzipped the bag. Everything was exactly where it belonged—my gym clothes, my running shoes, my toiletry kit—and I thought for a split second I was home free. It must've just been something in the toiletry kit. A razor clattering against the deodorant stick or something.

But then I saw it: just under the tongue of my shoe was a white plastic cap.

"Take that out." The boredom in Thibedeau's voice was long gone.

Holding my breath, I did.

And sure enough, it was a bottle of pills. Dilaudid, according to the label.

What the hell?

"These are not mine."

Captain Hamilton snatched them out of my hand and read the label. "No, they're not yours." *If looks could kill . . .* "They're prescribed to one Marcy Jackson."

"Marcy—" My jaw fell open. "How the hell would I be taking my ex-wife's drugs? She lives in another state."

"Not according to this." He turned the label so I could see it. Yeah, it was my ex-wife's name, but the address beneath it was mine.

"Captain, this is not mine. I've never taken—"

"Save it, Ruffner," Thibedeau barked. "This situation is now under investigation by Internal Affairs." He took the bottle from Hamilton. "And this is evidence."

"Sir, listen to me. I—"

"You're in IA's hands now," Hamilton said. "And, as of this moment, you're suspended." He held out his hand. "Gun and badge, and then get the fuck out of my precinct."

I couldn't breathe. I couldn't move.

And as an invisible noose slowly tightened around my neck, Trent just grinned.

CHAPTER TWENTY-EIGHT
DARREN

A ndreas had only been gone a few minutes when Marla called my desk phone. Her voice was barely above a whisper. "I don't know what you two did to piss off the captain and get IA involved, but word to the wise, Darren? Don't get involved."

"What?" What the hell was she talking about? Of course I was getting involved; I was *already* involved. My partner was in there being interrogated, his family was being threatened, and our investigation was at a make-or-break moment. I couldn't just leave Andreas to weather it alone. "No, I need to—"

"Honey." She might have been whispering, but there was nothing soft about her tone. "You need to listen to me right now, 'cause this is the best advice you're gonna get all day. I'm telling you: stay at your desk, keep your head down, and get to work. At least *look* like you're working. Because you hovering like a hummingbird right now? You're not going to help Andreas any, and you're definitely not going to help yourself."

"But Marla—"

"Get back to *work*, Detective Corliss."

She hung up, and I sighed. She had a point: I hadn't been called into the captain's office for a reason. If they came out and found me right outside the door ready to jump without knowing why, it might make the situation worse. Whatever the fucking situation *was*. Not to mention, I had plenty of eyes on me right now. The more I behaved normally, the less they'd look my way.

It wasn't long after her call before Hamilton and Andreas went trooping down the stairs, with Detective Thibedeau on their heels along with Trent. Shit, one of the least trustworthy cops in the entire city had sat in with Andreas and the captain. And the fucker from IA. The four of them disappeared down the stairs before I could catch Andreas's eye. What was going on?

"They finally got proof," one of the detectives at a desk near mine said, voice full of satisfaction. I didn't know his name, but I sure as hell was going to remember his smug fucking face. "It's about time that bastard went down for his dirty little habit."

"It's been an open secret for years," his partner agreed. "I guess the captain's finally seen the light."

"Or he decided Ruffner wasn't worth the trouble of protecting anymore. You can bet on it, Hamilton'll be out within a fuckin' month once IA starts pokin' into how he conducts himself. You know he wrote me up for goin' on a coffee break?"

"You were gone for three hours," his partner said with a chuckle.

"Hey, I'm a big guy, it takes me longer to get to the machine." They laughed until they noticed me watching them. "Aww, the baby looks like he's gonna cry! How's it feel to know your partner's a dirty cop, Baby-face?"

"I don't know, how's it feel to know that if Internal Affairs investigates the captain, they'll look through all our computers as well? Thibedeau's the thorough sort." I smiled sharply. "How will he react when he finds the porn you've been downloading when you should be filling in your reports?"

"Bullshit," the guy snapped, his square jaw flushing with heat. "There's nothing like that on my computer."

"Really? You sure?" I leaned in a little. "You do know that deleting your browser history isn't enough, right? Not with forensic computing the way it is. They'll dig *deep*. Are you prepared for that?"

"Fuck you, Corliss," he said, but he quickly turned his attention to his computer, fingers working rapidly. My shot in the dark had hit the mark, it looked like. Not that I could muster the extra energy to care right now. All I cared about was what was happening to Andreas. Drugs? They were searching for drugs? If they looked in his locker, they'd find his antiretrovirals. His status would be out in the open. That would devastate him after so many years of careful secrecy.

It didn't take very long for them to come back—no, wait. Not all of them. Where was Andreas? Trent and Thibedeau continued upstairs, probably to laugh maniacally together in the frozen halls of IA. Hamilton looked my way as he continued on to his office and motioned for me to join him.

Once his door was shut, I couldn't keep quiet. "What's going on? Where's Andreas?"

Hamilton sighed heavily as he slumped back into his desk chair. "Detective Ruffner is currently suspended for suspected use of narcotics while on duty. Where he is now, I don't know." He set a badge and gun down in front of him, his fingers lingering over the worn leather of the badge.

Suspended? "Narcotics?" I was so confused.

"Dilaudid. In his wife's name," Hamilton said flatly. "We found a bottle in his gym bag."

Oh, *what*? "This is bullshit. Who told you about this?"

"Detective Newberry brought it to the attention of Internal Affairs, which brought it to *my* attention. The question is," he speared me with a disappointed look, "why *you* didn't bring it to me first, Darren."

"Captain—"

"I could have done something if I'd had enough warning. Gotten the man into a treatment program, gotten him out of here without the dog and pony show. Instead I had to humiliate my best detective in front of witnesses, not to mention breaking out the HIV thing. Jesus Christ, Darren, why didn't you tell me? Or were you and Andreas still having issues?"

"I didn't tell you anything because he's not using drugs! His HIV status, okay, I did find out about that, but it wasn't my secret to tell. If he was using, though, I would have passed it along, of *course* I would have." Or possibly not, but he didn't need to hear that now. "You don't think it's a little suspicious that a detective not even based in our precinct is the one to bring the IA hammer down on Andreas? After years of people here envying him, wanting to fuck with him, but no one ever bringing charges because there was no proof, because there's nothing *to* prove. And suddenly Detective Newberry manages it?"

"The evidence is pretty damning."

"The evidence was planted by that son of a—"

"Darren." Hamilton sounded so tired. "Look, this isn't how I wanted things to go down, but I have to follow procedure, and procedure means suspending Ruffner pending a full investigation. Maybe you're right, maybe the drugs were planted, maybe his wife never had a prescription and we can prove it was faked. But that takes time, and it has to be done the right way. Do you understand? If you want your partner to have a future here, you've got to let us do things the right way and keep from rocking the boat. I don't want to hear any complaints about you from Detective Newberry, you get me?"

I could argue. I wanted to keep fighting, to battle over the point until both of us were bloody, but it wouldn't do any good. Andreas was suspended. That meant only one of us had an in with the cops right now, and that was me. I needed to . . . fuck, I didn't even know, but getting myself suspended along with Andreas wouldn't help anyone. In the end, all I could say was, "Yeah. I get you."

"Good. You're on desk duty for the rest of the day. The last thing I need is you 'accidentally' running into Ruffner while you're working a case."

I left on autopilot and headed straight back to my desk before I realized that if I had to keep listening to those two idiots sniggering next to me, I'd brain one of them with my stapler. I went looking for Paula instead. At the very least she'd be a sympathetic ear; at the most, she'd help me start figuring out a next step.

Naturally, Paula was out, investigating a new murder. The desk secretary gave me the info on it when I asked nicely, though; looked like the orchids I'd given her were paying off. The victim was female, midthirties, dressed too nice for the dirty place she was found. I didn't recognize the name, but the file said she was a public defender at city hall. She'd been shot twice through the head. Fuck.

I couldn't linger at the desk forever, no matter how hard I prevaricated. Thankfully, my area of the bull pen was fairly deserted once I got back. Looked like the captain had been yelling at everybody this morning.

The day dragged by at the speed of purgatory. I tried to keep myself occupied with files, going over witness statements, looking into anything that could possibly be used to incriminate Trent, but I couldn't find anything specific enough to be helpful. I only ate because

Marla forced a cellophane-wrapped tuna sandwich on me around one, as well as a cup of the hideous break room coffee. "It's not your mama's cooking, but it'll keep you going," she said. That was as close to sympathy as I ever got from Marla, and I appreciated it.

"Thanks."

Paula didn't make it back to the precinct by the time five rolled around, and I was in no mood to wait any longer. I left a message on her phone asking her to call me as soon as she could, then hightailed it out of the bull pen like my feet were on fire. Fuck, I wanted to leave, just go home and be with my family for a while and not think about what a shit partner I was, inevitably letting Andreas down because I was twiddling my fucking thumbs in the middle of—

"Darren."

Trent. Trent motherfucking Newberry was leaning against my car, the car I'd left in the precinct lot days ago because I'd been riding shotgun with Andreas ever since. I saw red. I wanted to rip him limb from fucking limb. I wanted to . . . not screw over our chances, faint though they might be, of wrapping this case up without more death, and Trent needed to be alive for that. Goddamn it. I needed to play nice.

I exhaled shakily. "Trent."

"Hey . . . how are you holding up?"

I laughed bitterly. "How the hell do you think I'm holding up? My partner has been suspended, I'm one ugly look away from joining him thanks to the captain feeling overzealous, and Internal Affairs is far from happy with me. I'm fucking peachy." Well, I didn't have to play *too* nice.

Trent stepped a little closer. "I'm so sorry for how things went down. I tried to keep you out of it as much as possible. Ruffner's a bad guy though, Darren. He was leading you down the wrong path."

"You're upset about us calling your family." I said it with an air of resignation.

He shrugged. "Well, yeah, but he's also a drug user. An addict. Who's to say he wouldn't get you hooked too? Especially since it seems like you guys were a little closer than most partners." I knew that tone of his, although I'd never heard it directed at me before. That was *jealousy*.

Trent was almost close enough to touch now. "Whatever he told you, it's not true." His big, blue eyes captured mine, wide and clear with perfect sincerity. "I'm not the bad guy here, Darren. I swear it. You know you can trust me. You've known me so much longer than him."

I never knew you. "That's true," I whispered. "But I can't—I can't talk about this right now. I have a lot of thinking to do tonight."

His hand rose, and I watched it come at me like a bullet that I was too slow to dodge. He set it on my shoulder and curled his fingers in toward my neck, and it took all my willpower not to shudder. "You don't have to think tonight if you don't want to." His thumb stroked over my collarbone. "I could help you put it off if you want to forget."

There isn't enough alcohol in the world. "I can't. Not tonight, I need to— Damn it." I shook my head and stepped back. "I need to go get my jacket. I left it upstairs."

"Okay." There was something like lust in his gaze, but he looked hungry for more than just me. He was on a winning streak, and fucking me would be the cherry on his sundae. I was just another goal, another way to beat Andreas. "If you change your mind, you know my number. I'm here for you, got it?"

"Yeah. I got it." I turned around and headed back to the stairs. I really had forgotten my jacket, but I didn't stop at the bull pen. I kept going all the way up to the fourth floor, not really thinking at this point, just so furious that I had to let it out somehow. There was one target for my ire that probably couldn't hurt me right now. If he was on Trent's side, I'd be screwed soon anyway.

Thibedeau's light was still on. I pushed my way into his office, so angry I could barely see. He looked away from his computer screen and sneered. "Well, well. If it isn't the world's worst detective."

"I think that title belongs to you."

"Oh really? I'm not the one who missed my partner's prescription drug habit. Or were you helping him hide it?" Thibedeau steepled his fingers in that stupid, condescending way he had. "Did he turn you so fast, Darren?"

"Who turned who?" I demanded. "Honestly, is this what you expected to find in Andreas's locker? A bottle of pills in his ex-wife's name, so easy to locate that you were back at your desk five minutes later? And you were so happy about it, weren't you? You finally get to check that little box on your form and file him away for good. But it's a lie, and I think that somewhere inside, you *know* it's a lie."

"Detective Corliss, listen to me—"

"No, *you* fucking listen." I'd had it up to my goddamn eyebrows with listening. "You've suspected Andreas of being dirty for years, and you've never found *anything* incriminating. You didn't even know he was HIV positive, and I bet there was a time you could have used that to drum him out of the force, or at least mandate that he be put on permanent desk duty," and yep, there was the blink of acknowledgment I was expecting, the bastard, "but you *didn't*. Because you had nothing. Now all of a sudden, you get some bullshit tipoff from Detective Newberry and you find the smoking gun? Halle-fucking-lujah? Did you really expect it to be that easy?" I narrowed my eyes. "Do you actually think it *is* that easy? Because if you do, you're way less intelligent than you'd like people to think."

"Are you here to tell me something new about your former partner?" Thibedeau gritted. "Because if not, you can leave, now. I'll be talking to Captain Hamilton tomorrow about your disgraceful attitude toward authority."

"Is that your problem with me? Do I not bend over far enough to lick your boots?" I shook my head. "No wonder you hate Andreas. But you're wrong about him. Your evidence is flimsy, the guy who gave it to you is playing you, and if you're really lucky, this won't be the beginning of the end of your career."

"Are you threatening me?"

"No. I'm warning you." My fire was dying, my anger spent along with most of my energy. I was exhausted. I could only imagine how Andreas felt right now. I wondered if he'd be at my apartment when I got home. Probably not—it was almost certainly under fresh surveillance after the scene at the precinct. "You're investigating the wrong man. I hope it doesn't come back to bite you in the ass."

I left with heavy feet and an aching head. I barely registered my surroundings as I drove to my apartment; it was kind of a miracle I made it back without stalling the car or running into a curb. I wanted to go home, back to my folks' place, to sit with my mother and eat with my brother and share a beer with my stepdad. But I didn't want to draw any more attention to them than necessary, so it was safer that I stayed away.

My apartment was empty. It figured. I turned on a few lights and drifted back into my bedroom to change. My bed was still a mess from this morning, and every crease in the sheets reminded me that last night, I'd slept here with Andreas. The night before that, we'd almost broken the bed frame. I couldn't remember the last time I'd been so happy. And now . . .

By the time the knock came at my door, I was into my second beer and halfway through a cold slice of pizza that tasted like cardboard as I checked my email over and over again, hoping for a message from Andreas and coming up empty. Andreas wouldn't bother to knock, and Trent wouldn't do it so politely. Maybe Paula had stopped by? I got up and opened the door, only to find—

"Detective Corliss."

It was Thibedeau. Fuck my life. "What do you want?"

"I want to talk to you about the *right* man." He looked about a second away from tapping his patent leather shoes with impatience. "But not in the hallway, if you please."

It took me a second to put it together, but as soon as I did—

"Let's go for a drive."

I couldn't leave my apartment without being followed, and I was about to go insane. I didn't dare call Darren. Or anyone, for that matter. There was no telling who was watching my every move and listening to my every call.

Which meant I couldn't go near Darren. I couldn't go near anyone involved in my investigation. We were at a critical juncture, a turning point that would make or break this case that I'd been working on for *years*, and if we didn't make our move soon, we'd be back to square one. If we made the wrong move, people could get killed. *Darren* could get killed.

But *we* weren't doing shit as long as that blue sedan was parked across the street from my building, or that lady kept passing down the sidewalk at exactly thirty-minute intervals. When I left around dinnertime to pick up some takeout, I was followed by a car and a bicycle. Shit, no wonder the precinct was short on resources— everyone was busy keeping an eye on IA cases.

If there was one faintly silver lining to having my every move watched, it was that if someone tried to target me in my apartment, there were cops watching. Not that I could guarantee they'd do anything about it, especially if they were in Trent's pocket. Or not cops at all.

Well. So much for sleeping tonight.

To my surprise, though, it turned out exhaustion had other plans, and I crashed shortly after midnight. I might've kept on sleeping—I had the time off, after all—except my phone woke me up at seven thirty.

Unrecognized number. Of course.

I picked it up. "Detective Ruffner."

"It's Thibedeau."

Now wasn't *that* a name I wanted to hear at the ass crack of dawn?

"What do you want?"

"I need to see you in my office. ASAP."

I mouthed some curses, then muttered, "Fine."

He hung up. No good-bye, no *I'm not kidding about ASAP.* Straight and to the point.

Sighing, I rolled out of bed and shuffled off to take a shower. Pity his straight-and-to-the-point-ness didn't include just cutting to the chase and telling me I was fired. At least then I could be prepared and bring a box with me to empty out my desk. Oh fuck that shit. I'd take one from the precinct. If they were canning me on trumped-up charges after all these years, they could spare a fucking cardboard box.

I showered, debated shaving, and decided not to bother. Then I got dressed and headed to work to find out if I needed to apply for unemployment.

The blue sedan was gone, but as I left the parking lot, a black one followed me. A middle-aged guy spoke earnestly into his phone and watched me as I drove past, so I smiled and waved at him. He instantly turned away.

Yeah, thought so, buddy. Say hi to my boss. Or Trent.

I shuddered and kept driving.

I took the back staircase from the parking garage up to Thibedeau's fourth-floor office so I'd cross as few paths as possible. By the third floor, I was well aware that my new prescription had not, in fact, completely killed the dizziness, but it was better. Sort of. I'd take it.

At his door, I glared at the lettering etched on the frosted glass.

Det. Mark Thibedeau

Internal Affairs Bureau

Teeth clenched, I knocked.

"It's open," came the terse reply.

Funny. I'd always imagined the gates of hell would take more work to open, but no, all I had to do was turn the knob.

As I stepped inside, he said, "Close the door and sit down."

I paused. Something in his tone was not what I'd heard on the phone. Without a word, I closed the door and sat down.

Thibedeau leaned forward and steepled his fingers under his chin. "I spoke to your partner last night."

My heart plummeted into my stomach. "And?"

He watched me silently for a moment. Then, quietly, he said, "Would you be willing to submit to a drug test?"

Nodding, I said, "You won't find anything."

"I'm . . ." He sighed, and I wondered where his usual bravado had gone. "I'm beginning to believe that."

I folded my hands on my lap. "What's going on?"

"The drug test will clear your name. Especially if you're willing to do more than a piss test."

"Such as?"

"Blood. And hair."

I shrugged. "Fine. Take what you want, but you're not going to find anything."

"Yeah, I don't imagine we will." Thibedeau drummed his fingers impatiently on his desk. No, not impatiently. Uneasily. *Nervously.* He glanced past me at the door, and when he spoke again, his voice was quieter. "I can't lift your suspension until we've completely cleared you. Which, even if your tests are clean, that doesn't explain how the medication got into your locker with your ex-wife's name on it."

I started to protest, but he put up his hand.

"I'm not finished."

I swallowed.

His eyes darted toward the door again. "The sooner you do the tests, the sooner I can clear you. It's going to take some time, but at least if they come back clean, I can work with your captain. See if we can bring you back to work."

"Even with the outstanding charges?"

Thibedeau fidgeted in his seat, folding and unfolding his hands. "I might have to twist Captain Hamilton's arm, but under the circumstances, I think it can be arranged."

"Under the—" I shook myself. "You've been after my hide for years, and now you're going to bat for me? What changed?"

"You can thank your partner for that."

"Come again?"

"Like I said, we talked. And after he left, I got to thinking, and I went through your files." He paused, drumming his fingers again. "And I got my hands on Detective Newberry's files from his precinct."

"Can you *do* that?"

His eyes narrowed. "Do you want me to send them back?"

"Uh. No. I don't think? What's going on?"

His gaze slid toward a thick green folder on the side of his desk, and his Adam's apple jumped. Facing me again, he said, "There's a lot of grime in that file. Complaints from fellow officers that never went anywhere. Allegations of criminal activity that were abruptly dismissed." He exhaled slowly. "Either Trent's a good cop who's got a lot of people that want to bring him down—"

I arched an eyebrow. "Can't see that happening."

Thibedeau shot me a glare, but went on, "Or he's a fucking dirty cop who's got someone covering for him."

"Am I right in assuming you think it's the second option?"

He nodded. "The question is, how is he getting away with it? I mean . . ." He tapped the thick folder. "I don't know what's happening there, but something isn't right. And somebody—somebody who has the power to call off IA investigations—is involved."

My chest tightened. "Oh shit."

"Oh shit is right. And now I've got *my* ass on the line because whoever that somebody is, it won't take much for them to find out I looked in Trent's file."

"Jesus." I rubbed the backs of my fingers along my unshaven jaw. So not only was Trent working with the mayor to run a complex crime network, he had a judge running scared, a shitload of blood on his hands, and now someone in his precinct's IA department in his pocket. And with Thibedeau putting his neck out like this, he could wind up dead if Darren and I didn't move fast.

"I'll do the drug tests," I said. "And then you'll talk to Hamilton?"

"Yes."

"And then what?"

"Then, hopefully, you and Darren can finish your investigation and get this fucker what he deserves." The slightest pinch of his brow added an unspoken *Please hurry.*

My stomach churned. You knew things were getting bad when IA was scared.

Thibedeau handed me a card for a local medical clinic. "To make sure everything is completely on the up and up, here's the place you'll go for the test." He nodded toward the card. "I took the liberty of booking it already. You're expected there in an hour."

Any other time, I'd have snidely asked how he knew I'd agree to the tests. And since when did drug tests require appointments?

I wasn't asking questions today. Not when I had this unexpected ally.

I took the card and tucked it into my pocket. "Thanks."

"Oh, and . . ." He reached into his desk drawer, pulled out a small white envelope, and slid it across the desk. "Darren asked me to give this to you."

I picked it up, but didn't ask what it was. It was probably for my eyes only, hence the sealed envelope. "All right. Thanks."

"Don't mention it."

I started to go, but hesitated. "There's, uh, one more thing." I faced him, thumbing the edge of the envelope, and took a deep breath. "If I'm not running low on favors."

"At this point, I think I owe you one or two."

I'd been waiting my whole fucking career to have Mark Thibedeau's balls in a vise, but it wasn't nearly as satisfying as I'd imagined. It was unnerving because mine were in the same one.

"My daughter is interviewing this week at city hall," I said. "For an internship. Apparently she was handpicked for it." I shifted my weight. "The day after Trent threatened me if I went near his family."

"Jesus . . ."

"Yeah. I can't tell her not to go because that'll just tip off Trent. And I don't know if you have access to anything connected to city hall. But if you can do anything, even if it's just postponing her interview and buying me some time . . ."

Thibedeau nodded. "I know some people. I'll see what I can do."

"Thanks."

I left the same way I came in, down the back staircase and out to my car. All the way down, that envelope burned a hole in my pocket, but I didn't dare open it until I was absolutely certain no one was looking over my shoulder.

Finally, when I was in my car with the engine idling—had to keep my followers on edge, of course—I slid my thumb under the sealed flap.

Inside was a folded piece of paper with Darren's handwriting on it.

Your contact reached out to me. Mtg tonight. 11pm. Same place as before. D.

"What?" I muttered, turning the paper over to see if I'd missed something. I read the words again. My contact? Same place? What did that even mean?

I looked closer at the letters, and realized his initial didn't quite match his handwriting. It was less of a *D* and more of a . . .

Bowling pin?

The pieces fell together.

Blake. He was meeting Blake. At the bowling alley.

I laughed as I stuffed the note back into the envelope. "Darren, you fucking genius." At least one of us could keep the ball rolling with Blake. I'd never forgotten the timer he'd set, and that every day we didn't make a move was one day closer to all-out war between Crawford's dirty cops and Blake's desperate drug dealers.

I'm counting on you, Darren.

This entire investigation is on your shoulders.

I wanted to send up a silent prayer that he wouldn't let me down.

But something told me I didn't need to.

The tests were simple enough, of course, and within fifteen minutes of walking into the clinic, I was on my way out. Now to go home and try to entertain myself until Thibedeau convinced Hamilton to let me come back to work. I did have a few TV shows I could binge-watch, assuming I could concentrate on—

"Andreas."

The voice stopped me in my tracks, and I looked down the hallway to my right. Darren met my gaze, then slipped through a doorway and disappeared.

What the hell? This medication didn't cause hallucinations, did it?

I glanced around to make sure no one was tailing me. A woman with a couple of toddlers was coming toward me, so I milled around for a moment until they went into a pediatrician's office a few doors down. When I was absolutely sure I was alone, I followed him.

The doorway led to a stairwell, and as soon as I stepped onto the landing, another door shut on the floor below this one. I followed, and when I stepped into the next hallway, yet another door closed, this time to a maintenance closet.

I hesitated. There was no window on the door. Was I sure it was Darren?

At the door, I put my hand on the butt of my gun—the captain had only confiscated my issued weapon, not my personal one. With my other, I reached for the handle on the door. Slowly, ignoring the relentless throbbing in my sprained wrist, I pushed it down and leaned into the door.

"It's just me," Darren said.

Releasing my breath, I stepped inside, and he immediately grabbed the front of my shirt, used me to push the door shut, and kissed me. Disbelief kept me still for a couple of seconds, but then . . . Jesus, it was really him. I wrapped my arms around him and returned his kiss with equal force.

"How the hell—" I panted. "I'm being tailed. I've got half the force following me around right now. You don't—"

"I know. That's why I got here before you did. And I won't leave until you're long gone."

I blinked. "But how did you know—"

"Thibedeau told me when and where your appointment was."

"He . . ." I held his gaze, then smiled as I started to relax. "You know, I really did underestimate you in the beginning."

Darren laughed. "Ya think?"

"And apparently I was wrong about Thibedeau too."

Sobering, Darren nodded. "Yeah. He told you about the shit he found on Trent?"

"Yep. And now he's got a target on his back, so we've gotta move fast."

"I know. So I'm meeting with—"

"Blake, I know. Smart move. And I can create a diversion. Keep everyone interested in where I am so they're not following you."

"They might follow me anyway."

"Maybe, but I think they're more worried about me. You're just the rookie detective, and everyone knows I don't keep my partners in the loop." I half shrugged. "As far as anyone knows, you're as clueless as they are about the case, so you're sure as shit not going off to meet my deep-cover informants."

Darren chuckled. "Who knew your reputation for being an asshole would pay off like this?"

I couldn't help but laugh. "Well, at least it's good for something." I paused. "Okay, tonight—I'll leave my apartment around seven. Drive around in circles, stop in a café here and there and make it look like I'm waiting for someone. Maybe pretend to be talking on a phone and drive them crazy because they can't track it. I can lead them all over the city for a few hours, so that should give you time to get to Blake and get out."

Darren nodded. "All right. That should keep them interested."

"We can hope." I rested my hands on his sides. "Whatever plan you and Blake come up with, start moving forward as soon as you can."

"Even if you're not back off suspension?"

"We can't afford to wait for that."

For the first time since we'd been partnered, some fear crept into his expression. He wasn't like a kid or a clueless rookie—more like someone who knew exactly what he was up against, and was beginning to realize just how much everything depended on him.

"You'll do fine," I said. "There isn't another cop in the city I'd trust with this."

"I have a feeling it'll go down smoother if you're there."

"Maybe. But that might not be an option. At this point, we have to assume you're on your own." I cupped the side of his neck and looked right in his eyes. "You up for it, Corliss?"

Darren nodded slowly. "If I have to do this myself, I will." He held my gaze with those puppy-dog eyes that had annoyed the shit out of me in the beginning, but were suddenly endearing now. "I won't let you down."

I smiled and drew him in for another kiss. "I know you won't."

CHAPTER THIRTY

DARREN

Setting up the meeting with the kingpin hadn't been as hard as I'd expected. In fact, it had been so easy that I was half-worried I was walking into an ambush when I went to the bowling alley that night.

I'd asked Andreas if he had any advice for dealing with Blake. He'd raised one eyebrow at me and said, perfectly deadpan, "Don't try to bullshit him." Great. Super helpful.

I had dressed down for the meeting tonight—no suit and tie, just me in jeans and a long-sleeved T-shirt. I was armed, of course—I wasn't an idiot—but the Kahr was a lot smaller than my service pistol. The whole thing fit, along with its holster, in my side pocket. I resisted the urge to run my fingers over the outline of it as I got out of my car and headed for the door.

I wasn't Andreas. I didn't have a history with this guy—I didn't have a feel for how to approach him. Fuck, I didn't really even know what he looked like—mugshots only showed so much—although his people clearly knew way more about me than I was comfortable with. Someone waved me through the smoky interior of the building over to a corner, and a minute later, I was sitting across from an ordinary-looking man, average in every way except for the sharpness of his eyes as he took me in.

"So you're Ruffner's Boy Scout, huh?" He didn't sound particularly pleased, but what could I expect?

"I'm his partner."

"Yeah? Even though he's suspended right now?"

"He won't be for long," I said confidently. "But yes, even though he's suspended. I trust Andreas with my life. And you obviously trust him with yours, or you wouldn't be meeting with me now."

"Eh." Blake shrugged. "I don't know about *trust*, so much as I know what to expect out of Ruffner. He's like a dog with a bone, that guy. He keeps at a problem until he cracks it, even if he's gotta break a few rules to do it. You, though? Kiddo, you're so new you still shine."

"Which is why I'm not suspended right along with him. People will listen to me if I need them to."

"Are you sure about that?"

"I am." *Pretty much.* "But it's a trigger I can only pull once, so if we're going to do this, it has to be done right. I need a setup, and I need it fast."

Blake stared at me for a moment, then nodded and reached for his beer. "All right. Montrose Airfield, you know it? It's a little regional airport, mostly caters to private citizens. There's next to nothing in the way of security out there. Once a month, a plane flies in late at night, no identification; unloads an unmarked shipment of drugs into a storage hangar; and then flies out again. The drugs are usually gone the next night. And the guy who picks those drugs up is a cop named Trent—"

"Newberry," I finished.

He mockingly toasted me with his beer. "Got it. He transports them in a police van to a warehouse on the edge of town, where my people take over. He never touches the stuff where anyone can see it, though, and he's got people around here scared good. You cross Trent, you're crossing the mayor, and that doesn't end well for anyone."

"Zoe Dugan," I recalled.

"Yeah, Zoe. She had her problems, but she wasn't going to snitch. Didn't matter, though, not once Carter started naming names." Blake sneered. "I hope he's enjoying his goddamn witness protection, after giving all the rest of us up to a bunch of dirty fucking cops."

I changed the subject as gracefully as I could. "So Trent moves the drugs the night after they're flown in. Alone?"

"Maybe with one or two other guys there, but he doesn't make a production out of it."

"And Mayor Crawford is never there."

"He doesn't stir from his hole in the city, not when it means he could get hurt. He's got brains, but he's a coward through and through. I don't know how you're going to get him out there, much less get him and Trent to go after each other, but that's not my part in this." He shrugged and sat back. "My part is to tell you that the next shipment comes in to Montrose Airfield tomorrow night. That's how long you've got to slap cuffs on these guys, because after that? My people won't wait for them to shoot first."

"I understand." I did, all too well. There might be dirty cops on the mayor's payroll, but in a gang war, it wasn't going to matter who you sided with: everyone would be fair game if they got in the way. "We'll handle it."

"You better."

Fuck yeah, I better.

I left Family Bowl in all its smoky, neon luster behind me and got back in my car. Tomorrow night didn't leave us a lot of time to get things in place, but at least I knew where I had to start.

Trent.

"Oh, Darren." A slim hand ruffled my hair, and I groaned as I picked my head up off my desk. "Hey there, sleepyhead."

I smacked my lips and rubbed the numb side of my face as I tried to get my eyes to open. "Paula?"

"Got it." She was smiling at me, but it was the kind of smile you made when you were trying to talk someone down from a ledge—way more worried than sincere. She set down a Starbucks cup in front of me. "You look like you need this more than I do."

"Oh my God, yes." I sucked down a third of the latte before my taste buds caught up with me. Soymilk, *ugh*, but fuck that, it was caffeine. "Thank you," I said gratefully. "I needed that."

"I guess so, if you're sleeping at your desk. Have I not convinced you of the many attractions of the break room sofa yet? At least it gets you horizontal."

I shook my head, then winced as my neck objected. "I tried, but I couldn't stop thinking about how many of my coworkers' asses had been right where I was laying my face." The bull pen was already filling up with those coworkers, in fact, most of them surreptitiously watching me, alone at my double desk.

Paula smacked me gently on the shoulder. "Hey, don't ruin that couch for me, it's my second home!" She looked at me sympathetically. "Having a rough time working your case while Andreas is out?"

"Andreas?" I made a face. "Jesus, don't talk about him to me, okay? I'm in a mess of fucking trouble thanks to that asshole."

"Hey, now." Paula's sympathy started to slip away. "Whatever else is going on, he's still your partner, Darren. And I'm sure he's not a drug abuser, whatever those jackasses found in his locker. He'll be exonerated, you'll see."

"That would be nice. It would be *nicer* if he hadn't gotten into that kind of mess at all, but I guess it's too much to ask for him to be a decent human being and not antagonize IA to the point of wanting to get rid of him. And maybe me, by extension."

"You think he wanted to drag you down with him? Come on, Darren, give your partner a break."

"He's not my partner right now," I said coolly. "And if I'm lucky, he won't be again."

Paula stared at me for a long moment before reaching over and grabbing the Starbucks cup again. "Well. Looks like your membership in our club is revoked, then. Also, bastards who turn on their partners don't get good coffee." She swiveled around and dumped the cup in the nearest trash can, then walked away without a backward glance.

My portly, red-faced neighbor sat down next to me with a whistle. "What'd you do to get on her bad side, Baby-face?"

"Get fucked," I said, then turned back to the file I'd fallen asleep on.

By noon, nobody was trying to talk *to* me, but a bunch of people were talking *about* me.

Well, actually, one person was trying to talk to me. "Darren!"

I started and looked up at the newcomer. "Trent? What are you doing here?"

"I heard you were having a bad day," he said with a little head shake. "I thought taking you out to lunch might help improve it."

I sighed. "No, probably not."

"Let me take you out anyway. It's a nice day. Some fresh air and sunshine will clear your head."

"I've got a lot to do . . ."

"There's always more paperwork to do, Darren. It'll still be here when you get back."

"Fine." It was the sound of a man who not only knew he'd been beaten, he didn't care. God, I was tired. "Whatever. I'll drive."

"Anything you want."

We ended up getting drive-thru at a Mexican place and parking down by the river to eat. I tried not to think about the parallels between the last time I'd been down here and who I was with now. We ate in silence for a few minutes before Trent said, "Are you doing okay?"

I laughed mirthlessly. "No, I think I can safely say that I'm *not* doing okay. Nowhere close, actually. Andreas has dropped me in the middle of a fucking hornet's nest, and now I have to deal with it all by myself."

"What are you talking about?"

"I'm talking about my partner being a goddamn vigilante!" I snapped. "I'm talking about the audio files I found—holy shit, did you know he even bugged *me*? His own partner?" Oh, I was definitely going to Hell. "I'm talking about the files he's got from the actual *mayor*, Trent. I thought something strange was going on when he kept following up on leads without me. He set up microphones all over the place—he's got audio files of the mayor talking about *drug shipments*." I didn't really have to feign the beginnings of hyperventilation.

"Drugs? What kind of drugs? What sort of shipment?" Trent asked sharply.

"I don't know what kind, but whatever they are, they're coming in tonight. Millions of dollars' worth, and apparently Mayor Crawford thinks things are getting too hot. He's going to go and get them himself, and Trent, I am not fucking prepared for this. I can't go after the *mayor*."

"No," Trent said distractedly. "No, you definitely can't do that. And . . . tonight? A drop? What's going on with that?"

"I guess it's supposed to be tonight, and the mayor said he was through fucking around with middlemen. Something about his right-hand man being compromised, I don't know—he didn't name a name."

I could almost hear Trent grinding his teeth. "Where were these files, Darren?"

"They were stored in a thumb drive, taped to the top of his desk drawer. I only found it because I was looking for evidence to exonerate that fucker." I dropped my head into my hands. "But nothing he's got is legal. I don't think he cares anymore. Trent." I reached out and grabbed him by the shoulder. "You have to stay away from Andreas. You hear me? He's at the end of his rope, there's no telling what he might do."

"And now? Where are the files now?" Trent's shoulder was almost vibrating with tension under my hand.

"I deleted them, of course," I hissed. "What else could I do? They were obtained unlawfully; they're no good as evidence of wrongdoing."

"That's . . . probably smart," Trent said after a second. He patted my hand and managed to look almost normal. "If I were you, I'd keep this information to yourself."

"Who am I going to tell?" I asked sadly. "I've been a detective for less than two weeks and I'm already a pariah."

"Yeah, I heard about your little tussle with Morris. Don't let her get you down, okay? Now." He hopped down from the hood of the car. "Drive us back to the precinct. I've got some stuff to do. We can talk more about this later though, all right?"

"Right," I agreed, getting back into my car. "Later." After I'd relayed a message to Andreas through Thibedeau.

The ball was in his court now. I only hoped he could get in to see the mayor in time.

There were a number of advantages to having informants at city hall. Today, one of those advantages came in handy—getting the mayor's schedule of meetings into my hands. With a little more help, I managed to slip into the building without anyone noticing.

As I made my way toward the conference room where Mayor Crawford was supposed to meet with a committee from the state's Department of Transportation, I kept my head down. There were cops around, some of them picking up overtime by working security at city hall, and a lot of them knew my face. Word had gotten around to multiple precincts that I'd finally been busted as a drug addict, and that I was suspended until further notice. If one person recognized me—one person who wasn't already in my pocket—I was getting escorted out of here. There was no margin of error today.

I stayed away from the conference room for the moment. There was security posted outside, and they'd get suspicious if I was hovering around. Fine. All I needed was to catch Crawford on his way to his next meeting. If my smuggled calendar was correct, that meeting was up on the sixth floor, which meant he'd be heading to the elevators in about five minutes.

Of course, the meeting ran late. When didn't they? To make myself look less conspicuous, I busied myself on my phone. If anyone bothered to look, they probably assumed I was returning text messages or checking emails. No one needed to know I leveled up twice on Candy Crush.

Finally, the conference room doors opened, and Crawford emerged with his usual entourage—security, an assistant, a few suits I didn't recognize—hot on his heels.

I stepped in front of the group. "Mr. Mayor, I need a minute of your—"

"Make an appointment," he said dismissively, and kept walking.

"Mr. Mayor, wait." I stepped in front of him "I'm Detective Ruffner. Twenty-first Precinct."

He halted. His entourage did as well, the security guys bristling at the edges, watching me warily in between glancing at the mayor, probably waiting for the green light to tackle me.

The mayor sighed, shifting his weight impatiently. "What do you want, *Detective*?" He spat out my rank with palpable distaste.

I straightened, setting my jaw. "I want to know what you're planning to do to stop what's going to happen at the Montrose Airfield tonight."

"All right, that's enough." One of the suits tried to step between us. "The mayor is very busy and—"

"Montrose Airfield?" Crawford narrowed his eyes. "What are you talking about?"

I scanned the others in the group, then met his gaze. "There's a plane coming in tonight." I shook my head. "I have no idea what's on it, but there's talk all over the street about the merchandise being stolen."

The rest of his entourage rolled their eyes and exchanged incredulous *can you believe this whacko* glances.

Crawford looked right at me. His features hardened, but the faintest shift of his tense posture didn't escape my notice. "Stolen?"

"Yes." I waved a hand. "Like I said, I don't know the details. I just know someone is going to be there to intercept the plane before the real buyers can get there, and—"

"All the illegal activity at that airport was shut down years ago. By *your* department." The obnoxious suit snorted. "Or are you worried your dealer's next shipment is going to wind up going to someone else, Detective Ruffner?"

I gritted my teeth. "If it is narcotics, then we've got the makings of a turf war, and—"

"Detective," the mayor growled. "Are you really coming to me to ask what I'm going to do about drug smugglers stealing from each other?" He laughed, but it sounded forced. "Have you lost your mind?"

Shifting uncomfortably, I clicked my tongue. "Mr. Mayor, please. This could be huge. And really bad."

"Then why aren't you talking to the cops?" the suit asked with a sneer. "Or are they still not talking to you?"

More snickering, head shaking, and eye rolling.

I swallowed. "No one there is willing to listen because they think I'm a drug addict. But someone is going to get killed unless—"

"They *think* you're an addict?" someone said.

Someone else laughed. "Wait, you said you're Detective Ruffner, right? That junkie detective they finally busted?"

Crawford glanced over his shoulder. Glaring at me again, he growled, "Is that true?"

I exhaled hard. "It's—"

"*Detective Ruffner.*" Captain Hamilton materialized beside me and grabbed my arm. "Just what the hell are you doing?"

"I'm—"

"Not a word," Hamilton snapped, and hauled me back a step. "Was I not clear when I said you were suspended? Did that somehow translate to giving you free rein to harass the mayor?" Before I could answer, he turned to Crawford. "Mr. Mayor, I apologize. This—"

"This *is* one of your men, Hamilton?" Crawford asked.

Hamilton sighed heavily. "Yes. I'm sorry. He's—"

Crawford glared at me, then stabbed a finger at the captain. "He's out of control is what he is. Get him out of here!"

"Will do, Mr. Mayor. Sorry for—"

"Junkie son of a bitch," the mayor muttered, and brushed past us. The rest of the entourage followed.

"Come on." Hamilton jerked my arm, and in silence, we walked to the elevator. Even inside the elevator, he kept his hand on my arm, and I kept my gaze down, avoiding the scrutiny of the bubble camera above our heads.

Silence followed us down to the parking garage and all the way to Hamilton's car. I slid into the backseat. He got in the driver's seat. As he drove, neither of us spoke until we were out of the parking garage and on the main road.

Finally, Hamilton glanced at me in the rearview. "Think he bought it?"

I looked out the window. "Let's hope so."

"See anything yet?" Darren asked.

I lowered the binoculars. "Nothing yet."

"Shit," he muttered. "That plane is due in fifteen minutes."

"And they probably don't want to be seen loitering around here longer than they have to." I peered through the binoculars again. "Patience."

He grumbled something under his breath, but I ignored it. I remembered my early years well enough. Nothing was more boring than waiting for something to happen when all you wanted to do was kick down doors.

We were hunkered in an empty hangar facing the tiny airport's tarmac. Across the street in a beat-up van outside an equally beat-up garage was the rest of our team—all of them hand-picked by Paula and operating under her watchful eye—who were monitoring the cameras I'd set up this morning before going to city hall. That was to say nothing about people I had planted all over the roads leading to the airport. If anyone came within half a mile of this place, I'd know about it.

And if shit went south, SWAT was standing by in a barn across the street and, in a nearby field, more SWAT was waiting in a helicopter that was ready to fly in on a moment's notice. I didn't like having this many people involved—no matter how carefully they'd been vetted, all it took was one leak to fuck everything up. We didn't have much choice, though.

My heart thumped against my ribs. All we had to do was wait, and hope to God everyone had taken the bait.

My earpiece crackled to life. "We've got confirmation the aircraft is headed this way. Over."

"Copy that. Over." I turned to Darren. "You catch—"

"Yep." He put up his own binoculars and scanned the area.

A second later, another transmission came through: "We've got a vehicle entering. Two individuals." Pause. "Looks like one is Crawford."

My heart sped up.

Two minutes later, sure enough, the mayor walked out onto the air strip. He was alone except for a single security guard. The guy was armed, but he wasn't one of the guards I'd seen at city hall.

In fact—

"Is that Officer Huan?" Darren whispered.

I looked through the binoculars. "I'll be damned."

"Jesus. Are there any cops left who aren't dirty?"

"Sometimes I wonder." And I hoped like hell none of our backup was dirty.

"He's a little light on security for something like this."

"The more security he brings, the more people will know what's going on."

"But if he thinks his shit's about to get ripped off . . ."

"He's a sitting politician," I said. "And he probably knows we're sniffing around. He can't afford more witnesses who might testify against him."

Darren exhaled. "Well, he's here. Question is, where's—"

"Ruffner," Paula said on the radio, "I've got a visual on Newberry. He's alone and three minutes from your location."

I chuckled. "That answer your question?"

"Yep." Darren fidgeted. "Is it just me, or is this too easy so far?"

"If you just jinxed us . . ."

"I'm just saying. Something doesn't seem right."

My spine prickled. It wasn't that I thought this had been too easy. Up until this point, I'd mostly expected it to be. But Crawford and Newberry were both damn good at keeping their hands clean. Even if they showed up here, there was no guarantee they'd incriminate themselves.

So help me God, if Trent tries to be a hero and make an arrest . . .

I tamped that thought down.

"I've got a visual on Trent," Darren said. "He's coming around the east side of the terminal on foot."

"And here comes the plane." The lights in the distance were coming in as fast as a little twin-engine could, and Crawford and Huan were watching.

Near the terminal building, Trent halted. Hidden by shadows—he thought—he watched too, and the whole world seemed completely silent except for the incoming plane and, when it touched down, the squeak of tires hitting the runway. Nobody moved while the plane taxied.

As the aircraft came to a halt in front of Crawford and Huan, Darren nudged my arm. "Trent's on his way in."

I turned my head. Yeah, he was on his way, walking fast and determined, and even from here, he looked pissed.

Huan saw him, and gave him a nod of acknowledgment. Crawford was busy speaking with the copilot, who'd just stepped out.

My heart beat faster as Trent closed in. "Paula, you guys getting all this?"

"Every word, hon," she said. "The engines are creating some background noise, but we're picking up—"

"Oh shit!" Darren hissed.

I shifted my gaze toward Trent.

Just in time to see him whip out a pistol.

"Fuck!"

The muzzle flashed twice, and the crack of gunfire echoed through the night. A split second later, Crawford slumped against the side of the plane. Then he crumpled to the ground, leaving a smear of blood on the white finish.

The copilot tried to scramble back into the plane, but Huan grabbed him. One swift kick, and the man dropped to his knees on the pavement a few feet away from Crawford.

"Out of the plane!" Trent bellowed, waving his weapon at the pilot. "Out of the plane! Now!"

"Shit!" Darren turned to me. "What now?"

I clicked on my radio. "Paula, we need—"

"Already on it, baby. SWAT will be there in four. Helo's going up as we speak."

"Good. Now we—"

Something cold and solid dug into the back of my head. I froze.

Beside me, so did Darren.

"Hands behind your head." The cold voice wasn't one I recognized, but it sure as shit wasn't friendly.

I slowly put my hands behind my head. "We're cops. We—"

"I know who you are, Ruffner." Beside me, Darren was pushed forward a step. "Hands behind your head, Corliss."

Darren swore under his breath, but obeyed.

"Now move." The thing against my head—the gun that was probably going to splatter my brains all over the tarmac—nudged sharply. "We're going for a walk."

CHAPTER THIRTY-TWO
DARREN

A drenaline was a weird thing. I'd been in exactly two truly life-threatening situations before I made detective, and my reaction to the adrenaline had been different each time. When I crashed my car into a lamppost at sixteen, everything had seemed to slow down, and afterward it had still felt like I was looking at the world through a thick, muffling fog for a while. When I'd had a gun pulled on me my first year as a beat cop, my hands had been shaking so hard I could barely put them up.

Tonight, everything became sharp. If things were slow, it was the world around me: I could hear Paula hissing over my earpiece, *Stop, pull them back, we have a situation!* I could feel every bit of loose gravel under the soles of my shoes as Andreas and I were marched out onto the tarmac, heading straight for the plane where the pilots cowered while Trent yelled at them. I could smell the acrid tinge of my own sweat, and a hint of blood on the cool night breeze. The mayor was a spattered mess. My heart beat was frantically fast, but my mind seemed curiously patient.

Wait. We had to wait. For SWAT, for the right moment, for anything that might give us an advantage. We had to be smart, and that meant trusting each other to do the right thing. *You have to trust your partner, Darren.* Vic's advice had never been more pertinent. No matter how bad I wanted to grab Andreas and run, I couldn't do it. Not yet.

The gun dug into the back of my head, pressing me forward. I kept my hands up, hoping that if I left them high, the guy might not remember to . . .

"I'll take *that*," he grunted, stepping up close and jerking my gun out of its holster. I could hear the other guy doing the same to Andreas, and I ground my teeth together. Okay. Options were changing. Just because they'd remembered to grab our guns—the obvious ones, anyway—didn't mean we were completely defenseless.

Just mostly defenseless.

"And there they are." Trent was facing us now, shaking his head like he was disappointed. "Darren, wow, you're just *everyone's* tool, aren't you? A few friendly words and you cut your own feet out from under yourself so you can fall faster in line. What did Andreas say to you to get you back under his thumb, huh? Or," Trent smirked, "did he not have to say anything at all? It seems like he's got a handle on what you like.

"And, Andreas, way to make a desperation play! Walking up to the mayor in broad daylight? Accosting him in front of witnesses, getting hauled away by your own captain?" His smirk turned into a grin. "You couldn't have made this setup easier for me if you'd tried."

Oh. He didn't know. He didn't know about SWAT or our backup or any of it. I tried not to visibly relax. Our odds had just gotten a little better.

"You don't want to set us up," Andreas said. Shit, how did he sound so calm? "How would that benefit you? With the mayor already dead and a plane full of drugs and two witnesses to the whole thing?"

"What, the pilots?" Trent shrugged as he glanced their way. "They've already served their purpose." He raised his gun.

"Don't shoot them!" I blurted out. Trent turned toward me, his expression mocking.

"What, you feeling a little sick to your stomach? Can't handle the business side of things? How did you ever expect to make it as a detective, Darren? It's a good thing you won't have to worry about that after tonight."

"You don't want to shoot them because they're the only ones who know where to get the shipments now," I said, talking fast. "You just killed the guy running this whole thing. I doubt he shared information about his sources with you."

Trent frowned. "I can find a new source on my own."

"But if you just talk to them first—interrogate them—you could save yourself the trouble." My voice hardly shook at all. I was oddly proud of that.

Andreas picked up the thread. "Nobody who heard me knows you're involved. We can make this into something good for your career, for all our careers." Paula was saying something over my earpiece, but her voice was so soft I couldn't make it out. Something about sight? The line of sight? Were they going to try a sniper? I could barely make out the barn from here. I had no clue whether I was obscuring the view or not.

"Or," Trent said, "I could pin this whole thing on a junkie ex-cop shooting up a dirty mayor, and incidentally killing his poor, misguided partner in the process. That would leave things nice and clean, because the only people here who know too much about me that I don't trust? Are you two."

"We should do it if we're going to," Huan muttered. He seemed nervous. "Cut and run before anyone else shows up."

Trent nodded. "Take the pilots to the car. Actually, no." He lifted his gun and, before I could speak out, shot one of the cringing men through the head. The body fell to the pavement with a wet *thwack*, and I could practically *feel* Andreas tense from two feet away. Trent grinned. "No sense in carrying along two when we only need one. We'll be there in a minute."

Huan nodded and got the other man to his feet with some difficulty—he had almost fainted. They left, and Trent looked back at us.

"There's no sense in complicating the ballistics," he said. "Looks like I get to do the honors. Darren, I always liked you." He gave me a wink. "So I'll shoot you first." The guy behind me backed off to the side as Trent stepped toward me. My breaths were shallow, my hands tingling with unspent energy, desperate to move. I had to move, there was no more time, but there was nowhere for me to go. I couldn't get out of this.

"Bye, babe," he said cheerfully as he raised his weapon. "It was fu—*huh!*" He toppled to the ground as Andreas launched himself across five feet of pavement and collided with Trent's lower legs.

There was no time to go for my little pistol, not while Trent's lackey still had a weapon on Andreas. He was taking aim by the time I got to him, but the shot went wide as I wrapped my arms around his waist and spun him to the ground. We hit hard, and the gun flew out of his hand. I got on top of him, but my own gunman was entering the game now. The first shot hit me in the back, and holy shit, that was going to *sting* tomorrow morning. The Kevlar did its job, though, and the bullet didn't penetrate. It did knock me forward, but I grabbed on to my opponent and rolled him on top of me just as the next shot came.

I was wearing a bulletproof vest. My assailant wasn't. I felt the vibration of it entering his body, watched his mouth open in a silent scream as the bullet shattered his spine. The second shot wasn't even necessary, probably a reflex on the shooter's part. The guy was already dead. And now I was caught beneath a corpse. I shoved him off and felt for my gun even as the shooter loomed over me, fury on his face.

He fell back just as fast as he'd arrived, a bullet striking his shoulder from out of nowhere and dropping him hard. Was that the sniper? I'd lost my earpiece in the takedown so I couldn't hear Paula anymore, but it seemed likely. I looked around in a daze for Andreas, and found him—

Flat on the ground, locked in a death grip with Trent over control of the gun. I wanted to call out, but didn't want to risk distracting Andreas; I wanted to shoot Trent in the fucking back, but we needed him alive or nothing would get resolved. I could help—somehow— but I had to get to my feet first, and that was tougher than it should have been.

Andreas was shaking, hard, so hard I thought he had to be hurt. Had he been shot? Had I missed it? Was it another side effect of his new meds? And, goddamn, his wrist was still injured. Fuck waiting, he was losing his grip on the gun, Trent would *shoot* him in another second, I had to—

I staggered over just in time to kick Trent hard in the face. He lost his grip on the gun and fell away to the side, and I leaned down to make sure Andreas was all right. All I needed was a second, just a look—I just had to be sure he was okay. We made eye contact, and I read the relief in his face and felt mine mimic it. He was fine. We were both going to be—

All the air in my body seemed to freeze as a sliver of ice sank into my back, punching through my vest like it was cardboard and into skin and muscle like they weren't even there. It slid between two ribs, lodging hard, and suddenly I was on my hands and knees.

Fuck, how had that happened?

I tried to take a breath, tried to lift my head and make eye contact again, but my lungs weren't working anymore. I exhaled with a cough, and it hurt so bad I almost collapsed right there.

Someone tugged hard on whatever was impaling me, swearing when they couldn't get it out. A hand fumbled in my pocket for— oh shit, my pistol, the little Kahr. If Trent got it, we were dead, and everything was fuzzy and I couldn't tell what the hell was going on anymore.

Two shots fired. The hand tugging at me vanished, and the knife— it had to be a knife—went with it. I wished that made me feel better.

"Andreas . . .?" My voice sounded thick, like I'd been drinking syrup.

"I'm here." Warm hands eased me down onto the ground, and I went with it because it was way easier than staying up at the moment. The movement jarred my wound, and for a second all I could see were starry constellations of pain.

"Trent?"

"He's down."

"You shot him?"

"Not fatally," Andreas ground out. "But he's not gonna be using his right hand for anything for a while." Now that he mentioned it, I thought I heard someone's choked-off whimpers. Or maybe that was just me.

"Sorry." I tried to chuckle, but it sounded too wet for that. "I lost my sit-situational awareness. But hey, at least . . ." Why was it so hard to speak? "At least . . . you're not the one who got knifed this time." All those guns going off, and I got put down by a knife. Vic would never let me live it down. "'Cause 'm awesome," I added. "Awesome partner."

"You'd be way more awesome if you hadn't been knifed in the first place." Andreas sounded mad, but I was onto him now—that was his worried voice. Which . . . shit. That wasn't good. "The paramedics are on their way. They're almost here, so keep your eyes open, Darren."

"Am." It wasn't my fault it was so dark; it was almost midnight, after all. I coughed again, and it hurt so bad I wanted to scream but I didn't have the air for it. I couldn't inhale. I couldn't breathe at all.

"*Darren.*"

His hand was the only warm thing in the whole world, like a brand against my shoulder. Everything else was cold, lancing pain, but it was getting fuzzier now, kind of distant. Distant was good.

Unconscious was even better.

CHAPTER THIRTY-THREE
ANDREAS

"**O**fficer down!" I shouted over my shoulder. "Officer down!"

Footsteps were coming my way. Or maybe it was just my heart pounding as Darren faded in and out in front of me.

"Come on." I tapped his cheek, smearing blood on his skin. "Darren. Open your eyes. Open your fucking eyes."

His eyelids fluttered, but didn't open. He was on his side, and I struggled to hold him steady and keep my wadded-up jacket against his wound.

"I'm not kidding." I pressed harder on the wound, my stomach sinking as blood saturated the fabric all the way to my hand. "You think I'm an asshole now, you're not gonna like me if—"

He coughed, his whole body jerking, and winced. Sinking back to the pavement, he moaned. Then he coughed again and tried to pull away from me.

"Darren?"

Before he could respond—and God knew if he could—a SWAT member dropped to his knees beside him with a small oxygen tank.

"You the medic?" I asked, thanking several deities that SWAT always had one.

He nodded. "Tell me what you've got."

Struggling to hold Darren still, I said, "He took a knife to the back."

The medic leaned over and shoved my hand out of the way. He lifted the jacket, and I thought he cursed under his breath as he pushed the jacket back into place. "Keep pressure on that."

I nodded and concentrated on holding it there, as if I could keep all this blood from spilling out of Darren and onto the pavement. Darren coughed and fought, and I held him as still as I could as the medic cut open his shirt and loosened the Kevlar vest enough to get a stethoscope under it, and I tried not to think about what might be happening on the inside. Or why the medic's features tightened when he listened to Darren's chest. Or whether it was a trick of the light, or if Darren's lips really were starting to turn blue.

All around us, there was activity. Voices. Movement. Handcuffs clicking. Shouting. Radios crackling. Sirens in the distance. *Way* too far in the distance.

But all of that barely registered over Darren's increasingly labored breathing or the painful-sounding cough that occasionally broke it up.

I didn't care about Trent. He was neutralized, so he didn't matter anymore.

Only Darren mattered, and there was nothing I could do to help him. There was nothing I could do except sit here, holding him as still as I could—*fuck*, he was strong—while he fought and coughed and choked and *bled*.

"His lung is collapsing." The medic turned and called out to one of the others, "Stretcher! We gotta get this guy outta here. *Now.*"

My own lungs turned to lead as another SWAT member sprinted to Darren's side, waved me out of the way, and knelt on the pavement. He hadn't been there thirty seconds before he spun around and called out, "Get that stretcher over here!"

The urgency in his voice turned my blood to ice.

"The ED is twenty minutes from here," the other said as he pushed an oxygen mask over Darren's face, ignoring Darren's attempts to shove it away. "Do we have that much time?"

The second SWAT member scowled, surveying the empty airfield. Those sirens were still too damn far away. "Put him on the helo. He doesn't have time to wait for a bus or a medevac." He switched on his radio. "This is unit 4-Alpha. I've got a stabbing victim with a possible tension pneumo. Bringing him to All Saints via SWAT helo. Repeat, SWAT helo. Confirm clearance. Over." To his partner, he quickly said, "The stretcher won't fit in that helo. Guaranteed. Get the backboard and we can use that instead."

The first medic got up and sprinted toward the ambulance while the second continued focusing on Darren. The radio crackled to life with a response, but my heartbeat drowned it out.

The medic was working fast, frantically getting Darren's shirt and vest all the way off. The blood-soaked Kevlar made my stomach lurch. Too much blood. *Way* too much blood. The fact that Darren wasn't fighting so hard now was not a good sign.

Come on, Darren. Come on . . .

The *thump-thump-thump* of helicopter blades had never sounded so sweet. As the helo touched down on the tarmac, everyone exploded into action. SWAT loaded Darren onto a fold-out stretcher, which they carried to the helicopter.

Blades spun. Voices shouted.

Everything was a blur of noise and activity except for me and for Darren.

I was completely paralyzed. Totally helpless. Absolutely useless.

And Darren . . .

Darren was getting weaker. His pale lips moved, mumbling something, but he wasn't clawing at the O2 tubing or trying to pull off the mask anymore. His hands feebly tried to push someone away, but even that didn't last long.

SWAT ran the stretcher to the helo's open door and lifted Darren inside. The medic followed.

He turned to me. "You coming?"

And finally, I could move. "Yeah, I'm coming." I hurried into the helo and stayed as far out of the way as I could while the medics frantically worked. I couldn't see his face. The oxygen mask covered most of it, and in what little light we had, I could see that the mask wasn't fogging up nearly as much as it should have been.

And he wasn't fighting anymore.

At all.

Shaking with the worst bone-deep fear and helplessness I'd known in a long, long time, I put a hand on Darren's shin. It was the closest thing to me, and there was still some body heat radiating through his pant leg.

All the way to the hospital, as the medics went from concerned to downright agitated, shouting into radios and at each other as Darren remained completely motionless, I held on to his leg and prayed like hell we'd make it in time.

It seemed like hours, but minutes after we'd taken off, the helo landed on the pad on top of All Saints Hospital. A stretcher and a trauma team were waiting. They pulled Darren and the backboard out, and before I'd even put my foot down on the helo pad, the stretcher, the trauma team, and my partner were gone.

"He'll be all right." One of the SWAT guys squeezed my shoulder. "These guys know what they're doing."

God, I hope so . . .

Everything had ground to a halt.

Bodies were cleaned up. Survivors were arrested. I'd lost track of everyone except for Darren, though Paula had updated me on the key players. Mayor Crawford was dead. Trent was in surgery, so no one could interrogate him anyway. Huan wasn't in much better shape, thanks to a bullet he'd taken amidst all the chaos. A couple of officers had been assigned to guard their rooms when they came out of the OR, and strangely enough, no one had nominated me for that role.

Paula had also told me arrests had been made, but none of that registered. Had the surviving pilot talked? I didn't know. Not that it mattered—I was in no condition to interrogate anyone anyway. I did manage a call to Captain Hamilton to let him know Darren had made it to the hospital, and vaguely registered that he was going to contact Darren's family and come down as soon as possible.

Beyond that, I was useless for anything except pacing in the waiting room and hoping for some kind of news. Not that there'd been any. Technically, they couldn't tell me anything due to HIPAA, but nurses and cops looked out for each other. The ER nurses sent me up to the ICU, and the ICU nurses told me they'd let me know the moment he was out of surgery.

Two hours later . . . nothing.

I shuddered at the thought that, right this second, Darren could be dead. God knew he hadn't looked far from it when they'd wheeled him away. Even now, I could still feel the near-panic of the EMTs as they'd frantically worked to keep him alive. He'd been in bad enough shape that using a backboard for a makeshift stretcher and putting him on a SWAT helo had been a reasonable way to get him to the hospital because they couldn't wait for the medevac.

But had it bought him enough time?

"Detective Ruffner?" a male voice called into the waiting room.

I turned on my heel to see a young nurse with a clipboard. "Yes?"

He gestured for me to follow him. We stepped out of the waiting area and into a hallway, and he quietly said, "Mr. Corliss is out of surgery. He's stable."

The words turned my knees to liquid. The dizziness from my meds had nothing on how violently everything spun now.

"Mr. Corliss is out of surgery."

"He's stable."

Darren's alive.

Oh my God, Darren's alive.

"Detective?" The nurse's hand met my arm and jarred me back into the present. "You all right?"

"Yeah. Yeah. I'm good. Is he awake?"

The nurse shook his head grimly. "Not yet. He's going to be under heavy sedation for a while even after he's out of recovery." His brow pinched. "If you want to go home and get some sleep, we'll keep you updated."

"No." I swallowed. "I'd rather stay until I can see him. Even if he's doped up."

"All right. It'll probably be another hour or two at least."

"I can wait."

It turned out to be three hours. I was a little fuzzy on the details, but he'd needed more time between recovery and the ICU. The only thing that firmly registered in my mind was when they finally told me—and his parents, who'd arrived an hour earlier—that he was situated in his room.

"He's still very, very heavily sedated," the nurse warned us. "He's mostly unconscious right now, so he won't know you're there."

Darren's mother pursed her lips. "Will he be awake in the morning?"

"In the afternoon, most likely. But he'll still be loopy and incoherent. It might be two or three days before he's up for conversation."

She looked up at her husband.

"We can come back tomorrow," he said. "Wait until he's awake."

"No." She steeled herself and turned to the nurse. "I'd rather see him now. Even if he's not awake, I want him to know I'm here."

I braced for her husband or the nurse to insist that was nonsense, but they both simply nodded. I cleared my throat. "I'd, uh, like to see him too, if that's all right."

His parents eyed me, apparently surprised, but Commissioner Corliss squeezed my arm gently. "Looking out for your partner. Good man."

I just smiled and left it at that.

The nurse led us to Darren's room. Outside the door, his mom paused for a deep breath. So did I. And she had my utmost sympathy—I was struggling enough with the prospect of seeing Darren like this. The thought of one of my kids in the ICU . . . I didn't even want to think about it.

She went in first. A moment later, I followed.

And we both stared at him in silence.

His left side was heavily bandaged, probably to immobilize his arm and keep him from dislodging the chest tube they'd put in. Tubes extended from the backs of both of his hands, his nose, and his mouth. Monitors kept watch over every vital imaginable, and the beep of the ECG actually comforted more than annoyed me. If it meant his heart was still beating, I could tolerate *any* noise.

His mother slipped her hand into his. The other was mostly bandaged aside from the IV, so I left it alone. Instead, I squeezed his leg like I had in the helicopter, and tried not to fall apart from both envy and parental empathy as his mom leaned down to kiss his forehead.

She turned to the nurse. "He'll be all right, won't he?"

"We're taking good care of him. He's stable, and we're watching for any signs of infection or—"

"But he'll be all right, won't he?" The question was more forceful this time. Less invitation for roundabout answers and carefully scripted bullshit.

The nurse took a breath. His eyes flicked toward me, then back to her. "I have no reason to believe he won't make a full recovery."

Darren's mother turned to her son again, stroking a few strands of hair off his forehead. I couldn't read her well enough to know if the nurse's answer had been enough. And on any other night, I might've lost my patience and tried to drag an impossibly precise answer out of the guy.

But, tonight, Darren was alive. It looked like he'd stay that way. There wasn't much more I could ask for.

The nurses weren't kidding about Darren being loopy for the next few days. Most of the time, he barely recognized anyone. When he could speak, he asked where he was, why he was here, when he could leave, and didn't seem to register any of us as separate entities from each other. To him, we seemed to be a group of floating heads who wandered in and out and refused to tell him when he could leave.

His parents stayed for shorter and shorter stretches. They desperately wanted to be by his side, but I didn't blame them for needing breaks, and it wasn't like they could leave his brother alone for long. They had one son who was quickly forgetting who he was, and another who couldn't remember *where* he was from moment to moment. Had I been in their shoes, I was pretty sure it would've killed me.

As it was, I was useless to anyone. The nurses gently encouraged me to go home and get some sleep, reminding me they'd call the instant Darren was truly awake or if his condition changed, but I couldn't sleep beyond brief catnaps. I couldn't drive. I was lucky I had my phone set to remind me to take my pills, or I'd have forgotten that too.

The nurses, being saints, started letting me crash in an office that wasn't being used. I'd doze for an hour or two, then come back and stay by Darren's side. Even after visiting hours were over, they never kicked me or his parents out. When all this was over, I owed every last nurse in this ICU a cup of coffee. Every day. For a month.

I'd managed to catch a little bit of sleep when someone gently shook me awake.

"Detective?" a woman's voice said.

I forced my eyes open. The stethoscope around her neck jarred me back into reality, reminding me I was in a hospital and why, and I jerked awake. "Is he okay? What's—"

"He's awake." She smiled. "His family is on their way now, but I think he wants to see you."

I sat up slowly, if only so I wouldn't pass out and have to stay away from him a second longer. "How's he doing?"

"He won't shut up about calling you and getting an update on your case. I'm assuming that's a good sign."

I laughed as I gingerly rose, my whole body aching and my injured arm throbbing just for spite. "Yeah. That's a good sign."

She took me back to his room, and as I walked in . . . God, relief had never been so profound.

He was sitting up, eyes open and some color in his face. There was still an oxygen tube in his nose and an IV in the hand that was pretty much pinned to his side, and he was using the other hand to shakily hold a plastic cup. Compared to a normal day, he looked like shit. Compared to how he'd been on the pavement at the airfield? He'd never looked better.

He set the cup aside and smiled weakly up at me. "Hey."

"Hey." I touched his arm as I leaned down to kiss his forehead. "You've had me worried sick."

"Wasn't really a picnic for me either. Just FYI."

"At least you got the good drugs," I muttered. "I'm still suspended for the ones I didn't even get to take."

His smile vanished. "Still? Even after Thibedeau cleared you for the sting?"

I nodded. "Yep. Things have been a little crazy for the past few days."

"The past . . ." He blinked. "How long have I been here?"

"You've been doped out of your head for about three days."

"Jesus. And I didn't even get to enjoy it."

I managed a laugh, but it took a lot of work. As I met his gaze, the shootout flickered through my mind, and all the ways it could have happened differently tried to show themselves at once. I shook them away and squeezed Darren's arm. "God, I'm so sorry about this."

"For what?" Darren brushed his fingertips along my wrist. "It was a sting gone bad. It—"

"I could've stopped him, though. He—"

"Andreas. Jesus." He shook his head. "There was so much shit going down from so many directions, you—"

"You're my partner. I should've—"

"Shut up."

My teeth snapped shut.

Darren met my gaze, his eyes tired but focused. "You stopped Trent from shooting me in the fucking face. I'll take this over that."

I shuddered, remembering all too clearly that moment of sheer rage when Trent had trained his gun on Darren. Easing myself down on the side of the bed, I slipped my hand into his. "That fucker wasn't taking you down without going through me first."

Darren smiled sleepily. "I know. I have never once doubted you have my back." He rubbed the side of my hand with his thumb. "I'm pretty sure if I'd been out there with anybody else, things would've been a hell of a lot worse."

That wasn't something I wanted to think about. My subconscious would run me through all those worst-case scenarios for the next few months whenever I tried to sleep, but that could wait.

"I'm just glad you're okay," I said. "You scared the shit out of me out there."

He laughed, but winced. "Says the man who was threatening to be even more of an asshole if I fell asleep."

"You heard that?"

"Uh-huh." Under his breath, he muttered, "Fucker."

I chuckled, which wasn't nearly as painful for me. "I was just trying to keep you there with me."

"Yeah, while I was trying really hard to pass out, you dick."

"Tell you what." I patted his arm. "Next time you want to go to sleep, I'll let you."

"Sounds like a plan." He swallowed and winced. "So what happens now?"

"That's up to your doctor, don't you think?"

Darren rolled his eyes. "I meant at work. The case. After this thing goes to court and everybody goes to prison . . ."

I looked down at our joined hands. "I don't know. I've been working this thing so long, I . . ." I shrugged. "I guess it depends on where the captain assigns us."

"'Us'?"

I met his gaze. "You don't want to work together anymore?"

"I didn't say that." He squeezed my hand. "I just . . . didn't know if you still wanted a partner."

"I don't want a partner. I want you." I touched his face and leaned in a little closer. "Before Hamilton assigned you to me, I didn't want to work with anybody because I couldn't trust them. I couldn't imagine a partner I'd trust with my life *and* who I could work with. But with you . . ." I traced his cheekbone with my thumb. "Truth is, I can't imagine doing this job without you now."

He blinked, and then a playful smile formed on his lips. "C'mere you big sap."

I laughed softly, but he silenced me with a kiss. And, God, it felt good to kiss him. I didn't have the energy to even think about getting turned on, and he was in no condition to be doing anything other than resting, but the relief of this long, affectionate kiss was enough to nearly melt me where I stood. The reassurance that we'd both made it through in one piece was insane.

I drew back enough to meet his gaze. "You know, maybe what should happen next is I should take some vacation time." I smoothed his hair. "Make sure you stay out of trouble while you're on medical leave."

Darren grinned. "You? Keep me out of trouble? That'll be the day." His grin faded a little, and he added, "But . . . if you really do want to take some time off, I wouldn't mind the company."

"Good, because I don't think you're going to be able to get rid of me."

He smirked. "Lucky me—only man on the planet who Andreas Ruffner *wants* to be around."

"That's about the size of it, yeah." We both laughed softly, and I pressed another long, gentle kiss to his lips. Get rid of him? Not a chance.

A subtle cough made the hair on the back of my neck stand up. Darren tensed too.

I broke the kiss and turned, and . . . goddamn it.

In the doorway, staring at us with bemused disbelief, was Captain Hamilton and Darren's parents.

Clearing my throat, I sat up, then stood. "Um . . ."

"Hey, Mom," Darren said sheepishly. "Vic. Captain."

"Uh, hi," the captain said.

Rolling his eyes, Darren muttered, "Every time I kiss you in a hospital bed . . ."

I smothered a laugh.

His mom eyed me, then looked at her son. "Well, they did say you were awake. We'd have been here sooner, but wanted to make sure someone was staying with Asher."

Darren sobered. "Does he know what's going on?"

"He's . . ." she began uneasily. "Not the details, no. He's worried about you, but we didn't want to bring him here and upset him."

"Good idea."

Beside the commissioner, Hamilton cleared his throat. "Ruffner." He motioned toward the hallway. "Can I borrow you outside for a second?"

"Yeah. Sure." I glanced at Darren, who nodded, and as I stood, I gently freed my hand from his. Because this whole time, as we'd exchanged awkward greetings with his parents, we hadn't bothered to let go. Whoops.

I followed the captain into the hallway and quietly shut the door behind me. "Yeah, Captain?"

"You know . . ." He gave me a puzzled look. "When I told you to get along with your new partner, I didn't mean . . ."

I laughed, heat rushing into my face. "Yeah. About that. It's—"

"It's not my business, Andreas." He put up his hands and shook his head. "I'm just surprised, that's all." Lowering his hands, he added, "Hell, I didn't even know you were gay."

"I'm . . ." I hesitated. I was too exhausted to explain bisexuality to my boss, so I just shrugged. "Surprise?"

He laughed quietly, but then turned serious. "So he's gonna be okay, then?"

"Yeah. He'll be hurting for a while, and he needs to take it easy, but . . ." I nodded. "Looks like he'll be fine."

"Good. Good." His eyes flicked toward the door, and more to himself than me, he added, "Good." Then he cleared his throat. "Listen, I brought something for you." He reached into the pocket of his overcoat, and when he pulled his hand back out, he extended it.

My heart skipped. My badge.

"Welcome back, Detective."

As I took it from him, I exhaled. "Thank you, sir."

"Your gun is in the armory. You can sign it out anytime."

I nodded, turning my badge over between my fingers like I'd never touched it before. Even though I'd been cleared for the sting, my suspension hadn't been officially lifted. I'd been reasonably confident things would work out, but it wasn't until now, with the cool brass and smooth leather in my hands, that I could finally rest easy about my professional future.

Hamilton shifted uncomfortably. "And I wanted to apologize. For not taking you at your word. I've known you too long to think you weren't as good a cop as we both know you are."

"Thank you, Captain. To be fair, you did see the morphine in my locker."

"Well, I'd like to tell you that was the first time I took the allegations seriously. But it wasn't. So, I'm sorry, Detective."

"Don't worry about it." I paused. "So what happens now?"

"Now, we wait for Trent to be released." He glanced at his watch. "Which, he's probably out in an hour or two, so we'll be bringing him downtown for a little chat." He met my gaze. "I don't think we'll have too much trouble getting names out of him. Paula rode here with him in the ambulance, and when she told him he was looking at life without parole upstate, he was already trying to make a plea bargain."

"Smart man," I said through my teeth. "I imagine there's a lot of people in that prison who'd like a piece of him."

"Exactly. So he says he's got a long, *long* list of names for us."

I arched an eyebrow. "He's still going upstate, though, right? No plea bargain for a minimum security—"

"As long as we can play the 'we're throwing you in with the general population' card, I'd say we've got the upper hand."

I couldn't help grinning. "Well, Paula knows the case almost as well as I do now. Turn her loose on him, and you'll probably have every name he's got."

"That's the plan." Hamilton paused. "Question is, are you up for going out and collaring the people he name-drops?"

"All of them? No. And actually . . ." I glanced at Darren's door. "To be honest, if it's all right with you, I'd like to take a few days off." I gestured at the room. "While he's recovering."

Hamilton blinked as if he'd forgotten about what he'd seen in Darren's room. "Oh. Well, with the next phase of the investigation moving forward—" He shook his head. "No, on second thought, you and your partner both need some R&R after all of this. And there's already a hell of a shit-storm in the press thanks to the mayor being killed, so the two of you may want to keep your heads down."

"I don't think that'll be a problem. At least, until the trial."

"Still, that should give you both a chance to recuperate. If I need your input on anything in the meantime, I'll let you know."

I exhaled, relieved to have at least some of this case's weight sliding off my shoulders. "There's one other thing, though."

"Hmm?"

I gulped. "What about the threats Newberry made about my kids? I already sent my youngest and her mom out of town, but—"

"Don't worry about them." Hamilton patted the air with both hands. "I've already got people on it. Near as Thibedeau could figure out, the only one who made any calls or arrangements about your daughter's internship interview was Newberry himself. He's digging deeper just in case, but it doesn't sound like there was anyone else involved. Your kids should be safe."

"Good." Still, I'd probably wait a few days before I gave my ex-girlfriend the all clear to bring our daughter back to town. Just to be safe.

"All right," Hamilton said. "I'm going downtown to help Paula wrangle this mess." He inclined his head. "Why don't you go home and get some rest? You've earned it."

"I will. But . . ." I nodded toward the door. "I'm going to stay here with him for now."

"Oh. Right." He looked at the door, chuckled to himself, and shook his head.

"What?" I asked.

"Just thinking." He clapped my arm and, as he started to walk away, threw over his shoulder, "Would've put you two together a long time ago if I'd known you wouldn't kill each other." I laughed, and he kept walking.

After he was gone, I didn't go back into Darren's room right away. For a moment, I just stood in the relative silence of the hallway, absorbing a sense of calm I hadn't known in ages. I stared down at my badge, tracing the edge with my finger.

Things were far from over. Once Trent started dropping names, the department would be collaring people by the dozen. Witnesses I'd stashed all over the country would be brought back in to testify. The trial would probably be a media madhouse, and it would probably drag on for fucking ages. Odds were, some more dirty cops would be revealed, arrested, and convicted. No, this was definitely not over, but for today, I could catch my breath.

Darren was okay.

My kids were safe.

My name was cleared.

Though I hadn't banked on the mayor getting killed, the crime ring he'd run with Trent was quickly coming unraveled.

I tucked my badge into my pocket. Things were going to get chaotic, but for the first time in a long time, I could believe they were going to be okay.

Relieved and relaxed, I pushed the door open and went back into Darren's room.

CHAPTER THIRTY-FOUR

DARREN

I could say this for being an invalid: I didn't want for food.

The ability to take a deep breath without feeling like I was courting an asthma attack? Walking as far as my apartment's bathroom and back without help? Sleeping in the most awkward positions imaginable because I couldn't put a lot of pressure on my back without feeling like I needed an IV of the good stuff? *Those* were things I wanted.

Time, apparently, would heal all wounds, but I really wished it could heal this one a little faster. I'd been out of the hospital for almost a week now, and I was so sick of being idle that I could almost scream.

"Fucking forms."

I *wasn't* so sick of it that I wanted to jump back into doing paperwork, though. I had a pass while I recovered, which meant Andreas was doing most of the legwork right now. Lucky me, he was doing it in my apartment too. It just made sense: I needed someone to help me get around, he had the time off, and staying with my folks wasn't an option right now.

Asher hadn't taken my injury so well. He couldn't retain what had happened, and every time he saw me meant learning I was hurt all over again. It made him angry and stressed, and that wasn't good for anyone. So, I stayed in my place and my mother indulged her caring instincts by bringing a new casserole over almost every day. Today's had been mac and cheese, usually only a holiday food because she put enough butter and cream in it to single-handedly support a dairy farm.

"You should take a dinner break," I informed him, stretching a little to ease the tension in my shoulder. "It's so good, seriously."

"Later. I have to finish filling this bullshit out in triplicate first. Besides," he gently tapped the end of his pen against my forehead, "you'd have to stop using me as a pillow, then."

"Ah, right. In that case, never mind." I settled a little deeper against the soft cotton of his sweatpants. "You'll just have to starve."

"Or I can wait five minutes until you're asleep again."

I moaned pathetically. "I'm so sick of sleeping."

"You're gonna wish you'd enjoyed it more when you get back to work. This case will be keeping us busy for months."

That was an understatement if ever I'd heard one. Paula had stopped by last night to drop off a pan of lasagna and bitch at us for a while about everything that was coming to light thanks to Trent's testimony. "Seven in-house arrests," she'd said gloomily. "And that's just in *our* precinct. Trent's is nearly double that. Plus Blake and his people, plus the officials at city hall . . . It's so hard to make sure everything is being done right. We can't afford any mistakes, not with all the attention this case is getting from the press."

"Thibedeau must be in seventh heaven," I'd remarked.

Paula had snorted. "Thibedeau has gotten his ass reamed by the higher-ups for not catching on to any of this any sooner. He's going to keep his job, but it's not pretty. It's a good thing he's got a new intern to help pick up the slack." She'd winked at Andreas.

"Don't remind me." His daughter, Erin, hadn't been pleased to find out that her "offer of a lifetime" had actually been a power play that had nothing to do with her at all. Andreas's ex had already bought the train ticket, and Erin had been packed and ready when Andreas broke the news to her.

It had taken some doing, but Captain Hamilton had eventually wrangled a similar internship for her in the precinct. It just happened to be working for Thibedeau. Erin had accepted, and I'd finally gotten to meet her a few nights ago. She had her dad's coloring, his thick dark hair and blue eyes, but she must have inherited her mom's sense of humor, because she was sweet and funny and actually seemed pleased to meet me. There was a lot she still didn't know about the situation, namely that her dad and I weren't exactly typical partners, but I had hope that she'd come around pretty quickly when she learned.

The rest of what she didn't know, well . . . that was entirely up to Andreas to divulge. I doubted it would happen anytime soon.

"I'm actually looking forward to going back to work," I said, ignoring the tangents that tried to carry my brain away. Stupid meds. "My first case as a detective, and it ends up changing the leadership of the city. Who knows what the second one will be like?"

"Probably something simple." The tip of the pen scratched familiarly against the paper as Andreas scrawled his signature for probably the fiftieth time this night. "Maybe a robbery."

"Yeah, of the museum, or one of the big banks."

"Or a smuggling case."

"Human trafficking," I agreed with a nod.

"Or just picking up a dealer."

"Because of the violent vacuum that's about to hit the city's power structure."

Andreas threw the pen onto my side table. "You're a ball of fuckin' sunshine, you know that, Darren?"

I rolled slightly and grinned at him. "I'm just trying to be realistic! Life's not going to be boring, that's all I'm saying."

"Yeah." The way he looked at me made me want to sit up, straddle his lap, and pin him to the headboard, which was another pipe dream for the time being. He leaned over and kissed me, warm and tender. Those weren't words I'd have imagined applying to Andreas a month ago, but we knew each other better now.

"It's definitely not going to be boring."

Dear Reader,

Thank you for reading L.A. Witt and Cari Z's *Risky Behavior*!

We know your time is precious and you have many, many entertainment options, so it means a lot that you've chosen to spend your time reading. We really hope you enjoyed it.

We'd be honored if you'd consider posting a review—good or bad—on sites like **Amazon, Barnes & Noble, Kobo, Goodreads, Twitter, Facebook, Tumblr,** and your blog or website. We'd also be honored if you told your friends and family about this book. Word of mouth is a book's lifeblood!

For more information on upcoming releases, author interviews, blog tours, contests, giveaways, and more, please sign up for our weekly, spam-free newsletter and visit us around the web:

Newsletter: tinyurl.com/RiptideSignup
Twitter: twitter.com/RiptideBooks
Facebook: facebook.com/RiptidePublishing
Goodreads: tinyurl.com/RiptideOnGoodreads
Tumblr: riptidepublishing.tumblr.com

Thank you so much for Reading the Rainbow!

RiptidePublishing.com

ACKNOWLEDGMENTS

Thank you to the usual suspects for helping with the police info, as well as the ever reliable Nurse Kelley for helping us dent and damage our characters in accordance with reality.

ALSO BY L.A. WITT

See L.A. Witt's full booklist at: gallagherwitt.com

ALSO BY CARI Z

ABOUT THE AUTHORS

L.A. WITT is an abnormal M/M romance writer who has finally been released from the purgatorial corn maze of Omaha, Nebraska, and now spends her time on the southwestern coast of Spain. In between wondering how she didn't lose her mind in Omaha, she explores the country with her husband, several clairvoyant hamsters, and an ever-growing herd of rabid plot bunnies. She also has substantially more time on her hands these days, as she has recruited a small army of mercenaries to search South America for her nemesis, romance author Lauren Gallagher, but don't tell Lauren. And definitely don't tell Lori A. Witt or Ann Gallagher. Neither of those twits can keep their mouths shut . . .

Website: gallagherwitt.com
Twitter: @GallagherWitt
Email: gallagherwitt@gmail.com

CARI Z is a Colorado girl who loves snow and sunshine. She likes edged weapons, prefers books to television shows, and goes weak at the knees for interesting men and exciting explosions (but not at exactly the same time—that would be so messy).

Blog: carizerotica.blogspot.com
Twitter: @author_cariz
Website: cari-z.net

Enjoy more stories like
Risky Behavior
at RiptidePublishing.com!

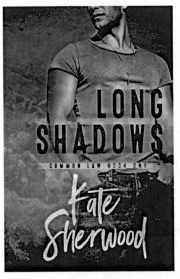

Long Shadows
ISBN: 978-1-62649-526-5

Can't Hide From Me
ISBN: 978-1-62649-444-2

Earn Bonus Bucks!
Earn 1 Bonus Buck for each dollar you spend. Find out how at
RiptidePublishing.com/news/bonus-bucks.

Win Free Ebooks for a Year!
Pre-order coming soon titles directly through our site and you'll
receive one entry into a drawing for a chance to win free books for
a year! Get the details at RiptidePublishing.com/contests.

CPSIA information can be obtained
at www.ICGtesting.com
Printed in the USA
LVOW10s2023060517
533536LV00001B/6/P